# FOUR NEW WORDS FOR LOVE

# FOUR NEW WORDS FOR LOVE

MICHAEL CANNON

First published August 2013

Freight Books
49-53 Virginia Street
Glasgow, G1 1TS
**www.freightbooks.co.uk**



A CIP catalogue reference for this book is available from the British Library

ISBN 978-1-908754-24-0
eISBN 978-1-908754-25-7

Typeset by Freight in Garamond
Printed and bound by Bell and Bain, Glasgow

the publisher acknowledges investment from
**Creative Scotland** toward the publication of this book

For Denise and Rachael – my girls

Michael Cannon was born and brought up in the West of Scotland and worked variously as an apprentice engineer, tax officer, various temporary occupations and oil worker before returning to higher education to study literature. He now works for the University of Strathclyde. His debut novel *The Borough* was published in 1995 and *A Conspiracy of Hope* followed in 1996, both published by Serpent's Tail. His novel *Lachlan's War* was published in 2006 by Viking to much acclaim. He lives on the south side of Glasgow with his wife and daughter.

"If equal affection cannot be/ Let the more loving one be me"

from 'The More Loving One' by W.H. Auden

# PART 1

Nick didn't take long. Quick Nick. I lay back and thought of Eng... I've no particular reason for thinking about Nick at this particular time. I'm in the flat, with Lolly. She's rolling her third spliff. The air's layered with strata of smoke, turned rust coloured in the late light. You can puncture two layers just standing. I don't touch the stuff but people have become passive addicts just being around her. With Lolly there's always a danger of proximity.

Sometimes I feel I don't actually have thoughts in this place, I *encounter* them, suspended in this haze. But then that sounds like the kind of intellectual wank you hear from students on the top deck of buses, putting the non-matriculated world to rights with their annoyingly loud voices.

Lolly's got two speeds: dead-stop lethargy and high-octane hustle. Both infect people around her in some way. I'm the only one here to bear the effect of tonight's sloth. It takes me all the effort I can manage to stand up and walk to the window. It's getting on for the magic minute. I always stand here and watch it, weather permitting. The sun's cast an oblong of light on the opposite wall, catching Lolly in its passing. She keeps herself air-hostess orange. Her colour looks even more ridiculous in the bronze rectangle.

Either it's the passive dope or she's radiating some kind of inner light, like a catechism picture of the Holy Ghost, sweating piety. Maybe there's more to her than meets the eye. But that's rubbish. There's exactly as much to Lolly as meets the eye and she spends a lot of effort making sure men spend a lot of time taking the sight in. She's got hips to breed gladiators and breasts like missile silos. She's got a theory of fat women. Some women are dumpy fat, some gloomy fat, some shy fat, some aggressively fat and some, very few, are erotically fat. There's no mistaking Lolly's category. She aims her breasts at men and they surrender. I don't know if it's got to do with genes or attitude, but it hardly ever fails. Maybe her reputation adds to her attraction. I can't say I understand it. But in a way I do. If I'm depressed I'll rest my head against her chest, and it's got the same effect as wrapping yourself in a duvet that's been blown dry in the fresh air.

She's put the spliff to one side and turned her attention to the camera. I groan. She insists I sit on the sofa. Every time something happens, or doesn't, she takes a picture of us. She's got shoe boxes of those stamp-sized photos you get in booths, black and white graduating to what passes as colour of the two of us, faces squashed together or at the wrong height because the seat won't screw up or down, cataloguing our reckless Saturdays through boiling puberty and beyond. She's always saying we should pour them on the carpet and sort them out. I don't think so. I usually deflect her attention. It isn't hard. I'm thinking of history. She's talking nostalgia. If you don't know the difference it can be fatal. She doesn't know the difference. I don't have the energy to explain. She doesn't have the attention span to listen.

I get crushed as she sits beside me. She leans forward to put on the autotimer. I get the full heft of her breasts in my neck. She's got no sense of private space, and I'm not just talking about rubbing her tits into the back of strangers on the tube. When I started to cry in the cinema toilets it was Lolly who kicked the door in and snatched the thing from my hand. We watched the line appear. 'Try another,' she ordered. You only get one in the pack. I sat crying on the pan while she left to get another and then she stood beside me, holding my hand, as I tried to accumulate enough pee for another try. And even then we got on one another's nerves. She told me crying leaked out the liquid I was trying to muster. 'Hardly,' I said, 'I don't think your bladder works that way. You've got your biology all wrong.' And she said, 'No. You've got *your* biology all wrong.' And even although she was annoyed, she was crying. And that's when I had an unkind thought. Why me? Why me and not Lolly? When it comes to men she's got no powers of discrimination that I can see. And I know her best. I know her better than she does. I knew who it was because there was no process of elimination. I spent all my time discriminating at the expense of the fucking obvious precaution. And the irony was that Quick Nick lived up to his reputation. I wouldn't have minded so much if it had been more memorable, but it lasted as long as a jolt with a cattle prod, which was the same length of time it took him to work out his exit strategy. I only found out his nickname later. Lolly told me. She told me she'd named him. I was too depressed to ask. Biology or not, I tinkled out another pee. We waited. The result was the same. She squeezed my hand. She's been near at every crisis in my life.

There are girls around here who use abortion as a form of contraception. I'm not religious and I'm not superstitious, but I've an image of those potential mothers, old women about to croak, going towards the white light when they realise there's a little queue waiting for them in the tunnel, a line of foetuses in various stages of development, eyes, when they have them, deep black with reproach.

I wasn't keen on telling Dad. Lolly's idea was not to tell him and let the news seep in.

'Are we talking about the same person?'

Dad's ability to pick up a signal is as good as Lolly's. His idea of a hint is a boot in the balls. They both live in a world where they confront, or are confronted. Facts arrive, they aren't foreseen. The reason I wasn't keen on telling Dad is that he's built this little fantasy round me to separate me, in his own mind, from Mum. He calls me 'Princess'. This has more to do with him than me. I don't need any fantasies to separate me from Mum. But he's fragile enough. If it takes this little delusion to keep him standing I wouldn't deny it unless I had to – like giving him the news that I'm pregnant.

Rumour has it that Mum in her prime could give Lolly a run for her money in the fornication handicap. Maybe she still can. She left us eight years ago, when I found out how I got my name. Dad said it was because of his favourite film star. 'Your namesake,' he said, 'my little Gina.' Dad and Gina Lollobrigida. A cosmopolitan Italian beauty and a skinny alcoholic Glaswegian ex-plumber with nicotine stains, shakes and a volcanic cough that sometimes spots the furniture with glistenings of lung. Some fantasies are so fantastic they're sad. Dad and Gina Lollobrigida. As much chance of that pairing as walking into the living room and interrupting the Yeti doing sums. It turned out that Dad didn't name me at all – Mum did. It turns out that she got her inspiration from some third-generation Italian waiter she was granting favours to, ankles behind her ears on the gingham table cloths. He was the owner of a trattoria up town, with his fake wop accent and straw Chianti bottles with candles in them. At least that was Dad's description, that came out much later when he had a bronchial infection that obliged him to dry out for two weeks. Mum's bit of stuff said he was going to the Amalfi coast to set up a place of his own and he'd send for her. Turns out the place was closed down by Health and Safety after the seafood pasta turned half the customers into double ended squibs, that Carlo's real name was Frank, that he'd gone as far as Newcastle to contaminate the locals there and shag hopeless Geordie housewives.

'Typical fucking wop,' was Dad's pronouncement, in front

of Mum, although we all knew he was no more an Italian than any of us. Maybe it was aimed to hurt, because she hurt him so much. Maybe it was because Frank was tainted by association. He pretended to be Italian so he was a 'fucking wop'. I live in Glasgow, with people. Dad's surrounded by 'fucking wops, fucking spicks, fucking chinks, fucking darkies, fucking pakkis and fuck knows who else.' A short sally for his half dozen cans and we're told 'It's like Liquorice fucking Allsorts round here now.' It wasn't like that back then, the glory days of national pedigree, before the population became this mongrel, whenever that was. I pointed out that he wouldn't have had Asian shopkeepers servicing his habit at half past ten on a rainy Sunday night back then, but he was past reasoning a thousand bottles ago. He's fighting to keep the ethnic purity of him and his cronies, so they can all lie gurgling drunk on their various piss-stained mattresses across the city.

I don't know if her shagging drove him to drink or if he'd have got there on his own anyway, but she timed her departure to perfection – just after Kevin's. She left, Dad imploded, and any pretence of being a family disappeared with her.

He answered the door before I could put my keys in the lock. Lolly was holding my other hand. We couldn't get in with him barring the way. From my hesitation he knew something was coming. He's never fully sober but he wasn't drunk. 'My little Gina...' He touched my face. I could feel the beginnings of a tremble, like a washing machine that's about to go into spin.

'She's pregnant.'

He dropped his hand. For a moment nothing about him seemed to change and then, very slowly, he looked like one of those sea-side inflatables at the end of holiday that's leaked just so much air, still afloat but you wouldn't trust your weight to it. And then he turned round and walked back into the living room and turned up the telly. Lolly followed shouting explanations. 'She knows who he is! She's not like her mother!' I bundled her out, grateful and angry at the same time.

I didn't see him for a week, but heard him come in in the early hours, coughing, flushing the toilet, shouting in his sleep, aggressive static caught up in whatever goes on in the jumble of that fucked-up imagination. I confronted him early afternoon mid-way from his bed to the toilet, hunched, vulnerable.

'Is this supposed to be role reversal?'

'This can wait till the morning.'

'You haven't seen the morning since Mum left. *I'm* the one who's pregnant. *I'm* the teenager – at least for the next couple of months. *I'm* supposed to be the one who misbehaves. *I'm* the one carrying the kid. *I* need support – not another passenger.'

He swayed a bit and sucked in some air. 'Gina, my Gina...' He touched my face. His eyes welled with tears and then he stood stock still, a thought struck him and the tears vanished, as if they'd been turned off at the tap.

'He's not a pakki is he?'

I didn't give him the satisfaction of an answer. He spends three days off the sauce and interviews me, looking like something that lives under a rock. It seems he's prepared to put the unknown ethnic background of his grandchild behind him. In itself this is no small thing as he tries to explain to me the change he's undergone. His liver must have gotten up at a count of nine while the booze was sent to a neutral corner. He says he has a calling to become a grandfather. We both know the fucked-up job he made of being a dad, although neither of us says so, and he sees this as a second chance.

'Well, Dad, here's a grenade in the guts: there's absolutely no fucking chance of me staying here with a kid to get the kind of upbringing I got – or didn't.' I don't actually say it but it's the first thing I think. If I say it now the bottle will come out the neutral corner and knock seven shades of shite out his liver. If this fantasy will keep him going till he gets some kind of normality, whatever that might mean, where's the harm? These are conversations I'm having with myself as he sketches out his plan, in fits and starts, over the next week. He's going to dry out. He's going back on the tools. We'll move – the city is no place for a young one. I get quietly angry. Why did none of this occur to him before? Why were Lolly and me allowed to smoke fags in decommissioned lift shafts when we should have been doing homework? Why did I have to bribe strangers to sign my report cards? Did he know anything about my whereabouts, never mind ambitions, between the ages of eleven and nineteen? Does he now? Any recrimination will crush this fantasy so I let it run on. As for moving from Glasgow, I know that Dad's internal geography consists of a series of drinking dens, linked by bus routes, with houses and the occasional shop between. Beyond this is an enormous, vague, threatening place called The Rest of the World, filled with famine, theme parks, unimaginable dangers, fucking wops, fucking spicks, fucking chinks, fucking darkies, fucking pakkis and fuck knows who else who, even if they spoke the same language, wouldn't understand his accent. It's a place you don't go but, according to Dad, we're going there with my baby. I think he's glimpsed bits and pieces from day-time telly and formed some image of a cottage with ivy, the friendly country parson, Mrs Miniver dropping in with warm scones. If there ever was such a place, and he went there, the residents' committee would have him turfed out before he could piss in the bus stop. Everyone has fantasies of some kind. Some can be achieved. Most can't, but it's the fact that they're just out of reach that tantalises and keeps you going. The distance of the gap in Dad's case startled me. I could imagine the sense of dislocation he must have felt, happily wandering round in his mind then opening his eyes. Out goes the cottage with the big-titted dairy maids, in comes the sofa with the burnt fag marks, the fridge sprouting algae and the final demands for the electric. I don't know if drink drove him to imagine something impossibly better, or the realisation of the distance drove him to drink. While he ranted he was eating more or less regularly and I debated with myself the advantages of a staple diet versus the danger of letting the fantasy run. The decision wasn't mine.

'You're wanted at the Social,' Lolly said.

'What for?' he asked.

' Cause she's trying to get a place fixed up.'

'They're staying with me.'

'I'm only the messenger.'

'Actually, Lolly,' I said, 'you're a fucking newspaper.'

'Gina... My little Gina...'

He welled. Anybody crying in the same hemisphere sets her off. She spoke between pants. She was going for the big one.

'I've caused untold hurt.' She got that from the re-run of *Crown Court* on afternoon telly.

'Put a sock in it. The hurt isn't untold because I'm telling you about it. It's not difficult to see who's the brains in this outfit. Dad, you stop too. You were never going to leave here. You in the countryside? The only plumber in Brigadoon. When you're on the sauce you can't change a washer.' I spread my arms encompassing the sofa, the scarred table, the flat, the lock ups, the circle that enclosed all those piss-smelling pubs he lives in that burp out drunks at closing. 'This is all you know. I'm not going far. Me not being here doesn't mean you won't see your grandchild. You can come round. You're miserable sober. I'd rather my kid had a happy granddad who takes a drink than some gloomy sober bastard.'

He wiped his eyes. I pressed home the advantage 'And no, Dad, he's not a pakki.'

'Let's have a cup of tea,' Lolly said. After he'd gone she said she thought we should give him the benefit of the doubt about trying to dry out.

'We could give him a nudge. It might make a difference. We could look it up in the phone book and get him to go. One of those groups where all the dipsos get together and tremble, but don't say what they drink.'

'They do say they drink. That's the whole point. If they admit it to the others then they've admitted it to themselves. That's supposed to be the first step to getting them off the sauce.'

'I thought the whole point was to keep it secret.'

'Keep what secret?'

'What they drink.'

'It doesn't matter what they drink. It could be anything. It's the end point that's the point.'

'I thought it was anonymous.'

'It's the alcoholics that are anonymous, not the alcohol. How much stuff have you been smoking lately?'

One thing I lied about was getting a place near him. I'd intended getting as far from Bridgeton as I could. It turned out to be not very far. There's a reason why housing is readily available round here. I went down to the Social and threw a crying jag, claiming Dad had turfed me and my unborn child out. He backed me up. I'd scripted it for him: shame on the family... bastard grandkid... no daughter of mine... Lolly went along to feed him the prompts. There was another reason too. She said it went badly from the start. The social worker was a woman, so pointing tits at her didn't work. She seemed to think she was some kind of custodian to the slums she was in charge of, and she wasn't impressed by a trembling drunk stammering badly rehearsed lines about the shame of it all. Nothing in Lolly's armoury worked, and she did cause untold hurt by calling her a hatchet-faced cow who could stick her slum accommodation up her arse.

I went down next day and demanded to see the boss. He was a man. I *started* in tears. It was a blinding performance. I didn't find it difficult. I've got a whole stock of sad things I can think about to turn it on at any time. If all else fails I think about Kevin.

It worked. But it turned out that either I'd overestimated my powers of persuasion or the range of available housing stock. I imagined a balancing act: good flat in a crap area or crap flat in a good area – high ceilings versus good schools. I got a crap flat in a crap area with the disadvantage of being within stumbling distance of Dad. Write down this address on any employment questionnaire and watch your chances go down the toilet. Local shops have bars on the *inside*. There are attempts at what the local rag calls 'encroaching gentility'. I live on the fourteenth floor. If I go on to the roof with a telescope I *might* be able to spot a delicatessen within visible radius. I don't know what direction gentility is encroaching from, but it's running as fast as fuck away from me, Dad, Lolly and everyone else *I* know.

Of all people it was Dad and his gargling cronies who came up trumps. Pool their resources and I thought all you'd get would be a collection of tumours, but, hats off, they came up with cutlery, a sofa, saucepans, a radio, a telly and loads of other stuff. The cutlery had GCC stamped on it. Glasgow City Corporation went out of existence before I was born. That was the oldest of the knocked-off stuff. The sofa gave off cartoon noises when you sat or stood, and unless you knew about it there was a crevasse just off-centre that could lead to sudden intimacy, or spillage. I got to know its quirks and didn't mind using it till Lolly said I might have been conceived there. *I* can scarcely imagine, and that's saying something, that collision. I get as far as the two of them approaching one another through a pea-super of mutual fag smoke, then there's an image of Dad's hand, with its crescents of nicotine, vibrating like a tuning fork, touching Mum's face and the image derails in a hot flush of horror.

Patrick, one of Dad's cronies with the same grog-blossom nose that seems to be the badge of the gang, turned up one afternoon with towels, still damp and with a stray sock in one of the folds. He told me it might not be a good idea to visit the laundrette for a couple of weeks. There was no need because the next day Dad, Patrick and another of the gang I don't know, turned up with a washing machine. The third man was introduced as Tam, and he made Dad look healthy. It's obvious they didn't catch a lot of daylight. They stood squinting in the afternoon sun, Tam looking like Nosferatu turned vegan, coughing up some kind of resin. Looking down on them from the fourteenth floor unloading the thing he seemed to have surrounded the washing machine with pats of shining frog spawn. The lift, miraculously, worked that day. Perhaps there is a God. Lolly and me manhandled the machine in and out. The fittings were there. Lolly got on all fours and plumbed it in while they unashamedly studied her arse, standing around like redundant porters. I produced a can each of the cheap stuff I kept for Dad and they opened them in frothy plumes. They all agreed that the beer was too warm. Lolly straightened and said they should see about getting me a fridge then. They did that too. On first opening, the washing machine gave up a sock. It would have been too much to hope for it being the mate of the one delivered with Patrick's towels. Perhaps there isn't a God.

The only thing I can guarantee was bought was the Lladro shepherdess, complete with Bo Peep outfit and a bona fide receipt, that Dad delivered in a box. It was hideous. He was so proud of it he didn't trust himself to take it out the tissue. God knows I could have used the money instead, but I trotted it out with the lager and the custard creams whenever he came round.

So Lolly and I saw in my twentieth birthday in a council high-rise on a burst sofa surrounded by a load of dodgy gear. I didn't look pregnant, although I'd had the doctor confirm the cinema toilet result. It was too much to expect empathy, but what I wasn't prepared for was Lolly's non-stop use of the flat. Until then indoor sex depended on someone's parents being out, although in summer any dry flat surface will do and she's got a genius for erotic improvisation. But I felt resentment rise as night after night I could hear her gymnastic climaxes from the next room. The inside walls feel as if they're made of compressed egg boxes. It doesn't leave much to the imagination. My temper snapped when a big show-down I was waiting for in *Coronation Street* was blotted out by another supersonic shriek. I banged the wall and shouted to her that I had to see her *now*. I didn't have long to wait. She normally packs them off as soon as they've served their purpose: post-coital fag, slam of a door, gone. I don't even know if the same one reappeared or it was a succession of new ones. They all looked the same anyway.

'I'm not running a fucking knocking shop. Here's me, abandoned. That'll be the baby's nursery. You're desecrating it.'

'Listen to yourself. Abandoned? Who by? Does he even know? Have you tried to tell him? The truth is that you don't like depending on anyone except the Social and only then because it's not a person. You like the idea of being some lonely heroine in a tower even if it's a fucking dump with a broken lift. It makes you feel different. And what's so different? You're up the stick and unmarried. Look around! Even if you had someone who'd stick around, he'd probably slap you about a bit every time his team lost, like half the poor fucking cows around here. "Abandoned"? "Nursery"? "Desecrating"? I must've stumbled into 1940. Let me know when the all clear sounds.'

I didn't deserve that. I think she'd been bottling something up too, although God knows it wasn't sexual frustration. She wasn't right about everything but she was right about a lot of it. She knows me better than anyone. She's not bright, but she's got the sharpest instinct I've ever come across. After that tsunami her big orange chest was heaving up and down. I could see the half inch roots of her parting, and it suddenly occurred to me that if she'd only stop barbecuing herself on sun beds, and saturating her head with chemicals, she'd be the pale, pleasantly-plump grown up evolving from school photos, not this tangerine caricature in shag-me shoes. And somehow, looking at her just then, I saw all the increments she'd grown out of, like an insect shedding skins, each stage captured by the countless photos we'd taken together:

the skinny kid, the pale pubescent, the top-heavy teenager, the chip shop sex bomb, and now this. I'd fallen into her fatal habit of nostalgia. But I'd seen all of her stages and I loved them all.

'I love you,' I said, and burst into tears. My hormones were all over the place.

'I love you too.' Her sobs are volcanic. When I'm with her I understand what the phrase to fall into someone's arms means.

'It's a pity we're not lesbos. It would make life a lot simpler.'

'I like cock too much,' she said. We both burst out laughing, uncontrollably, till it was near hysteria. I looked down. The bump was visible. It might have been the tears but I swear my ankles looked swollen. I faced a vista of support tights drying over radiators on loveless nights.

'I'll never find anyone now,' I said and burst into tears again. That set her off. We were just two heads, four arms, four breasts and two bodies convulsing. Looking over her shoulder I could see the whippet-thin specimen that she hadn't yet kicked out, standing in the hall. He was swaying from foot to foot, looking frightened. His instinct was to run, but I think he still thought it worth hanging around in case another go on the swings was still on the cards. His eyes were on stalks at the mention of lesbians. I think he thought all his Christmases might have come at once. He coughed to let her know that he was still there. She made an irritated flick behind her back, without turning round, waving him to bugger off. He looked punctured and closed the door behind him. I stopped crying. So did she.

'Why do you always go for them?'

'Why do you think?'

'No I mean *them*, the under-nourished specimens.'

'I don't know. Staying power? I didn't think there was a type.'

But there was, and I don't think their selection had anything to do with stamina. They were all the colour of sticking plaster gone through the wash. They all looked like illegal immigrants. There was something of the panting fugitive in every one. I thought of them as bowling pins, knocked over by her orgasmic onslaught, once seen easily forgotten, interchangeable, dispensable. She did too. I've a theory their selection was unconscious, a genetic thing she doesn't understand, Lolly's slob fat genes screaming out for slob skinny genes to make a normal slob, and those deluxe ovaries of hers destined to be thwarted by the barrage of precautions she took.

The truth was that I was jealous and not just for the company. My libido see-sawed wildly with my mood swings, and I needed something to stop my plunging self-confidence. I felt I couldn't be less attractive and I made the mistake of telling her. She moved towards the door.

'What are you doing?'

'Calling him back.'

'*Even* if I did find him attractive, I draw the line at your cast-offs.'

'Please yourself. Get changed and then we'll go out and get two more.'

But I don't get changed, the way Lolly does, have a shower and put some slap on and leave your whole history behind you with the pubes in the plug hole. I'm not going to trawl myself round town pouring drink down my neck and stunt my baby just to forget why I got here. I don't undergo Friday night transformations. I'm the sum of my past, the way Lolly isn't.

She took the hint, not just about that night but about my situation. She only ever brought men back when she'd run out of all other possibilities, and she was as quiet as someone with no interior life, and the bedroom manners of the Hulk with a hard-on can be. I spent a lot of nights in. Sometimes, if it was late and I was already in bed, I would hear the key scrape in the lock and then she'd be in my kitchen, by the sound of it banging together the only two pots I owned, although God alone knows why because she can't cook a thing. And if I suddenly felt more lonely, more unattractive than I normally felt, that uncanny instinct of hers would smell it, the clattering would stop and I'd hear her have a quick pee and a quicker brush of her teeth, and then she'd climb in beside me and say 'budge up', while the weight of her bulk had already pushed me onto the cold bit, and she'd put her arms around me and I'd say something like: 'I hope his intentions were honourable. And by the way, can you at least bring your own fucking toothbrush next time.' And she'd say something like: 'If you ever hear me sounding as old as you, feel free to kill me in my sleep. Please.'

At that time I'd a part-time job in town working as a window dresser, cash in hand to avoid the Social. Thinking back, it shows the kind of blunt stupidity I'd normally credit Lolly with. Who's more likely to be seen by a benefit spy than someone who spends part of their time on display? I wasn't a natural. All my artistic flair was taken up by the flat. I use an upturned crate as a coffee table. I have my own style – fucking skint urban rustic. It's a minimalist approach that has to do with minimal money and the need to hide everything at short notice from the police. I did what I was told in the shop. One afternoon I was half-way up a ladder when suddenly I knew that something wasn't right.

I walked home, which was stupid. I called Lolly, which wasn't any cleverer. Her medical expertise is all used up by remembering to take the pill. She called the doctor. Even before she arrived I'd started to bleed. She called an ambulance. Lolly came with me. All of a sudden I wasn't pregnant any more.

They kept me in for three days. They were very nice. They told me it wasn't as uncommon as I might think. I didn't think – the frequency of miscarriages hadn't occurred to me at all. They told me that as far as they could tell 'It wouldn't compromise your chances of conceiving again'. When you're single and twenty and broke, that isn't really the consolation it's meant to be. They said that none of the complications that can result had occurred.

'Everything,' they said, 'had come away cleanly'. 'Everything.' None of this was said unkindly. I thought: a discharge without complications then. I didn't feel anything, except a sense of dread that the vacuum was about to be filled by something worse than a sense of emptiness. There were four of us in the room, Lolly's hand welded to mine, and I didn't want to give way in front of strangers. One day you're pregnant and the next day you're not. A discharge without complications. All the complications have been removed. So they discharged me.

'Everything' hadn't come away. 'Everything' was the half of it. I started crying on the landing before I got to the door. Lolly fumbled the keys because she couldn't see the lock. She bundled me in as if trying to barricade all the accumulated grief on the outside. Everything made me cry. Everything. I don't mean kid's stuff because at least I'd had the common sense not to buy anything till nearer the time, when I would have been surer of the outcome. The things a dead child leaves behind must be the saddest furniture in the world. Imagine moving a sofa and finding a dusty bear, haemorrhaging stuffing. It would kill you stone-fucking dead on the spot. Or even worse – it wouldn't.

I didn't have that to put up with. I didn't need it. The excuse for tears was all around: the spatula stuck in the cold fat of the frying pan that I'd intended cleaning after work; the balled-up tights thrown in the direction of the washing basket; the toothpaste Lolly had squeezed from the middle although I always tell her not to; the discarded cap with the hard crust. These were all mementos of a past life three days ago when I had a baby inside. The fridge magnets made me cry. The Hoover made me cry. Lolly had actually gone out and bought food of some description. She hasn't a penny. The generosity of all that ready-made tat, stacked like bricks in the fridge, made me cry. I wasn't crying for the life that wouldn't be, the Disney scenarios that Dad dreamed up. I wasn't crying at being thwarted because I thought I'd some vocation as a mum. It was some kind of purge. When I wasn't crying out loud I was crying silently. Lolly said I cried in my sleep. When I got out the bath it was deeper. Dad came round and stared at the crap carpet, being all silent and strong. He's got a face like a roadmap anyway but the lines had formed themselves into a mask of complete misery. He didn't say a single thing until he felt himself about to cave in, so he got up and left. Except that he turned round at the front door and said, 'Was it a boy?'

'I don't know.'

'That's what I had hoped for, a boy. I wanted you to call him Kevin.' Which wasn't deliberate but was just about the worst possible thing to say to me just then. He's not selfish but I've never met an alcoholic who isn't the centre of their own needy world.

After that I cried all through afternoon telly. Lolly joined in. The sofa became a blancmange. I fell asleep at *Countdown* and woke up during the late news. We were sitting on an atoll ringed with paper hankies, an ankle-deep reef of tears and crisping snotters. I'd been crying for a week. I took stock.

'Enough's enough,' I said.

'Do you want to get changed and go out then?'

'You got over that quick enough!'

'I think you'll find half of those fucking hankies are mine!'

But I didn't want to go out just then, or the day after that, or the day after that, or the number of days it took me to reach some kind of balance. So Lolly went out to get some fish suppers because the pre-prepared crap in the fridge didn't appeal, and I bagged the hankies and, among the debris, found the remote that had somehow got lost during that lost week. I ate at her nagging and flicked the channels. I didn't have the attention for anything. Her patience lasted a whole minute.

'For fuck's sake let's watch something! I don't care if it's *Gardeners' World* but let's watch something!'

'Lolly.'

'What?'

'Thanks.'

'Any time. Give us the remote.'

So she stayed, again and again. And I did go out in a series of excursions, to the corner shop, the cinema, the radius widening with each trip. And although Lolly's dope smoke makes impartial thought almost impossible I do think, standing here by the window, that I've reached some kind of balance. Unless I'm here the minute will pass with no one to appreciate it and all that beauty will go to waste.

She's fussing with the camera's self timer, balancing it on the crate, and there's a lot of breathing and swearing. She insists I sit on the sofa. The flash goes off as she turns towards me. Her arse has filled the foreground and that's all she's succeeded in taking a picture of. She turns back. There's more fussing and swearing. She touches the button and throws herself on the sofa. It lets out a groan as I'm levered off the cushion. There must be two clear inches of daylight between my arse and the fabric when the flash goes and captures me levitated, Lolly's arm halfway round my neck.

'Try and remember the maths next time. Fat girl jumps on sofa equals skinny girl airborne.' But she's not listening. She'll spend ages setting up a photo and lose interest the instant it's taken. I go to the window and step out onto the balcony. The minute has arrived. The smell of warm tar and cut grass rises up from the street below with the sound of kids playing football. The high-rise across the way has turned crimson, the windows flashing like sequins. The bend of the river is a molten curve. The whole landscape looks as if it's been dipped in honey, hiding, for the length of the illusion, the litter, the syringes, the half-submerged trolleys. 'Come and look,' I say, but when I glance across at her she has this underwater look, as the last sucked-down lungful hits. I turn back for the last heart-breaking thirty seconds, standing on this platform in the saffron air. The ball below hits a car, setting off the alarm. An adult shouts.

The kids scatter. The spell breaks. The colours fade.

'It's the only free show in town.' I say, to no one.

* * *

I'd never been in the flat before without being pregnant. I wasn't sure if my subsidy depended on it, but I decided not to tell the Social anyway. Lolly said I was very wise. I still spent too much time watching day-time telly. I'm sure there's a link between that and mental deterioration. I took stock. I reasoned that it doesn't have to be like this. I've said before to Lolly that I'm the brains of the gang, but that's being damned by faint praise. Miss Proctor, who wrote that 'Lorraine suffers from a chronic inability to understand, or to want to understand, anything that does not interest her' was the same woman who sent me home with a letter to my parents telling them I was squandering my gifts. I used to forge Lolly's mum's signature on her report card. Because she couldn't do joined-up writing Lolly wasn't able to return the favour. Dad couldn't do joined-up writing either but for other reasons. I used to stick the report card in front of him and he'd sign, without reading, in a series of spastic jerks that looked as if he'd done it on top of a spin dryer. Other parents might have taken the hint at the mention of squandered gifts. I didn't expect my homework to become a family enterprise but, looking back, it wouldn't have been unreasonable to expect the telly to have gone off for half an hour.

It's too easy blaming someone else. At some point the statute of limitations runs out on your childhood. No doubt I'd have made more of a go of school if either Mum or Dad had shown an atom of interest, but the truth is I didn't want to make more of a go of it. I knew how crap my education was, but I went on sitting in front of day-time telly getting stupider. I had to break the cycle.

I went back to the shop and asked if I could work further back from the pavement. I didn't want some window-shopper from the

Social seeing me. I spent a fortnight in the stock room. Their system was obsolete. Understanding it was both boring and difficult. I replaced it, kept less stock and moved it quicker. The woman I'd filled in for came back from holiday to find her week's work could be done by Monday afternoon.

'What does this mean?' she said.

'It means you can get on with doing other things.'

Up till then she'd always put on an air of superiority and had let it generally be known that she only worked for pin money, as a break from the women's guild or whatever. But when I said she could do something more she came out with language you don't hear on the BBC. 'Careful,' I said, 'one doesn't want this getting back to Philippah on the badminton committee.' By mid-afternoon she was two steps up a ladder in the front window, complaining heights made her dizzy and trying to work up a case for constructive dismissal.

They asked me to work full time. I told them to make me legit and then told the Social I'd just found a job. The fact that I wasn't pregnant came out in the exchange. They let me stay in the flat minus the subsidy. I earned a pittance. Tax hadn't occurred to me. It's never touched anyone I know. The first official wage packet listed the deductions. I felt no better off than before, except that I was one of the faceless drones paying for the likes of Lolly and Dad.

My social life still stretched no further than the cinema. I was working myself up to a quiet night down the pub. Lolly appointed herself social convener. A quiet night is a failed night by her reckoning. At that time there was still a liner of sorts anchored in the Clyde, used as a floating casino and dance club. *HMS Fornication*, a rust bucket of emergency fucks kept afloat by sheer exuberance and a life belt of spent condoms. The licensing laws allowed all-night drinking. A whole social stratum of Glasgow was banged into existence against the cracked port holes on that boat. Young girls tripped up the gang plank in slingbacks, hearts full of high hopes, handbags full of illicit drink, and lurched down four hours later, stomachs full of Bacardi, uteruses full of cooling spunk, the future single-parent families of the city. To the right-minded city fathers and the hard-line religious types, it was Sodom and Gomorrah on the quayside. It was either going to sink or get closed down. The breaker's yard beckoned. The boat's days were numbered. Word got around. The final weeks were frantic. Girls wearing outfits that wouldn't keep them warm in Tenerife stood at the dockside in a wind that would cut cardboard, trying to talk their way past the bouncers.

'I've got tickets for the boat on Saturday.'

'I thought we were taking it easy, going to a quiet local pub.'

'There aren't any quiet local pubs round here. And even if there were, they'll still be here when the boat isn't.'

She turned up on Saturday to help me get ready. She'd topped up her tan and squeezed herself into some corset arrangement that squeezed everything up and out like a market garden display. I felt like the desperate sister they let out the attic when the gentleman caller comes round. Lolly went through my wardrobe full of 'this won't do's and 'is this a sack?' and 'too dull for Mrs Menopause' and 'this is sexual kryptonite' and that sort of thing. Her compromise solution was for me to keep on what I was already wearing and leave most of the buttons undone. But I didn't spill out strategically the way she did, and I didn't want to either. She insisted on a photo. I look like a maiden aunt who's run out the burning house without stopping to get properly dressed.

We had to wait on the quayside even though we'd tickets. The wind funnelling up the Clyde estuary was vicious. The buttons didn't stay undone. I'd had the presence of mind to put on a coat. Even though I'd three times more clothes on than Lolly, I was freezing. She wasn't. It wasn't just natural insulation, she's got some kind of hormone that kicks in when drink, fun and men are involved that makes her immune to cold, exhaustion, embarrassment, subtlety or any of the other things that inhibit the rest of the world. My hands were plunged into my coat pockets. When she handed me my ticket I was shocked at how cold her hand was.

'Sometimes you've just got to teach your body who's boss.'

The bouncer looked at the heft of her bag. 'Full,' she said, 'like your balls.' He smiled and waved us up the gangplank. We walked into a wall of noise. Music spilled out from the dance floor, flaking rust, and pulsed its way into the casino where Chinese waiters were going frantic round the tables. Lolly ordered two glasses of tap water from the bar. The guy put them down with a bang. This didn't cover the overheads. We went into the toilet and Lolly fished out the gin and mixers from her handbag. The place was crowded out with girls doing the same. Dope smoke was rising out two separate cubicles like talking smoke signals, adding another layer to the smell of hairspray and cheap perfume. Girls were renewing their lippy or mascara already. The noise was tremendous, with about fifteen simultaneous conversations and disembodied shouting from the booths. You could get drunk on this alone, and I watched Lolly take a giant breath and joyfully expand. She was in her element in that bouquet of ripe, ready women. It affected me too. I felt light headed as we walked back towards the music and looked around. Lolly leaned against a pillar and watched me looking, a half ironic look on her face. She has technique she usually employs, like one of those angler fish you see in telly documentaries, down miles deep, where there's no light, suspending her bait. Once a victim gets too close to see what's flashing it's too late. But she wasn't doing that yet.

'He's not here yet,' she said.

'I don't know what you mean.'

'You're not a very good liar.'

'I think I must be too old for this place. I don't see the attraction any more.'

'Here it is coming.'

I turned to her and we both managed a quick refill, pouring from her handbag like a goatskin, before I turned back and pretended to look anywhere but in his direction, as he weaved his way through the bodies towards us. He staked his claim without a word. That annoyed me. I let him stand for a long time before pretending to notice.

'So you're back in circulation.'

'I'm not a corpuscle, Nick.' Lolly's nodding approval behind his back, because this is one we haven't rehearsed.

'Want a drink?'

'I've got a drink.'

'Want to dance?'

'That's why I brought my handbag.'

'Want some fresh air?'

'You're fresh enough.' Lolly gives me the thumbs up.

'I only heard about it afterwards. Gina, I'm so sorry...' He lets his voice tail off with his falling gaze, puts his drink on a nearby table and pretends to study the floor for about twenty seconds. Of course it's complete fucking rubbish. You'd have to live in a submarine at the bottom of the Clyde not to hear about anything that goes on round here. Nick's emotional range is about as deep as his intelligence. He has a series of poses he strikes, like something out a mediaeval tapestry, that are supposed to represent sadness, reproach, regret or whatever. I don't know if he's actually capable of feeling anything. He tries to match his appearance that he's always aware of to what he thinks other people think he should be feeling, groping his way towards a combination, like a colour-blind electrician. At least he does that as long as he's trying to get something, like sex or promotion. The rest of the time he doesn't give a fuck. This attempt looked like constipation.

'You know me, Gina. I don't walk away from my responsibilities. If only I'd known.'

I'm distracted by Lolly sticking her fingers down her throat and miming a hurl. 'Three's company,' I say, across his shoulder. She leans towards me in a conspiring sort of a way. I'm assuming it's a joke at Quick Nick's expense, some dig at his spurt problem, but it's just to give me another refill. I've been drinking in big nervous gulps since pretending not to see him. He waits till she goes before coming out with a real fucking howler.

'Somehow, Gina, I think whatever comes out of you and me being together can't be bad.'

Is he talking about the act of him making his deposit or the end product? Does he even know what he's talking about? You can't assume Nick's words mean anything because it's almost impossible to overestimate his superficiality. But I know what to say to him right then and there: 'Well, that's all right then. You wouldn't have minded my varicose veins and heartburn and piles and tiredness and clothes always drying over the radiator and you doing two nights and a Saturday to make ends meet and my cracked nipples and the teething and the sleepless nights and the resentment that there's someone that isn't you monopolising my tits and the realisation that if you're any kind of a parent at all you've got someone depending on you for the rest of your life.' But I didn't say any of that. I felt dowdy, surrounded by all these multi-coloured, high-octane girls. He's very handsome. Wherever we went he was the focus of attention, girls always looking at him and now girls looking at us, obviously wondering what he saw in me. Because it was me he'd crossed the room of all those glances to talk to, and not just for old times' sake. And I stood basking in his gaze, wanting to believe in its sincerity, because for the length of time it was focused on me it didn't seem to matter that I looked as if my clothes were held together with safety pins. I wanted to be wanted, and he wanted me, and although these ambitions weren't a perfect fit I was prepared to live with the overlap because, like the song says, he made me feel like a natural woman.

'Friends,' he said, offering his hand. I took it. I'd never shaken his hand before. I'd held it. Touching it again I felt a surge of hormones at the memory of his handling me that made me want to lean into him.

'Friends,' I said.

'Live and let live,' he said.

'Forgive and forget,' I said.

'Let the good times roll,' he said.

So we let them roll in the back of his work's van, parked fifty yards from the gangplank, suspiciously furnished with a roll-out carpet, and in my flat, his parents' house, the cinema, on top of the after-hours fabrication bench at his work and anywhere else that the mood took us. Once you got the first one out the way he developed the staying power that didn't deserve his nickname. When he looked into my eyes I wanted to believe what I saw, although I knew he was only watching me watching him. When I think back I believe that people were only real to him to the extent that they reflected him to himself.

And we did forgive and forget. I once forgave him six times in a single night. I forgave him standing against the wall till the radiator burnt my arse, on top of the Ikea bureau that threatened collapse, in the shower, on the floor and I can't remember where else. And in all that forgiveness, although I thought I was diligent on forcing reluctant condoms, there was something that gave, or I simply forgot. Lolly was in the flat when I came out the toilet with the reading. I told her not to say anything. Within two days everyone who was anyone knew.

And then Nick forgot me.

Lolly said that although I might be the brains of the outfit, when it came to men I didn't have the sense of a dog. I began an inventory of her past men characterised by the only thing that distinguished them from one another: bad feet, bad teeth, bad hair, bad breath, socially bad, psychotically bad. She stopped me with one of her flat-footed pronouncements: 'All I ever do is fuck them.' And I realised the depth of my stupidity. She saw people for what they were and didn't care. I wanted to invent Nick to justify to myself I wasn't just a fuck, when deep down I knew he wasn't even likeable.

I'd done enough crying for the rest of my life. I was calm. I'm only twenty, I told myself, and I'm in this for the long haul. I went to the shop and found out that given the length of my official employment, rather than the time I'd worked there, my 'statutory rights' as the manager called them amounted to fuck all. Then there was another meeting with the Social, which I immediately escalated by demanding to see a man, not the hatchet-faced cow from the last time. I didn't throw a crying jag, I was all silent tears, Madonna-like suffering, patience of a monument, the full nine yards. It worked.

I left Nick a voice message saying now was the time to prove he didn't walk away from his mistakes, and to make me an offer. I left another message in case he didn't understand the first. I said I didn't expect a white wedding, or any kind of wedding at all, or even for him to stick around, but that he had to provide some kind of financial support for his kid. Lolly was for the pre-emptive strike, 'calling in the authorities' as she put it. She's got a total disregard for all authority until she needs it. I wanted to give him the chance. But it turned out that Nick had evaporated, left home, moved job, maybe had plastic surgery and was now a woman with big tits in Rio de Janeiro as far as getting hold of him was concerned. Lolly said that if he had a pay packet the bastard could be tracked down. When my wellbeing was at stake she was fierce – all bets were off. I told her he could go and fester. He'd emigrated to that limbo land of no responsibility beneath notice or worth caring about. He might bump into Mum. Dad's reaction was predictable.

'He's not a pakki is he?'

'No, Dad. He's the same useless bastard as last time.'

And then he said something so unexpected it threw me.

'Are you thinking of telling your mother?'

'Firstly, I've no idea how to go about it, and even if I had, why would I allow someone time with my kid when they haven't shown a shred of interest in me for eight years?'

'She might want to give something.'

I could imagine what 'something' might be. One of those giant furry animals you see miserable kids walking round zoos with, in tow with the absent dad, making up for all those lost moments with some big unsuitable gesture and too many sweets.

'I don't want her chucking conscience money at my kid to excuse all the things she didn't do for me.' It was brutal and true and it shut him up. If she was still alive she'd be the type of person who gives a gift and wants instant and disproportionate thanks, and when she doesn't get it, sulks. 'We don't need anything given grudgingly.' That was the first time I'd said 'we'. Early as it was I already felt a sense of 'we' that I hadn't the first time round. We against the world. People come and go. We'd get by.

And all the things I'd predicted in that mental list I should have delivered to Nick, did happen. I got piles, heartburn, hot flushes, everything God designed to make pregnant woman unattractive. Sometimes I'd get into my dressing gown for an early night by half past three, and it was catching myself in the mirror, in that merciless mid-afternoon slanting light, that I had one of those stop-your-heart moments and realised the difference between love and romance. Romance is flowers and chocolates and sex on tap and the novelty of another body you're not used to. Romance isn't compromise because you haven't had time yet to find out all the things you don't like about the other person. Romance is thrilling because you know it isn't real, and you know it's more intense because it's temporary. Love is in it for the long haul and staying because of, not despite, all the irritating things about the other person because the good things outweigh the bad. Six months ago my fantasy would have been Nick with intelligence. Now it would be a man whose face I can't quite imagine because he's defined by what he does, not what he looks like. He gets me the stuff when my heartburn comes on. He isn't irritated by my clumsiness, my size, my instant tiredness, my banished libido. We lie like spoons in a drawer and he tells me things. Stupid little things. The amalgam of nothings that add up to the day. Do men like that exist? I've grown up around people who think sensitive men are really women. Any man with those credentials around here hid them till they died. Or if they didn't they were treated like you might imagine. And that last thought cut me in half, because I realised that finding the kind of man round here I thought I deserved was as likely as dad and Gina Lollobrigida.

Lolly came with me to the antenatal classes. I nominated her my birth partner. She turned squeamish at the explanation of childbirth, which I thought a bit thick, considering all the traffic she'd seen in the other direction. The men who turned up with their partners were a mixed bunch. There was a vegan couple who looked as healthy as Dad except they looked as if they'd knitted their own clothes with egg noodles. There was a rich-looking couple in their mid-twenties who both looked very, very clean. He looked like an oversize preppy American schoolboy and I'd have given hard cash to see his face when the fun really started. There were two normal guys, Tom and Duncan, who turned up with their partners and obviously found the whole thing embarrassing, especially being lumped with the vegans. They linked up and stood outside, smoking and farting and talking about football as a relief from the Zen music and aromatherapy birth plans. I know this because Lolly went outside to join them and tell them we weren't lesbians. I looked up from the half-hearted pummelling she was giving in back rub classes, to catch her trying to give Duncan the glad eye in the mirror. Her reasoning was straightforward – the nearer the time the more grateful he'd be for a bit on the side. 'Have some morals,' I said. 'Put yourself in her position. She's got enough to contend with without finding her man's playing away from home.'

But she wasn't capable of thinking herself into someone else's position, and it didn't matter anyway. He didn't respond. Either he was frightened or had more morals than she gave him credit for. Personally I think he was one of those men who refused to see the attraction in a fat orange Amazon. Someone with taste. For whatever reason he made it clear that she left him cold, and the more he ignored her the more she wanted him.

'Wouldn't it be nice to have someone faithful like that? Not like Nick and all those other bastards. Someone you could settle down with.'

'So why are you trying to sabotage his marriage when it looks as if that's what he's already got? Are you jealous?'

'Of that boiler? Have you seen her?'

'And if you had him at her expense then he wouldn't be the kind of person you're pretending to look for. You'd lose interest in him quicker than Nick did me.'

'I suppose.'

My time came closer. My belly was like a drum. When I got tired it was like turning the light out. I peed in spoonfuls. Lolly said that if your waters break in Marks and Spencers you get a fifty pound voucher, or a hamper, or something. I told her it wasn't enough of an incentive to hang around and get fallen arches. We were watching *Emmerdale* when my waters did break. I already had the bag packed and told Lolly to call a taxi. She turned all fingers and thumbs and I had to take the phone from her.

'This is the easy bit. I'm going to need you to hold it together a bit better than this. Check the lift's not broken and hold it on the landing.'

They wouldn't let her stay overnight with me but promised to call the instant things started happening. For some mysterious reason, having closed off her mind to all the details, she now thought the whole thing couldn't happen without her. I didn't make any bones about it and told them I wanted every drug going. Rumour had it Mrs Vegan had opted for a home birth. I could imagine her, with the first mediaeval pain, realising that aromatherapy and her hand-knitted husband weren't going to be of much use when her vagina looks like a python eating a sheep – in reverse.

They called Lolly in the wee small hours. I knew from her instant arrival that she'd been smoking in the car park, chatting up the A & E porters. I'd been so uncomfortable I'd been persuaded to have a bath. I was sitting in the water like a convulsing egg, contractions coming thick and fast, when Lolly burst in brandishing her phone like a police badge.

'They said it's happening.' She looked disappointed at the lack of drama.

'No they didn't. They told you to come in. I was there when they called. Turn off your phone.'

I lumbered back in my paper dressing gown. There was some complication that delayed the pain intervention and I heard myself making inhuman noises, until I was swept up by a blissful wave. I looked down, between my thighs, and saw Lolly staring, wearing a look of paralysed horror. The doctor arrived, all business, brushes her aside and draws an imaginary equator across my stomach. 'I work from here down,' he said to her, 'you stay up north.' He's young, assertive, reasonable looking and he must earn a mint.

'We're not lesbians you know. I'm just her birthing partner.'

He completely ignores her. I have no idea how much time passes. I'm soaked in sweat and the paper gown is stuck in patches. The doctor says something I don't hear and leaves.

'We're going for a ventuse delivery,' the midwife explains.

'Where's he gone?' Lolly shouts, beating me to it. There's an edge of panic in her voice that starts my heart hammering.

'To get his boots on – for traction.'

He reappeared between my legs like he'd sprung up out a

trapdoor. A whole new cast has appeared with him. Suddenly, from it being just me, Lolly, the doctor and the midwife, there are now two female paediatricians wheeling a machine and someone else too – I've no idea who. Aside from the paediatricians they're all wearing different coloured uniforms. It's like panto. Lolly's peeking south and what comes after I get from hysterical description that grew with each telling.

Evidently I've some kind of tarpaulin stretching from my arse to the floor. The doctor returns with what looked like a sink-plunger, which he pushes into me followed by, according to Lolly's account, two feet of handle. I understand the need for the boots when he begins a tug of war with my organs. A small head appears between my legs. The doctor detaches the sucker. Lolly told me the next bit. I made her take out the embroidery. The little face is looking down the slipway of the tarpaulin. The eyes open and eerily look at the new world. One of the paediatricians intervenes and sticks a tiny tube up the new nostrils and mouth to suck out all the stuff. I'm panting and pushing. The doctor gets some kind of grip and, also according to Lolly, the baby comes out like an artillery shell, smeared in blue grease and without making a sound. The doctor gives the baby to the two paediatricians who take it over to the machine, shielding the action with their backs. I don't remember crying for my baby but Lolly said I was howling, shouting and sobbing like an accordion that's fallen down a flight of stairs.

They turn back and hand the blue bundle to me, tell me I have a beautiful baby girl. The exhaustion vanishes. The universe contracts to this little face no bigger than the 'O' I can form joining my forefinger and thumb. They've been cosmetic in their use of the blanket. When it slides back I can see the sucker ring on the top of her head, like a monk's bald spot. Lolly said the doctor was still at it, elbow deep, like a vet in a safari park. He hands a large bloody pancake to the midwife. He apologises to me for having had to do an episiotomy. I'm so happy and pain-free I wave this away.

Having no idea what her perineum is called, Lolly takes a look. I'm not convinced that what followed was spontaneous because she manages to miss the tarpaulin and any sharp edges and fall on top of him.

* * *

It's strange, all kinds of skills are monitored and tested. You need a licence to drive a car. I'm sure you have to have some kind of certificate to teach swimming. You're not a real plumber unless you're registered with some body or other that can vouch for you. But you don't need to pass any kind of test to be a parent. Look at mine.

No one really teaches you anything about having a child. It's not negligence, it's just that nothing really prepares you. You can read about the tiredness and the stretch marks and the soreness, but they're all surface things. One night, when Millie wouldn't sleep or feed and cried right through for seven non-stop hours, Lolly said you could understand how parents could become child-beaters, couldn't you? And I said no – you couldn't. Don't get me wrong – much of looking after a baby is sheer boredom. There were times I craved adult conversation so much I tried to drag out the midnight exchange at the corner shop, making idle chit-chat through the bars as he checked the camera to make sure I wasn't casing the place, before sliding across the Sudocrem. And it's not as if you get a lot back at first – all you are is a mobile feeding station. And no one can seriously say they *like* changing nappies. If you're half-way normal you can admit that you find your own kid's shit less objectionable than you thought you were going to, but any other kid's as revolting as you imagined. And I can't stand those *professional* mothers, not mothers with professions but those ones who can't wait till they're *outside* to breast feed, brandishing nipples like periscopes, changing their kids' nappies on park benches, who make a virtue of letting themselves go because it's wholesome to look like a sow with ten kids, breasts like tubers, sitting smiling in a hurricane of noise and snotters.

What none of those books or classes tells you, because they can't tell you, is that if you're any kind of a parent at all you not only love your child, you fall in love with her. Big things fit into small things. I gushed with more love than I thought the universe could hold and she just drank it all up. I've never forgiven Mum because I never really tried to understand her. What kid does? But all I have to do is to stare at Millie for five seconds and her leaving us is even less understandable. When I told Lolly I couldn't understand child-beating I was deadly serious. Dad's as good a grandfather as someone of his habits can be, better than he was a father. But he didn't hesitate to raise his hand to me when I was a kid. I don't know anyone treated differently. Maybe it was a generational thing. But there's being hit, and there's being hit. Not all beaten kids grow up to be child-beaters. No one's *ever* hitting Millie.

I wouldn't say life was easy, but I didn't have it as hard as most of the single mothers round here. I was a veteran for a start. Seventeen is the average. There are thirty-year-old grandmothers in this block, who dress the same way as their daughters. And I didn't try and do the same thing as some of the seventeen-year-olds, trying to lead *exactly* the same life as a year ago except with a kid in tow. I'd been on the receiving end of that arrangement. Dad asked me what I needed his cronies to steal. At first he turned up every second night with the shakes, because he'd spent the day drying out expecting to see her. I let him hold her for about a minute at a time, Lolly and me either side, propping him up like human scaffolding, my hands inches from Millie. The strain of staying off the sauce every other day was telling on both of us. I told him to drink more and come round less. The next week he looked radiant, swaying over her cot with this smile on his face I don't ever remember being directed at me. The only thing I really minded was his new habit of bursting into tears at the sight of her, setting Millie off.

I breast-fed for nine months and stayed with her practically every minute of that time. Lolly was a star. She kept offering me nights out. I told her our ideas of a good night out were different. I said my idea of a night out had nothing to do with men. She lost interest in the detail at that point and offered her services as a baby sitter. I accepted. I was expressing milk when she arrived. I was excited about the prospect of getting dressed up, even though it was only a girls' night. Lolly squirted some of the milk in her mouth.

'Have you tasted this stuff? It's disgusting.'

Then we had the five minute talk, starting with my mobile number, written headline-size beside the phone, moving on to Millie's sleeping routine, and household hazards and how to avoid them. She was wearing a scarf she pretended to hang herself with, sticking out her tongue and rolling her eyes. Millie was asleep by the time I left. Standing waiting for the lift I heard the creak as Lolly prised the letter box open.

'Put the bleach down!'

I refused to give her the satisfaction of seeing me smile. I was meeting Moira and Ruth. They'd been at school with Lolly and me, and sometimes we'd make up a foursome till other things got in the way. Of the two, Moira is the one everyone remembers, which is funny because she's half the size. She never exercises and keeps her shape by starving herself. She tans herself to light coffee-coloured, to stand out against all the pale people – like Ruth. Most people describe Ruth by all the things that she isn't.

Moira can't imagine life without a man, but not the way Lolly does. They both use men for different reasons. They're polar opposites. Moira's spent her life plotting how to get out of Bridgeton, but none of it involves self-improvement, or sacrifice on her part. She's *always* had boyfriends, as far as I know she's been faithful as long as it's lasted, she's *always* chucked *them* and moved on, without ever breaking her stride or looking back, and she's *always* had the next one lined up. I don't know if there was ever an overlap but you wouldn't get a chink of light between. She's demanded a higher spec at each move, like some social-climbing sales rep choosing a car. I think of her various boyfriends as relay horses. She's ridden a dozen nags with her eyes on a thoroughbred – a mason with a good trade, who can install her in a house with a patio. She gets her status, even in her own eyes, from the boyfriend she's with at the time. And she obviously thinks a woman without a man, like me or Lolly, since Lolly's men are accessories, has no status at all.

Ruth's quiet. I'd call her homely. Lolly says that in Ruth's case 'homely' means she's the type of girl most boys only want to fuck at home so they don't have to meet their friends with her. Lolly says that's the way men think. Lolly says that if a man ever asks you to describe a friend, and you say she's got a lovely personality, then you might as well say she's a farmyard animal for all the chance the poor girl's got. Lolly says men are merciless.

Ruth was always on the edge of things, even in the playground. When there were sixteen simultaneous games played in the same space and it meant there wasn't a spare square inch, she always seemed to find herself a quiet bit, watching hopscotch. She's chronically shy. She never skipped ropes because she didn't want to draw attention to herself, while Lolly, although she hated it, skipped just to make her skirt fly up and give the boys a chance to see her knickers. Ruth was always going to be one of those picked last choosing netball sides. Choosing any sides. Everyone recognizes the type, especially themselves. She's a bit overweight. We're back to Lolly categories here, not erotic fat but sad fat. Lolly says Ruth has fat in the wrong bits. Lolly says flat chest and a big bum is the double dunt – you're fucked both ways. When I think back it was never really a foursome, it was me and Lolly and Moira with Ruth two paces behind. You often find good-looking girls have plain girls in tow. Moria has Ruth. Moira uses Ruth. Ruth was the messenger. 'My pal fancies your pal…' stammered out in the playground, while she's looking at the pavement chalk and dying a death, because she likes the boyfriend's friend she's been asked to talk to, and as far as he's concerned Ruth's just a piece of talking furniture as he scans the bodies looking for Moira, wishing he was the one that Moira fancies. Women are merciless.

'Where's Lolly?' Moira asks. She never drinks locally and insists on meeting in a wine bar in town. They have wine bars near where we both live. They're bars that also sell wine, one kind that comes out a barrel and arrives in half-pint tumblers, and leaves people like Dad, with cast-iron livers, slumped across the table by noon. But that's not what Moira has in mind. She has the kind of place we're now sitting where people in those half-circle kid-on leather sofas actually pay money to drink foreign water. It's just after seven. The guys in suits have that Friday attitude. They're on to their second or third and are loosening ties. The music is cranking up and it's getting to the stage where you have trouble hearing the other person, unless you look at their lips at the same time.

'Looking after Millie.'

But she doesn't hear because she isn't interested. She's looking round and I can practically hear the calculation, like a Geiger counter as she catches the flash of an expensive watch, and it occurs to her that a mason and a porch might be selling herself short.

'That's lovely,' Ruth says. She's been looking at me so I turn my attention to her and it occurs to me, very unkindly, that the military don't need to spend all that money on camouflage. All they need to do is take tips from Ruth. It's astonishing how easily some people are overlooked, and it's got nothing to do with size. I start to talk to her about Millie, and after a couple of minutes of having hogged the conversation I feel vaguely ashamed. I've never really, in the true sense of the word, had a conversation with Ruth. And all I'm doing now is using her, the way Moira does, as something I can pour all my pent-up conversation about my favourite subject into. She could be anyone. But then I tell myself she couldn't be Moira, who has a supernatural ability to divert any topic back to her. And as I look at Ruth I can see she's listening, really listening, and not just because I'm the only one in the place thinking she's not just a bundle of tired clothes. There's a seriousness to her that puts men off. That's Lolly's diagnosis. That and her voice and her clothes and her face and the fact that she's boring. But Lolly's not going to trawl for hidden depths. Most of the questions I'd had from friends focused on how Millie had changed my routine, not about Millie herself. You could see they were imagining themselves into the role, and coming up with a judgement of maybe in ten years' time, or never. But her questions weren't like that. They were about Millie. And looking at her again, I suddenly wondered why it was that I saw through the Day-Glo tan and the scaffolded tits to the real Lolly, and yet somehow I'd missed Ruth. And the next thing I thought was that if there's substance to Ruth, why does she hang about with a worthless social mountaineer like Moira?

'What are you talking about?' Moira says, over her shoulder.

'Millie,' I say.

'Who's Millie?'

'Gina's daughter.' Moira still hasn't turned round. She's directing her attention like a lighthouse beam into corners, looking for more glints of money. After a second sweep she turns back to us with a blank expression. It's our turn to talk to her because she's giving us her attention. Ruth suddenly dries up. With equal suddenness everything about Moira gets on my nerves. We were supposed to meet for a chat and because of her we've come to this place that's making talk difficult. I'm not in the mood to make it any easier for her so I turn my attention to Ruth, and speak pointedly about Millie for the next couple of minutes, the kind of rubbish that obsesses new parents and leaves everyone else completely cold. It defeats even Moira's talent for steering the topic back to her. 'Kids,' she says, knowingly, takes two bird-like sips and again, 'kids.' This annoys me even more.

'I like kids,' Ruth says. Moira looks at her blankly then looks at me, as if wanting me to agree with whatever random thought has arrived.

'I suppose it's not beyond the realms of possibility,' Moira says, meaning that it's possible for her if she wants, but not for Ruth.

'Take my advice,' I say to Ruth, 'don't listen to a thing anyone says.'

'I thought everyone wants kids – eventually,' Ruth says.

'Or gets them whether they want them or not,' Moira says.

'Don't you want kids, Moira?' I pretend to be curious. 'Your mason might have his own ideas after a hard night at the lodge with only his apron for comfort.' She shoots an accusing glance at Ruth who shakes her head. 'Keep your knickers on. Ruth didn't say anything. We can all see them skulk into the hall with their little bags. Everyone knows who they are.'

'Putting out doesn't mean putting up with kids. Ask Lolly,' she retorts.

'It would seem kind of empty,' Ruth says, 'with your house and your husband and all your things if there weren't any children.'

'You planning on finding a husband then?' She's retaliating for the fact that Ruth's paid more attention to me than her. The calculation in the remark leaves Ruth staring hurt at the carpet. None of the boys Ruth ever liked ever paid her the slightest crumb of attention with Moira around and we all knew it. Moira turns away to scan new arrivals. 'Ruth with a husband and me with kids. Like I say, nothing's beyond the realms of possibility.'

'A child isn't an accessory.' There must have been something in my tone, or volume. She turns back. Other tables are staring across.

'So you're an expert?'

'You don't have to be to know a kid isn't for decoration.'

'I'll take your word for it. I don't know either way. Maybe you've got the maternal instinct, or whatever it's called.' I can tell from her tone that this is an offer to make things up. But it's not just to keep me quiet. She loves attention, but not this kind.

'I knew it before Millie came.'

'I hope you're not going to become one of those professional mothers who bores the tits off everyone just because she's got a kid.'

A steam whistle went off in my head, while two locomotives collided to the backdrop of an atomic bomb detonating in an erupting volcano.

'Perhaps some people are just less suited to having kids than other people. Perhaps some people just have an aptitude…' Ruth tails off. She's been following the exchange like a tennis umpire. There's something pleading in her look. Moira must have seen it a hundred times and enjoyed ignoring it.

Moira says: 'Just because someone's life is ruled by a kid she chose to have, or didn't, there's no reason why it should rule everyone else's life. Folk get jealous of other folk's freedom. Lolly's got the right idea.'

I say: 'Even if you don't choose to get pregnant and do, you can choose to live up to your responsibilities. The reason Lolly isn't here is because she's looking after my daughter.'

'Good for her.' People are staring. Her mentioning Lolly annoyed me even more. She couldn't hold a candle to her.

'That's the same Lolly who turned her life upside down for a kid who isn't hers, the same Lolly who can't stand you.'

'Do you want to move on?' Ruth says into the gap between us.

'Lolly's a tart.'

'Only for the fun of it. She's not a career shagger like you.'

'What would you know about careers? Did you see one sailing past your single-parent high-rise?'

I turn to Ruth. 'I always gave her the benefit of the doubt. Lolly was right – if you don't like the look of someone there's probably something wrong with them. Only stupid people don't judge by appearances. You've got more going for you than she has. Why are you hanging around with her? She only keeps you around because it suits. Once she's settled in her bungalow with her mason, you'll be lucky to get a call once a fortnight.'

There's nothing more insulting than being ignored. Ruth understands this better than anyone. She's toying with her drink and thinking furiously. It's a new experience for Moira to be spoken about as a third wheel. She looks as if she's been slapped. When I lean forward to stand Ruth mirrors my movements. 'Coming?' I ask, hopefully. She nods. We stand. The background noise has made this a mime by now. Everyone's watching. Moira's furious. She doesn't want to be a lone woman in here because that's the kind of thing Lolly does. For the first time Ruth, her safety net, is going out a door ahead of her. She brushes past to give the impression of having taken the initiative.

'And by the by,' I shout to the whole room, 'the reason we all know he's a mason isn't because he was spotted going into the lodge. He did a turn with Lolly last month. She put on his apron when he was asleep. Keep your eye on YouTube.'

The only response is the tension in her back. There are steps up to the pavement. We arrive moments behind her, but she's already gone. The air's thick with fumes of loitering double-deckers, waiting a change in the lights. They're all going in our direction. Moira's sandwiched herself in the canyon between two, trying to wave down taxis in the outside lane and ignoring the gestures of the driver in the rear bus. Just as he slides down his side window a taxi stops. She disappears into it. The lights change. With much grinding of gears the caravan moves on.

'Moira doesn't like public transport,' Ruth says.

'That says it all. Even if you'd never met her, that glimpse would be enough. It didn't matter to her that she was holding up a bus load of people. She's gambling on the driver having more patience than she did and not crushing her skinny arse flat. She's spent her whole life gambling on the generosity of other people. Good fucking riddance.'

'She's not that bad.'

'Give me one instance of her generosity.' We stand for a minute in the dispersing fumes. People brush past. I don't know if she's stuck for an example or she's just gummed up again. 'Don't be a stupid cow all your life. Stop being loyal!' But she is loyal. She only sided with me because of the specific cruelty of tonight, and I can see that she's already prepared to forgive it. She's loyal the way Lolly's loyal, and I like her for it.

'Is that true about Lolly and the mason?'

'No. But he's a shit anyway. He tried to come on to me when I was three months gone because he thought I was desperate. Let her surf and stew. Maybe she'll have the strength of character actually to be on her own for a while. Maybe not. Maybe it's better if they stay. They deserve one another.' We fall in step. I look down at her shoes. 'I know I'm no one to talk but you really ought to do something about your appearance.'

'Moira doesn't mind.'

'*I* don't mind. *I'm* thinking of you. *Moira's* thinking of *Moira*. You know what a foil is?'

I don't know if she does but she stops and looks at me and I see a face that looks as if it's been pulled in with a drawstring. I know if I don't do something to keep the momentum going she's going to cry. I take her arm and begin walking again. 'We could let Lolly loose on you. No – ignore that. I'm just thinking aloud. Lolly could cheapen anything.'

'Lolly doesn't like me.'

'She can't stand Moira. She doesn't dislike you.'

'I've spent my life not being disliked. You have to stand out, even a little, to be disliked. Not being disliked isn't the same as being liked.'

I stop us and swivel her round to face me. 'Well stand out then.

Even a little. Take a risk. I like you. Lolly loves me. She'll come round.'

* * *

'But she's boring.'

'She's nice.'

'But she's boring.'

'Not when you get to know her.'

'How would you know? It's half past fucking *ten*. I sent you out at seven. You haven't been round her for long enough to know how boring she could become. We grew up with her and she was boring then. Boringness is like having a stutter or something. It *clings*. And it's catching. Moira's a cow but at least she's not boring.'

'If it's catching then how come Moira didn't catch it? Because you're talking crap, that's why. By the way, I told Moira you couldn't stand her.'

She makes that irritated flicking gesture. She cares even less for Moira's opinion than she does for Moira.

'Why her? Why Moira? We've always known what a selfish cow she is. Your first night out in ages and you choose her.'

'I've been asking myself that since seven o'clock.'

'Half past fucking *ten*! Three and a half fucking hours! I wanted you to come back tomorrow morning, rogered senseless by Mr Right.'

'You don't find Mr Right in three and a half hours.'

'Mr Wrong then.'

'People have different ideas of what a good night is.'

'Something's happened. You caught the wrong bus, got contaminated by those old bingo trolls and came back sixty.'

'Until I started talking to you I actually thought the night had been okay, because of what I salvaged.'

'What?'

'Ruth – of course.'

'I swear to God if there was a poker round here I'd beat you to death with it.'

'She said she would come round and babysit so that we can go out.'

'If tonight's anything to go by I don't know if I can keep up.'

But I knew she was pleased at the thought of a night out. I think she thought it was going to be the way it used to be and I didn't want to put her right – yet. Ruth was as good as her word. I thought she might go back to being one of Moira's satellites, but she didn't. She stopped being frightened of Lolly when she saw her with Millie. There's nothing more irritating than someone who tries to worm their way in by being nice to other people's kids, but Ruth took to Millie the way Lolly took to puberty.

My first night out with Lolly I go for a first pee at half past nine, and come back to find her with a man who wasn't there two minutes ago. He's stretching to put a casual arm round her waist.

'This is Tam.'

'At this rate I'll be home even earlier than last time.'

'Tam's got pals.'

'I'm sure he has.' And looking round I could spot them. All hormones and bravado. But I couldn't complain. She'd toned down her behaviour for long enough, and it suited me not to be within half a mile of the epicentre when Tam found one of her many G spots. She didn't want to let me go home alone, and I didn't want to spoil her night, so she hit on a compromise by pointing at one of Tam's pals and telling him across the room to see me to the taxi rank. He looked like Tam, typical Lolly fodder. I didn't know his name. What's sadder, I didn't want to find out. With the speed he jumped up he obviously thought him walking me to the taxi rank would have the same ending as Tam walking Lolly.

The rank was full of the usual hoi polloi you see everywhere: trogs wanting to fight; a hen party pumping out oestrogen like nerve gas, the bride-to-be wearing L plates and hiccupping like a metronome; more students, still putting the non-matriculated world to rights; a posh bird on her mobile at a volume that even drowned out the students, who kept saying 'Ciao' till she silenced the phone with a poke, only to start all over again till I wanted to slap her.

The truth is that there wasn't anything wrong with the queue any more than normal. It was me. I never wanted what Lolly wanted and somehow tonight made me feel that although, with the exception of Millie, I didn't know what I wanted, I was further away from it than ever before. Tam's pal was leaning against me in an unnecessary way, talking about his car or job or something, some crap attempt to impress, when suddenly I thought if that girl says 'Ciao' one more time it'll take an archaeologist to retrieve my shoe from her arse. The taxi arrived just in time. I body-checked him, climbed in, called out the address and watched his disappointed face slide past. We crossed the river, the strung lights on the embankment mirrored wavily in the dark water. All over this city, under this dark sky, people are eating meals, or holding hands, or being ecstatic or just watching telly and being companionable. Maybe there's a given quota of happiness, like cinema seats or minerals, and it's all booked up or mined out at the moment. I don't know what I looked like when I got home, but Ruth took one look and said 'cry if you want to,' and with no intention of doing it – I did.

I don't know if crying in front of Ruth was a watershed or not, but it seemed to work wonders for her confidence. Lolly noticed it and said I was responsible for turning her from a doormat to a lippy cow. The drawback was that they began to compete for my attention, and Millie's affection. I arrived with groceries to find them at either side of the sofa, Millie in the middle, both calling her name. She was watching the telly, ignoring them both, but that's not the point. I showed the wisdom of a Sunday-school Solomon by dropping the bag, covering her ears, and telling them both to get the fuck out my flat. Bad temper has no more effect on Lolly than bad language. We've fallen out with one another three times a day since Primary One. But Ruth looked shocked. She went out, going back to that apologetic crouch she used when following Moira around. Lolly slammed the front door with a bang that rattled the letterbox. I could hear her rage on the landing, saying they should let that ungrateful cow stew in her own juice, and is this fucking lift *still* broke? When she paused for breath I could hear Ruth say she could see my point. Lolly started again as they walked down, a rant halted by stops for breath. I'd had a change of heart by the time they reached the fifth landing, but I wasn't about to tell them that. I took a peek from the balcony. By the time they'd reached the street *they* looked companionable.

Lolly came round the next day with a packet of chocolate digestives, which is code for an apology. We didn't mention last night. I didn't hear from Ruth for a week. She sent me a letter. I'd had bills but I'd never had a letter before. Lolly was more touched than I was, not by the prose but the effort. This represented a strain on the attention span she could only guess at. Lolly thinks punctuation is embroidery, and I could see that Ruth came from the same school of thought. The letter was one sentence long, which wasn't an attempt at style, and must have cost her as much effort as it would have done Lolly. She was sorry she hadn't been as good a baby-sitter as she should have been and she understood why I was angry and she hoped Millie wasn't upset and she hoped I could see my way to letting her try again and she could understand if I'd rather not and she hoped Lolly and me would make up because she didn't want to be the cause of a friendship that long ending and I was to kiss Millie and forgive Lolly for her and it limped on like that with an 'and' at the beginning and end of every line till it wheezed itself to a standstill. Lolly, who can't read without moving her lips, began reading it out loud till she got to the part about kissing Millie and forgiving her. Her voice broke, she burst into tears and threw herself on the sofa to more catastrophic noises. I packed Millie in the pram while the purging waterworks continued. I come back to the living room to find Lolly brandishing the crumpled note.

'I hope you're satisfied. That poor – Where are you going?'

'Ruth's.'

'Can I come?'

'No.'

I left her consoling herself with the chocolate digestives. Ruth lived with her parents in a stone-built terrace in Cathcart, two miles as the crow flies, light years socially from the pre-fab high-rises most of us grew up in. It was eleven in the morning when I got there. The place had a pleasing solidity to it, not like mine, occupying a space that birds flew through thirty years ago and will again when the structural faults turn chronic. I stopped to drink it in, this perfume of leafy suburbia, when I noticed the upstairs curtains twitch. A woman, maybe sixty, looked down. She had an expression like she'd trod in dog shit and was obviously annoyed at being caught peeking. I was staring up at her staring down at me when the door opened and Ruth, whose face only ever seemed to hold back some secret worry, smiled like a sunflower and fell on Millie with an avalanche of kisses. I enjoyed watching it run its course.

'So are you going to invite us in?'

I'm shown into the parlour, as I've heard they used to call them, with Millie, while Ruth disappears elsewhere. There are net curtains, flock wallpaper and the full nine yards. One minute you're in Cathcart, the next you're in the 1970s. God knows I'm no snob, couldn't afford to be even if I wanted to, but I'm looking for string pictures and plaster ducks, symmetrically receding. I'm distracted by a movement from the hall and I see Ruth's mum, with her back to me, put something in her housecoat pocket. She does the same thing again and stands aside. Ruth comes in carrying a tea tray. There's a bowl of hot water to heat Millie's bottle, which is thoughtful, two mugs of milky tea and a *big* plate with *two* Bourbon Creams. *Two*. From her upstairs assessment the old woman has decided we aren't important enough to merit more. I feel inclined to walk out there and then but that would have defeated the purpose. Besides, walking out had already separated Ruth from Moira, and it's not as if Ruth has a social life to fall back on. Looking around I felt quite bad when I realised that depriving her of a distraction, even if it was Moira, had probably condemned her to spending more time in this museum. No wonder she was keen to babysit.

She noticed I'd noticed the miserable biscuit quota. She went red. I chatted to cover the embarrassment, studied the room some more, and looked out the back window that gave on to one of those narrow terrace-house gardens, a strip the same width as the house, that extended to the back brick wall. Half the garden seemed to have been given over to vegetables. A man in his sixties, in a comfortable looking cardigan, was tending some kind of furrowed crop with a hoe. Sensing he was being watched he looked up and smiled, one of those apologetic downward-looking smiles, till Ruth stood beside me and held up Millie. Then his face broke into the same sunflower grin we'd got minutes before on the doorstep. Like father like daughter. I defy any mother to dislike someone who shows genuine happiness at their child. A breeze lifted his comb-over like the flip lid on a sauce bottle. It's impossible to take someone with a comb-over seriously. I might have laughed. He licked his hand to slick it back and busied himself with the hoe to cover his embarrassment.

'Your dad's nice.'

The door opens and Mrs Miniver, fifty years on, enters. Either she was wearing the full regalia under the house coat or she's managed a remarkably quick change. 'What a delightful child,' she says. It looks to me like she's evaluating the pram rather than taking Millie in. I'm wondering if 'delightful' is a word often bandied about in Cathcart, or it's one of the set pieces. There follows a couple of minutes of idle chit chat that involves some blushing on Ruth's part, and almost nothing on mine. The few questions she does ask are put in just for the sake of form. This is a one-way story. I learn in minutes that she's a grammar-school girl and that she met Dennis, the poor bastard with the hoe, at the Borough Hall dance. She makes it all sound like good Christian fun, but it's obvious she hasn't a Christian bone in her body. I'm nodding every ten seconds to show I'm listening; while trying to work out her age against Ruth's. If she married late it's possible she had to. She breaks off to go to the window and make some kind of secret gesture, because Dennis comes in and starts nodding faster than I am, like one of those toy dogs on the parcel shelf going over bumps. She starts talking about the garden, mentioning one or two plans. He's obviously been called in to do lots of agreeing. It's hard to reconcile her ambitions with the view from the window. She makes it sound like Hampton Court Palace, instead of the little suburban khaki strip, exactly the same as all its neighbours.

I'm astonished. Why does she feel the need to impress a single mother she's thought fit to allocate only one Bourbon Cream to? It could be that she's so starved of company that any chance to talk about herself is welcome. The more likely explanation is that it's automatic, a role she can't help herself adopt, like a comic-book hero in times of crisis. The doorbell rings, she slaps on the emergency make-up, and steps out of the house coat already in costume: Genteel Suburban Woman. Dennis and Ruth are exchanging sympathetic glances, and I can see the obvious affection there. There's an old car at the front door. The sofa, although ten times better than mine, is threadbare through the cap sleeves. The vegetables in the back garden aren't cosmetic. Whether she's intended to or not she's set out her stall: Dennis hasn't provided the lifestyle a grammar-school girl can reasonably expect, and Ruth's an obvious disappointment to her. Poor Ruth – small tits, big bum, manic mum.

The Bourbon Creams are long finished and the plate stays unreplenished. I stand up while she's still in full flood and use Millie as the excuse to leave, which is feeble, because she's asleep. The mother looks momentarily hurt. It hasn't occurred to her that other people aren't riveted by the sad story of her life falling short of her aspirations. Welcome to the club. I came here to talk to Ruth, not to be at the receiving end of some middle-class lament. Dennis seizes the chance to return to his vegetables. Ruth gets her coat, promising to get us to the right bus. Without a potential audience Ruth's mum loses interest in me and my delightful child quicker than Nick did.

'Your dad's nice,' I repeat, once we're out of earshot of the front door. She pulls one of those rueful smiles which causes one of those tiny, mid-stride desolations in me. We both know what I mean, and suddenly I like her mother even less, because it occurs to me that that fucked-up overbearing old snob might have established some kind of prototype in Ruth's mind. Why else put up with Moira? I'm thinking as I'm walking, and looking at Millie's beautiful hands, everything in miniature, dimpled knuckles. Sometimes I just hold them up for the wonder of them. As usual Ruth's keeping quiet and I look up to see, not the bus stop but the vista of her future: an ageing virgin in Cathcart looking after two increasingly doddery parents. A dad who will thank her with his eyes and a mum whose resentment will keep pace with her dependence. She isn't obviously pretty. What's good and attractive in her needs to be drawn out. She needs to circulate or she'll wither behind the twitching curtains. It's curious that I can see the panorama of other people's lives and yet, since Millie arrived, the view of my own future stops short at the next pair of shoes Millie will need.

'You know that Lolly's somehow managed to get a flat downstairs from me?'

'Yes.'

'Well she thinks she can afford it but she can't.' We pause at the bus stop. She stays silent. At this rate the bus might come before she picks up the hint. 'I'm gambling on the fact that you work shifts.' Still no recognition. 'For God's sake, Ruth, I'm suggesting that you and Lolly might try sharing. Lolly plus no one equals eviction in three months. Lolly plus you together all day equals one of you being dead by the end of the week, and my money would be on Lolly surviving. Lolly and you keeping separate hours, and agreeing whose turn it is to do the dishes and buy toilet paper, just might work.'

'I don't know...'

'It would be a trial period. You might not like it. She might not agree.'

'I don't know...'

The bus rounds the corner catching the low autumn sun in a string of flashing panes. I can feel Millie about to wake. This is it, I thought, a casual mid-morning exchange at a suburban bus stop, this is one of the pivotal moments in Ruth's life, and if it isn't settled by the time the bus arrives then the moment will have gone and she'll go back and fossilise.

'What else is there for you? That?' I point to the terrace. 'You'll die in instalments.' It's brutal. The bus is imminent.

'Yes,' she breathes, and then covers her mouth as if catching herself speaking treason.

'She might say no,' I caution, picking up Millie and collapsing the pram in one motion.

* * *

'No!' It's a bark that comes back before I'm finished the sentence.

'You can't do this on your own.'

'You did.'

'I had help from the Social, and a lot of nicked stuff, and you.'

'I'll get help from the Social.'

'You need a kid, or one on the way, to qualify for the kind of help I got. You're not their priority. I'll help as much as I can, but I can't spend the time on you that you did on me. I've got Millie. Look, I'm trying to put this as nicely as possible, but you're not a whole person.'

'Pardon me all over the place. What the fuck are you talking about?'

'What I mean is that you're not a whole person *yet*. You're the fun side magnified, and you can only be that way because other people do for you the things you don't want to do for yourself, things everyone eventually does for themselves. You think you're independent, but you're not. You eat at your parents. You eat here. You've never cooked anything in your life except pot noodles, and you don't know what anything costs. I'm not saying you're not generous – you're *too* generous. You're generous the way only a person who doesn't look after themselves can afford to be. When you think I'm short of stuff you go out and buy things, and it's a load of tat. Three dozen Jaffa Cakes isn't a balanced diet.'

I can see tears well. They're only partly genuine. She wants me to join in. This is all too close to home for comfort. I resist for her sake. I produce a pad and a pen and force her to sit and make up a list of her potential expenses. She always slumps at the prospect of writing, and her bottom lip shunts out like a cash register. It's the same pose as the nine-year-old I'd to pass the arithmetic answers to. Watching her write is torture. I could *inscribe* faster. She finishes, slams the pen down and leans forward, head on crossed forearms resting on the table. She can dance, drink and fornicate till the cleaning staff arrive, but any kind of mental exercise exhausts her. I slide the paper out from under her.

'What kind of employment do you imagine you'll have to get to fund this?'

'Dunno. Vet? I like animals?'

'You have to go to university to be a vet. And you have to pass exams to go to university. And you have to write fluently to pass exams.'

'Well, something else then.' To be fair to her she's not work shy.

'I'd say that's advisable. Lower your horizons a bit. And this list,' holding it up, 'leaves a few things out.'

'Such as?'

'Such as furniture –'

'Your dad's pals can nick it for me.'

'Such as furniture, that can't all be nicked or why would I be lumbered with this rubbish? Such as food, and rent, and gas, and the electric. Do you want me to go on? We'll just insert a few figures there then shall we?' She studies the totalled accounts over my shoulder. 'Your business plan's right down the toilet, and I haven't even included anything for social activities. If you get a half-decent job that's wildly beyond your capabilities you might *just* make ends meet if you stay in every night.'

'As long as she understands and we follow my rules.'

'And what rules are they? Pay up, wash the dishes and leave the living room free in case you want a shag on the hearthrug?'

'Pretty much.'

'She's been put upon her whole life. I didn't suggest this just so she can become your unpaid domestic. She's not going to replace the other people who do all the things you don't want to, to let you stay the way you are. You'll have to change, both of you. Be nice.'

'We'll see.'

'I mean it.'

And I did mean it. It was a kinder calculation than either of them knew. Ruth alone would contract round a routine of rust that would last till she was eaten by her cats. Lolly alone would live the life of a porn movie in fast forward till she combusted. I thought they might complement one another. I also had hopes for Ruth. Not all the men Lolly comes in contact with are the usual fodder. I'd an image in my mind of some quiet sidekick of Lolly's latest, drinking a solitary lager in the living room, while Lolly and his mate pummel the bedsprings next door. This lonely guy would be a satellite, like Ruth, and they'd meet and exchange shy 'hello's to a backdrop of Lolly's shrieking instructions, and Ruth would meticulously plate the chocolate digestives, to avoid eye contact, and they'd stammer out cringing small talk, and he'd strain every last sinew of his confidence to ask for her phone number, and they'd lay the groundwork for something meaningful and permanent, while Lolly comes like a factory steam whistle through the plywood partition. It's probably telling that most of my long term plans and kindest aspirations are for other people.

The first week they had about four spats which consisted of Lolly storming upstairs, bursting in, waking Millie and saying things like 'You'll never guess what she's gone and fucking done *now*!' And I never did guess, because it was usually something as trivial as Ruth storing the brillo pad under the sink, which wasn't really the reason but the excuse, because something else, probably nothing to do with Ruth or the flat, had annoyed her, and all it took was one tiny, unpredictable trigger.

'You're a human being, Lolly, not a bear with furniture. She's the most accommodating person you're ever going to get. You'll have to learn to get on.'

At which point her allegiances would instantly reverse, and she'd storm downstairs to a dismayed Ruth, and I could practically hear, welling up through the gaps in the linoleum 'You'll never guess what she's gone and fucking told me to do *now*!'

The interruptions tailed off, and the two of them settled into a kind of quiet mistrust, that neither would admit grew into friendship. Lolly can't be alone for any length of time. Her reliance on me borders on unhealthy. I've always known. I've never minded and I've always coped for the two of us but now with Millie as a priority I needed some help. I was glad of Ruth, as much to divert a bit of the attention. And there was another good consequence for me. I took advantage of the offers to babysit. I needed to work, and not just for the money. I needed something else beyond the round of toddler group, groceries, flat. Ruth worked mostly back shift. Lolly's attempts to find work hadn't yet paid off, probably because of her total lack of any qualifications. I organized a rota that allowed me to work part time.

I applied for a job offering loans over the phone. It was the kind of company that boasted how they got clients from all walks of life. Criminal records of potential customers didn't put *them* off them. Neither did the fact that the hapless bastards had been turned down by everyone else. The voice-over, on their telly advert, speeded up at the last part, like the commentator on the final furlong. It was the verbal equivalent of small print, the part that reveals the eye-watering interest rate, and the fact that your house *will* be taken away from you when you default. And the sad bastards always do. The guy who interviewed me looked about fifteen. From the job description it seemed to me that all it involved was assessing the gullibility of the poor morons who called, and distributing the leads to the sales people. The interview room was shabby, and that's the part they *let* you see.

'Can I see the workplace?'

He looked shocked, mumbled something, disappeared, came back and waved me to follow. It turned out the interview room is the garden spot of the place. The area was open plan. There was only one office, and that had glass walls so that the whip-cracker inside, a balding flat bloke with a crumpled shirt, could look out. Most of the people at the desks were on their feet. 'House rule,' says the teenager, 'you take the call standing so he,' nodding towards the fishbow, 'can see who's working.'

I'm not claiming to be a saint but I'd some misgivings, even before I arrived, about selling expensive money to the people who can't afford it. The appearance of this place didn't dispel my doubts.

The woman on her feet nearest me had a kind of pleading look on her face, there's no other way to put it, and you just *knew* that if she didn't con some even sadder bastard and make her target she's out, just like you knew that the guy behind the glass would grope you in the stationery cupboard.

'No thanks.'

The next interview was a music shop in town. My idea of a music shop is a place pumping volcanic noise into the street with most of the customers my age or younger. I dressed accordingly, that is to say in the only kind of clothes I own. The place had thick carpets not flattened with chewing gum. I felt my clothes looked gaudy and cheap, probably because they were. There were two girls on the other side of the counter who looked as if they'd come straight from the gymkhana. They had that kind of money smell you just can't buy. But they smiled at me, the quiet lift I needed as I followed the guy leading me into the back office. They were using this as an interview room. There was a woman in her fifties, and a late twenties early thirties man sitting the other side of a small low table. The middle-aged man who'd shown me through waved me to a vacant chair with a posh 'please' before joining the others at the other side of the table.

'Reminds me of the children's panel.' This was met with a blank silence. The younger guy kept staring at my clothes. The older guy gathered himself.

'What do you know about music?'

'Nothing. At least nothing about what *you'd* call music. How much do you need to know? This isn't a mega store. I thought the punters browsing in here would have a good idea of what they're looking for. I didn't think anyone impulse shopped for a sonata.' It happens to me sometimes. I'm seized by nerves and can't stop, no safety net between brain and gob. 'No offence, but why do you need to know? You don't need to know about Mars Bars or lentils or whatever to sell *them*.'

'But… there's a qualitative difference…' This from the older guy.

'Maybe so. I don't know anything about that and I imagine Zoë and Philippa don't either.' This is probably the nearest I'll approach an out of body experience.

'Who?'

'The two girls out there – whatever they're called. They're not exactly hard on the eye. You're not telling me *they* got the job because they know loads about classical music.'

They all look toward the older guy and so do I, and pick up the family resemblance. I now have nothing to lose. He clears his throat. 'We're not saying it's essential but it wouldn't be a handicap.' He has a fruity BBC Royal Correspondent delivery.

'I can't sew to save myself but I sold more stuff in my last place than anyone else.'

'I didn't see that on your CV.'

'I don't have a CV. I wrote a letter. If I did have a CV it would have been shorter still.'

The younger guy clears his throat too. His pose mirrors the older guy's. 'We called her in on the strength of the letter.' He hands this across and his finger taps the top corner, pointing at the Bridgeton address I'm guessing.

'Reference?' asks the woman.

'If you phone Tommy I'm sure he'll vouch for me. He might not be as quick to commit himself to paper. Most of it was on the black.'

'Black?'

'Black economy,' the younger guy translates.

'If you give me a chance I'll do my best to punt shed-loads of that classical stuff. That's really all I can say.' And it was.

The woman smiled at me kindly. 'We'll let you know.' The girls were equally kind on the way out. One of them looked at my top and said she couldn't have gotten away with it. I think she was sincere.

I anticipated a letter, the kind that arrives on bonded paper and begins 'We regret...' I gave it a week. Still nothing. In my book that's just plain rude. The following Tuesday I just *happened* to be passing with Millie and I wheeled her in. I wouldn't normally take a pram into town, but I wanted to make a point. Precisely what point I'm not sure.

'We expected you yesterday,' one of the girls said.

'You're expected to turn up to get turned down?'

'Simon offered you the job.'

'First I heard.'

'We tried to reach you on the number you put in your letter. We left a message and a text asking you to come in.'

My mobile is pay-as-you-talk, and I've been too broke to top it up. They offered to look after Millie while I went into the back to apologise. Simon turned out to be the younger guy. I think he didn't commit the offer to paper because a text was his small revolt against their ancient procedures. He agreed I could start a week late.

* * *

I'd been in the shop for a fortnight before I realised the thing that distinguished most of our customers – beards. Perhaps you can't really appreciate classical music without one, which is tough for women. I had a secret theory that a lot of them *pretended* to like it because they think it's the right thing to do, like those wankers who pretend to like modern art. Having said that, most of them were nice. They weren't the type I've met before who would try and grope you *and* shoplift at the same time. They were patient with my inexperience. They asked me my first name and didn't forget it. They seemed disproportionately grateful when I returned the favour. They said my 'frocks' were 'pretty'. They kind of patronised without realising they were doing it. In a completely disarming moment, in relation to nothing at all, one showed me a picture of his grown-up daughter and asked me about Millie. I gushed. He nodded, holding on to the CD racks, and then he walked right out without a backward glance. Simon told me she'd died. I cried on the top deck the whole way home. After a month he still hadn't overcome his embarrassment enough to come in. I found his address from our mailing list and sent him a note, saying there was buy one get one free on Rachmaninoff. He came in, smiled sadly, and said he couldn't see the offer on display.

'I lied,' I said.

The worst were the jazz fans, or, as Simon called them, 'aficionados', who could sit in a booth for half an hour and listen to a noise that sounded like someone sawing a trombone in half. This, one explained, was an 'improvised set'. The soloist was a 'genius'. I agreed. Anyone who can lure hard cash for those emperor's new clothes isn't stupid. Even the jazz types weren't that bad. In fact I liked most of them too.

I laid out my stall to the girls on the first day. Gabrielle, shortened to Gabby, and Naomi, that couldn't really be shortened (it had to be names like that, when you come to think about it – no one with that kind of expensive teeth work is going to be called Agnes). 'Look, girls,' I said 'I'm not going to hold it against you just because you grew up with money and wield the right cutlery.' They took this in the spirit it was intended. It didn't take a genius to work out that neither of them was overburdened with brains. Daddy and Mummy probably spent the price of a car each year on their education. They were probably getting French verbs drummed into them while mum was getting fucked across sacks of polenta, and you have to go some, with that amount of coaching, to wind up in a shop you don't own – or at least manage. They both looked like toothpaste adverts. They both smoked and swore with poise. They had a style, bought early enough to look natural, and even if they were shit thick they knew enough to know that. And although it sounds terrible, I got the impression that in the eyes of the customers they were interchangeable. Ask either and you're going to get the same well-pronounced useless reply.

It turned out that Gabby knew the owner. In fact it was her dad, the older guy at the interview. I never found out who the woman was. Naomi's dad was a friend of Gabby's dad. They probably went fly-fishing, or truffle-hunting, or some other posh thing together. Neither girl could sell a thing. They never knew where anything was. All their organisational skills were used up turning up on time with the teeth and the hair and the skin.

A point that's been brought to my attention more than once is that my intelligence is chronically underestimated by people who don't know me. If it's anyone's fault it must be mine more than theirs, because they change and the general opinion doesn't. It might be because I don't have any qualifications to speak of. Or it might be because I speak in a simpler way than I think. *Or* it might *possibly* be that I'm the feral product of an absent mum and an alcoholic dad, left to drag herself up in a council high-rise, with no idea of how to act or dress except what I've picked up on the hoof. New people take one look and usually underestimate me. But Simon took a look and he didn't underestimate me.

Within a few weeks of me starting Simon grew a beard – of sorts. I remember the physics teacher at school put up a picture of Einstein, the famous one with the electric hair. You'd need to be a bona-fide, twenty-four-carat genius to get away with hair like that. He did. His hair looked like a by-product of all that mental energy. It's the same with beards. Darwin could carry a beard. Simon couldn't. It wasn't even a proper Old Testament beard. It looked more like the kind they use to advertise facial trimmers, the type vain wankers grow to look cultivated. I might have kept my opinion to myself if he hadn't surprised me. I was doing a stock check, and sighing for something I could recognise as music, when I straightened and he was right *there*.

'Fuck me, a musketeer. You must be pathos.'

He looked startled, touched his chin and disappeared as quietly as he'd arrived. On castors. The next day he's clean shaven. 'Suits you better.' He went through the mime of pretending not to understand, as if my joke and his shave were a coincidence.

Gabby told me I got away with murder. Gabby had the hots for Simon. Anyone could see it, the way anyone with a shred of intelligence could see that nothing was going to come of it. He had an easy number, listening to music, dabbling with work and acting posh in the company of two big-bosomed lame-brains he could enjoy feeling superior to. He wasn't about to risk all that for a poke at the boss's daughter, or even the boss's best pal's daughter. Besides, there was something else about Simon. He chose his words *too* carefully, and he was careful to pronounce them all. Like I said, I speak in a simpler way than I think, but that's not the impression I got from the girls. They employed their full vocabulary, and it wasn't impressive. They made this noise when they didn't know what to say, which was often, that sounded like a small engine idling. Or they could say 'Yesssssss...' for five fucking seconds. It's the arrogance of people who assume you've got all the time in the world to listen to them form a thought. I didn't get the impression there were any profound nuggets struggling to get out. They both did it, even to each other, and neither realised. He tried to be like them, but he was too clever and didn't start early enough.

He wasn't bad looking, and despite my lack of self-confidence he didn't seem to think I was that hard on the eye either. All that attention that Gabby craved came my way. And we had reason to be together. I think the unspoken bargain with the 'management', in other words Gabby's dad, was that the girls were the cosmetic lure. Once they'd attracted the punters they'd filled their part of the bargain. I wasn't employed for my dress sense, and it suited me to work. I'm easily bored. I reorganised things the way I had in the last place, and he found every reason to stand near me. I can't say I minded. It had been a long time since Quick Nick, and my confidence about my appearance was at a bit of a low ebb. He suggested I develop a taste for music 'with substance', and when I asked why he said it 'might better qualify' me to sell it. I bit back the obvious about the girls because I was flattered by his interest. My neglected ego, that abandoned car with the poked-in windows, coughed a few times and trundled itself off the waste ground. Lolly noticed it.

'Why the make up?'

'I'm going to work.'

'What's his name?'

'Why does it have to be a man?'

'Because you used to go to work looking like one of those women protestors living in a tent outside a missile base, and you're answering a question with a question.'

Simon pretended to educate me and I pretended to be impressed by his Sunday supplement sophistication. But there were certain things I couldn't let pass.

'Don't tell me you *like* jazz.'

'What's wrong with jazz?'

'No one *really* likes jazz. They only *pretend* to like jazz.'

'It can have its merits.'

'What kind of answer is that? Your arse must get sore.'

'How do you mean?'

'Sitting on that fence. Jazz is the emperor's new clothes. People *pretend* to like it because they're frightened of missing what other people *pretend* to appreciate.'

'There's not much room for doubt in your scheme of things, is there?'

'There's not enough time. I don't have the energy not to mean what I say.'

And so it went on like that for a couple of months. He found more reasons for being with me. He asked my opinion on the smooth running of the shop, which was easy, and then went on to ask my opinion on anything else that happened to occupy his mind, which was nicer still. Given I was the only part-time employee, I had a disproportionate effect on the running of the place, and he seemed to think that because I was competent at this I'd be competent at other things too. He'd find me, hand across a mug of coffee I hadn't asked for, unfold *The Times* and point out – well, anything – from another crop failure in Africa to dwindling literacy rates in the Home Counties. And I'd have to abandon whatever I was doing and muster some half-baked opinion. And he'd look at me while I was talking, and I'd know he was listening, really listening, not focusing on my tits and taking inventory the way most men do when they pretend to listen. And it was as if he was always struggling with the problem of my appearance, this diamond in the rough.

He never made the girls coffee or asked their opinion on anything. Gabby accepted defeat gracefully, and I was tempted to console her with the fact that there wasn't anything in it, we weren't going anywhere. If I didn't have Millie I might have thrown caution to the wind and asked him out, even though work relationships are a bad idea. A child in the picture changes everything. Nothing's ever really casual after that, unless you're a parent like one of mine. I was reconciled to it stagnating into friendly chit-chat, till he found someone else, when he asked me out. It caught me completely flat-footed.

'I'll have to arrange a sitter.' He looked blank. 'For Millie.'

'Millie?'

'My daughter.'

'Of... of course...' he looked confused, as if I'd just invented her as an excuse not to go out with him.'

'She's the person I talk about all the time. The reason I only work part-time.'

He looked relieved, as if she'd just been wheeled into the shop like some court exhibit to prove a point.

'Well of course you must find a sitter for Millie.' And he smiled. And I had an image of him pushing a supermarket trolley with her in it while I chose posh biscuits from an aisle that stretched on for miles that didn't sell anything else. And we all smile at my choice.

Lolly offered me the loan of any of her outfits. I'd have looked like a starved tart. Ruth said I could try any of hers. The most alluring thing she had looked like a tent with a drawstring. I went out and bought a classic short black dress. Ruth, God bless her, said I looked like Audrey Hepburn. I humoured her and said the resemblance was uncanny: Holly Golightly, except not quite as good looking, living as a single parent in a Bridgeton high-rise. I'd still been expressing milk for Millie on the days I worked. Most of my bras were maternity washed-out hammocks. Lolly can identify a cup size on a moving bus at a hundred yards. She arrived with a present. 'It's a front-loader, rounds them up and herds them out. You'll actually have a cleavage. Spray some perfume in between so he can stick his face down there and draw up a lungful – works for me.'

They both arrived at five on Saturday evening, having struck a truce in the middle of one of their on-going arguments, to boost my confidence. I was already nervous, and the sight of this alliance for my sake made me worse. The three of us together gave the situation a seriousness it shouldn't have had. If you hang around Lolly for any length of time some of her reputation rubs off. But despite what the rumour mill might have thrown up, I haven't had many boyfriends. Two one-nighters. The only man I've had sex with more than once is Nick. Here was a chance maybe to start something with someone who might actually care for *me*. It was the only offer I'd had, beside the kind of bottom-feeders who see single mothers as an easy mark. The very worst thing I could do would be to let him know how much tonight meant to me. Maybe all the poor boy wanted was a meal in company. Lolly broke the silence with 'It's only a date,' walking up to me and spraying perfume she'd found in the bathroom down my new cleavage. Ruth found something to occupy her at the window. She'd never been on a date and there wasn't one on the foreseeable horizon. I knew *exactly* what she was thinking: people are meeting people and no one's meeting me. I wanted to squeeze her hand and break a plate over Lolly. Millie stirred. I wiped off the perfume and gave her a last feed. Lolly left on 'only a date', using up yet another of the finite meetings of this night. Ruth stood at the door, making small talk while I waited for the lift on the landing. It pinged on arrival. I told the surprised old lady inside to hold the door and rushed back to kiss her.

My heart was hammering on the bus. I got off two stops early to feel the air on my face and calm myself, walking through another metropolitan sunset, the sandstone buildings drinking in the last of the light. He was waiting at the bar. It was an Italian place, one wall covered by a kind of mediaeval painting that looked as if it had been done by Disney. They had a display of straw Chianti bottles that would have driven Dad berserk with rancour at the memory. He was perched on the edge of a stool, wearing clothes that looked as new as mine. His cologne hit me from about five feet, and I was heartened by the thought that he might be as nervous as I was. Our overlapping smells made a passing waiter blink. When I was about to sit on a stool he took my arm and steered me to one of the booths. He could have pointed. He didn't need to touch me. There was a good electricity. He sat with his back to the wall. I had a view of the mural. From the size of his pupils I could tell he'd already had a few. My spirits rose even more.

'Funny looking painting. Punch and Judy... or something...' I'd started talking about something I knew nothing about and I was aware my hands were moving too much, like at the interview. Short of sitting on them I didn't feel able to stop them.

'Pantalone. He's one of the stock characters of the Commedia dell'arte.'

'Fancy.'

'The soap of its day.'

'*Emmerdale* for serfs.'

Gesturing at absolutely nothing, I managed to knock over the little glass vase with cut flowers in water. He tried to right it and made matters worse. Then there was twenty seconds of confusion, while we shouted apologies at one another, and the staff replaced the cloth and the water-logged breadsticks. I ordered a gin and sucked it down in one noisy gulp before the waiter had moved two paces.

'Again, please.'

'Do you want wine too?' Simon asked, smiling.

'What the hell – you choose.'

The waiter hovered to prevent further breakages, recited the specials and offered advice. I smiled non-committally. He took the hint and drifted away. I confided in Simon.

'I can navigate round an Italian menu because my mum fucked off with an Italian waiter.'

'I'll have to manage best I can without those qualifications.'

When the wine arrived he sniffed the cork. You could tell they weren't impressed, given it was one up from the house plonk. I think sniffing the cork is the equivalent of kicking the tyres in a garage – they'll rub their hands and double the bill. This sophistication was wearing thinner by the minute, which made me feel even better. I ordered artichoke salad, followed by spaghetti and clams, and swallowed the wine in big thirsty gulps. He seemed to enjoy the sight. I don't know if it was for the thing itself or for the fact that I didn't pay any attention to etiquette. Ever since Mum and her fake Latin lover I can't take Italian restaurants seriously.

'Millie would like that,' I said, nodding towards the mural.

'It's strange, I only ever see you arrive alone. I don't think of you as a mother.'

'But that's the one thing I think of myself as, more than anything else. First and foremost. I'm not *just* that...'

'I didn't mean to offend.'

'You didn't.'

'After all, you don't *look* like a mother.'

'How does a mother look?'

'Not like someone who could get away with that dress.'

I could feel a blush rise up from my new cleavage, and turned my attention to the dessert trolley. They actually had a trolley that they wheeled across. I attacked the tiramisu while he watched, and then I took the initiative and ordered us both espresso and grappa. They were pushed for tables and asked if we'd mind drinking at the bar, where they'd throw in another grappa. We went back to where he'd been standing and sat on high stools, knee to knee. I started tittering at nothing. The espresso would have woken the dead, and I felt my heart lurch when it hit my bloodstream. Then I knocked back the grappas. It was stupid really. I'd wanted to savour the minute and now I'd used up the reason for sitting there. He finished his and suggested we could go on elsewhere for another.

'I can't. Well I can't have any more to drink. I'm still feeding Millie. I've had too much already. I feel like an arse, saying all that stuff about first and foremost...'

Perhaps we'd given the impression we were leaving because they appeared with our jackets. I automatically took mine and we found ourselves out on the pavement by ten. Then there was that awful bit I always hate, when you both stand not knowing whether to risk an invitation. I stood it for three seconds, and was about to throw my hat into the ring when he beat me to it.

'Would you like to come back to mine?'

'I – I would. But I've got to think about Millie's next feed and the babysitter. Why don't we go back to mine?'

He smiled. My heart took another espresso lurch. He lifted his hand and conjured a cab from over my shoulder, like a coin from behind an ear. I gave the address and we crossed the river again, back in the direction I'd come from, sitting forward to see the lights reflected in the water. It's another sight, like sunset, I never tire of. But as I kept looking out I noticed something I hadn't noticed before: the lighted window displays, and bars and restaurants growing scarcer as the spaces between buildings became the rule and not the exception, gaps filled with rubble and sprouting vegetation – broken teeth on the parade. And aside from the mosaic of lights from the high-rises, the only illumination is the sodium street lighting.

In the time it took me to eat a meal the lift had broken. I've hauled a pram up the stairs without seeing them the way I was seeing them now, with him beside me. And there was the strata of smells, fried food, stale piss and God knows what. Ruth was on her feet at the first sound of the key in the lock, standing in the hall as if intercepting a burglar. She went all shy, as I did the introductions, so I pointed him towards the living room. The kitchen's large enough for one person to stand in as long as you don't open the cutlery drawer at the same time. She followed me in as I searched the fridge for something for him to drink. She stood, almost touching me, vibrating with suspense.

'Isn't it stupid, I never bought anything for him to drink. I never saw him back here. But then I suppose I must have, unconsciously. Why else the good underwear I wouldn't mind being run over in?'

'Who are you talking to?'

'You. Me. *I* don't know.'

'What happened?'

'He's here. That's what happened. And he didn't allow me to pay for anything. Maybe he thinks the more he forks out the better the chance of getting his end away. I could have told him to save his money.'

'Why?'

'Why do you think? The last man who noticed me was Nick and it turned out he was only paying attention to himself. *He*,' I point through the wall, 'likes *me*.' I pointed at my cleavage. 'I'm taking every precaution science can devise, but it's going to take a fucking earthquake to stop sex happening in this flat tonight.'

'He might not want to have sex.'

'Lack of experience aside, and no offence intended, unless you crawled out of a flower, when have you ever head of a man not wanting to have sex?'

'You're shouting. He might hear.'

'I don't care. I'm home. He's here. I'm fed up being nervous and lonely. How was Millie? Hold on a minute.' Underneath half-rotted broccoli I found part of Dad's cache, three cans of cheap corner-shop lager. I wiped one clean, and delivered it with a spew of froth that swiped his groin. I absently wiped the mound of his tackle till I realised what I was doing, apologised and ran back to the kitchen. Once I'd heard Millie was fine I led Ruth to the door, picking up her stuff on the way.

'I hope it goes all right. Come down with Millie tomorrow and see me.'

I gave her the second impulsive kiss of the night through the closing door. If Lolly had asked me to come down she'd have demanded a blow-by-blow anatomical account of Simon's technique. Ruth meant it in a misty lens, flowers and chocolates kind of a way. I leaned my back against the closed door and thought for a second about how some people are too nice for this world, took a deep breath, plumped up my tits and strode into the living room. He was crouching over my music collection, that I play on my stolen stereo, trying to hide the wet stain in his trousers. I sat on the sofa, waiting for him, posing myself to look sophisticated. Realising I lacked a drink to complete the effect, I stood just as he sat down to yet more catastrophic noises from the upholstery. This sounded structural. Remembering I couldn't have another drink I put the kettle on. When I came back with a second beer I sat down as gently as I could. The sofa groaned again and gave up any pretence of lumbar support. We lolled together in the saggy bit. 'Two frogs in a lily pad,' I said. He just smiled. 'Cosy,' I said. His smiled widened. 'Do you want me to open your beer?'

'No thanks. I can pour it over my testicles all by myself.'

He put his arm round me, taking advantage of the dynamics of the sofa, reaching over my shoulder and taking my breast in his right hand.

'I see you're employing the cinema technique tonight. A bit previous isn't it?'

'Are you complaining?'

'No. There's another one here too.'

'I noticed.'

I swivelled round to kiss him. With more skill than I'd have given him credit for he unclipped the front loader and slid his hands in. A few seconds later he slid them back out looking worried.

'Sorry,' I said. 'Leakage. I thought I'd given Millie enough but I seem to be producing more.' He looked at my breasts as if they were water cannon, pointing at him. I had the strangest feeling that the romance of the moment had been lost and I had to do something, decisive and tender, right now, to get it back. The wail from the bedroom started right on cue.

'Sorry,' I said again, heaving myself up from the synthetic pit. He stood too and I left him for a moment, contemplating the corpse of the sofa. Millie was lying with her eyes wide open. She latched on like a docking spacecraft. I gave her a few minutes and then moved her across to the other. The kettle rose to a slow boil. It's not electric. It's a whistler, something you could identify in the pitch dark a hundred years from now. I was hoping she'd finish before it became too insistent, but I had to move through to turn off the noise. He obviously had the same thought. He caught me in the hall. My dress was still undone, my front-loader open. Millie was sucking rhythmically and there was a pearl of milk on the other nipple. For some reason she jerked away. Perhaps he thought that there was a single jet, a feeding syringe, not the sprinkler arrangement that showered the side of her face till she turned back and latched on with the same suddenness. He stopped dead and took all this in. I reached into the kitchen, shut off the noise, wiped her cheek and covered up. When I looked at him again he seemed morose, studying the patchy linoleum, a mosaic of off-cuts running back to the living room with its ridiculous furniture, and it was as if he was weighing up the pros and cons and calculating whether a fuck was worth the squalor and the consequences.

'I – I'm sorry...' he said. 'I'm really sorry. This is all too much reality to take at one sitting.'

'What do you want me to do, expose you in instalments? Maybe I could wheel the sofa into the shop and you could practice sitting on it a couple of times without the whole fucking ambience.' The instant I swore I knew it was a mistake.

'I'm sorry. It's not just...' and he gestured in a vague way to indicate the whole fucking ambience. 'Then there's the baby...'

'But there's always been the baby. You knew about the baby when you asked me out.'

'Yes... but. There's knowing and there's *knowing*. I didn't really...'

'I shouldn't have sworn. I'm sorry. She'll settle in a minute and we can both have some tea.'

'I'm sorry.'

'You don't have to keep apologising.'

'I made a mistake. A mistake.' He looked down, not wanting to meet my eye, and reached for his jacket at the same time.

'Please. Don't go. Not like this. If you still feel the same way in five minutes...'

It didn't stop him. All that supposed passion, dwindling to the offer of a cup of tea and a plea not to be left alone. He wouldn't look back and said sorry at least twice more. In his hurry to go he accidentally slammed the front door. It didn't catch and ricocheted open. I stood at the entrance, listening to his feet on the stairs, till

I heard the bang of the lobby door echo up the stairwell. Millie fed throughout, her sucking amplified by the concrete acoustics.

She fell asleep still latched on. I put her down and went to pick up the dead cans from the living room. I looked at the sofa. With the exception of Millie, the only good thing to have happened to me, this broken ugly thing seemed to epitomise my life to date. I wouldn't let someone else's opinion of me form my view of myself, but I'm looking around and I saw what he saw. Someone I thought me and Millie might just have had a future with looked at me and my situation, totalled the sum of my parts and decided that I add up to the square root of fuck all. And right now I can't pretend to myself that it doesn't hurt.

# PART 2

When he wakes these mornings Christopher can feel the weight of his organs. When he has time to reflect, which is all the time he has, Christopher has contemplated the aggregate weight of his parts, and concluded that he is mediaeval. In that blissful moment, when the return to consciousness is unforced, Christopher is now obliged to take stock. He knows *who* he is but mentally reconnoitres to establish *where* he is. This is a relatively recent phenomenon. Thousands of previous mornings didn't require orientation. Age has cast him frivolously adrift, a trailing fair-ground balloon grasped too late.

He notes, with renewed surprise, that he has slept only on his allotted side, despite having the mattress to himself. Solitude has not yet accustomed him to the expanse. With an automatic gesture he retrieves his bedside glasses and the room swims into milky focus. He imagines himself on the other side of the gauze curtains, suspended above the dewy lawn, ascending like the truant balloon. And in that retreat the context of his diminishing world would be revealed, like a child entering his address in an exercise book: suburban street, near London, England, Britain, the World, the Solar System, the Milky Way, the Universe.

Movement is the order of the day. And it has become an order. The automatic transition of impulse to motion has gradually become a thing of the past. Now it requires the marshalling of forces. 'And that's another thing...' Christopher says aloud to himself. The other thing is the previously invisible functions of his body which now clamour for attention. Previously Christopher considered his body, if he considered it at all, to be like a seaworthy ocean liner. Provisions were taken on board and the rest saw to itself. The boilers were stoked, the propellers turned, a multitude of things went on below decks, without supervision or consciousness, and the ship sailed stately on. Now the interior workings, with sighs, palpitations and eruptions, are becoming vociferous.

With the momentum of habit Christopher locates his slippers, left parallel in readiness, slides his feet into them, and stands. Retrieving his dressing gown from the door hook he bends to tuck a heel into the flattened pile of one slipper, and bangs his head on the knob.

'Fuck.'

He is shocked. Where did that come from? 'Fuck' is not an item in his vocabulary, or Marjory's, or the reactionary parts of the BBC he is accustomed to. It's a word from the world Marjory took pains to exclude, and now it has intruded.

He pads to the bathroom. Her merciless combination of reflective cabinet and fixed mirror give him back himself in unwanted detail. His hair lost its youthful vigour with its colour. Although thinning, Christopher's hairline has remained adamant; he does not sport the liver spotted scalp of his contemporaries, and the impression of abundance is only debunked at close quarters. The Prussian haircuts of Marjory's cajoling followed her to the grave. This new licence has nothing to do with vanity but absent-mindedness. Propelled in sleep by a mysterious static, the untrapped portion radiates in unpredictable permutations. A penumbra is cast by the overhead light. The flattened section, stuck round the vicinity of his ear, forms a curious crop circle, giving him the hallowed silhouette of a just struck match in a high cross-wind. He sits.

Twenty years ago Marjory would tut disapproval from the bedroom at the torrential noise, as he pumped a steaming arc down the toilet each morning. It was a small but satisfying rebellion to direct the jet for maximum acoustics. And now, first thing, he sits to pee. There is now a hesitancy; his bladder has become inexplicably shy. After the first he is fine, but his last standing early morning attempt coaxed a trickle over his slippers. And that's another thing... There is also the issue of his bowels. Previously the mere act of getting up set in train the motions. Now there are rumblings and issuings with little method and perilously brief forewarning; another rebellion below decks.

He purges himself, cleans, flushes, stands. He lets the dressing gown and pyjama top fall to the ground. Full nudity in this hall of mirrors is too gruesome a prospect. He is only fully naked when condensation draws a veil. He runs a basin of warm water, lathers his face and pulls the shaving mirror on its extending bracket till his face shudders into view. He had been over-enthusiastic and looks like a bespectacled polar bear. He swivels the mirror to its magnified side and notes, with macabre curiosity, fissures, broken veins, the wattle, stubble emerging from the foam like soot on snow.

He shaves in long practical sweeps, rinses the basin and climbs into the bath. Turning on the shower he luxuriates under the warm cone, after all these years still childishly pleased with the novelty of hot water on demand. Marjory has left a pumice stone, another small find, and he stands, stork like, forehead pressed against the tiles, water pleasurably cascading down his back while he files the scurf from his heels. He climbs out and dries himself before the condensation clears, collects the bundle of clothes and returns to the bedroom. An astringent closes the pores on his face. He dresses in a shirt and tie. Hound's tooth trousers complement the leather carpet slippers. The dangling braces snap satisfactorily into place. Taking up two paddle-shaped brushes he tames his hair with a cursory glance in the mirror.

'Splendid. Splendid.'

This is repeated in a kind of litany as he goes downstairs to the kitchen. Contemplating the prospect of cereal or kipper, Christopher sits at the table and, stretching across, turns on the radio. It's an old fashioned set, a vestige of earlier times, shared with his mother that he refused to relinquish in the onslaught of Marjory's improvements. A circular dial controls a vertical stripe that drifts between wavebands calibrated with the names of foreign cities. He is floating in the ether between Budapest and Vladivostok, when a voice asserts itself through the static. It is the shipping forecast, a catalogue of wind velocities, compass directions and quadrilaterals of sea incomprehensible to him. An image floats into his mind: Hebridean seamen shrouded in gleaming oilskins, a pitching bow and tumultuous seas – and disappears as mysteriously as it arrived. A rich, plummy voice replaces the first, the comforting familiarity of received pronunciation, concentric ripples of civilisation with the BBC at its epicentre. A second and third image are conjured: ragged expats sweating in pith helmets; sophisticates on a colonial veranda, sipping sundowners beneath mesmerising revolutions of a slow fan. It's the World Service. It's the news. It's five thirty a.m.

'Splendid. Splendid,' Christopher says as his forehead makes slow contact with the table, and he immediately falls asleep.

* * *

A list of stock-market prices, delivered in deadpan monotony, awaken him. For the second time in five hours he has to locate himself. He looks at the clock. Ten fifteen. The image of a kipper pops up in his imagination like the displayed price in an old-fashioned till. His timing is perfection. The butter melts into the kipper, curling beneath the grill, as the poached egg is scooped from the water. He completes the ensemble with toast and a pot of Earl Grey.

Fifteen minutes later he is walking in the direction of the newsagent. A cluster of small shops still face one another across the High Street, embattled remnants of the village purveyors he knew as a child, till London came knocking. The bell announces his arrival. He prefers a less obtrusive entrance. Scanning the newspapers his eyes are drawn to the upper shelf. There is a young woman whose breasts defy gravity. His scrutiny is curious, not prurient. Even the Edwardian corsetry that pre-dated his mother wouldn't provide the superstructure for this display. Is it nutrition? The bell rings again. From his peripheral vision he is aware that his glance vies with another. George Coleman is studying the same detail with quite a different expression. He turns to look at Christopher in a sudden exchange of grubby complicity. The glance is gone as soon as it arrives. Christopher turns away. He doesn't like George Coleman and feels contaminated by implication. He buys his paper and retreats, exchanging a cursory nod with George as the bell rings him out. Both know this is an association George is keener on than Christopher. Christopher imagines that George imagines some fraternity of louche outings.

The kitchen tap has developed a persistent slow drip, a water torture to calibrate suburban afternoons. Despite lacking all practical skills, Christopher takes a detour into the ironmongers, regretting his decision as the aproned figure turns to serve him. The young man of contagious gusto is intermittently replaced by the old man of corrosive cynicism. Christopher has seen enough cynicism in his life. He came here more for the pleasure of the chat than the need for washers. Enthusiasm is a draught. And there's another reason why he dislikes the old man: he's a veteran bigot, who treats Christopher with the reverence of a belligerent drill-sergeant for an officer who exemplifies the callousness he's trying to instil. God knows, Christopher has given him no cause. He shares none of his opinions, but that doesn't seem to matter. It's a trend Christopher notices in those around him who have reached a similar age: they presuppose a common pool of shared prejudices.

Mrs Griggs has visited during his absence. All evidence of the kipper is gone. A salad beneath clingfilm has appeared in the fridge. He tears chunks of wholemeal bread and eats with relish, vine tomatoes popping like party balloons in his mouth as he scans the letters page. After lunch he takes a soft chair and turns on the television. Christopher watches the cavalcade in bewilderment. His chin touches his chest.

He wakes with a start, silences the television and makes for the kitchen. The wall linking kitchen to dining room has been knocked through, the only one of Marjory's improvements he agreed with. The room has pleasing, spacious proportions. The rear wall is glass, French windows leading on to a patio with two steps descending to the accommodating privacy of the long narrow garden. It's early evening, perhaps seven, and glorious. The shadows are lengthening. He walks out to the perfume of cut grass. The adjacent garden has an oak placed just so, to filter sunlight for the benefit of anyone standing here, at this time of night, at this time of year, with the earth and sun standing in these relations, a configuration he can almost believe got up for his appreciation. Insects mill in the diagonal beams. The accumulated beauty strikes him like a blow. He breathes ten times, twenty, and looks at his feet as if expecting to find something has sloughed off.

He returns inside. The structure of his day has revolved round the purchase of a newspaper and senile naps. The structure of his life folded like wet cardboard on his wife's departure, and it's not as if he can blame this on deranged grief. Was the seed of apathy always there? He sits for a moment at the kitchen table, taking stock, dredging memories like strata. A tender child, with a tender mother, taken absurdly early at a tender age. Which age,

Christopher thinks, until the abstraction of senility, isn't tender? The rapid instars of teens and adolescence. The groping hesitancy of excruciating courtship. Marriage. The career trajectory that flattened before achieving the degree of respectability his wife craved. Disappointment generally: with work, that wasn't quite going to improve the world by even the subtlest of increments; with a marriage that seemed to petrify once the rings were on; with the vicarious frustration of his wife's thwarted social ambitions, left consciously at his feet to augment his own disillusionment. His growing detachment. Resignation to fate and the intermittent consolation this affords. Marjory's death.

He looks again at the day's newspaper and scans it with morbid fascination. He can't remember a single thing. In a corner, in a pile denied the cleaner, stands a column of folded newspapers, bundled and tied in readiness for recycling, daily strata of history. He can't remember any of that either. He can't look at any theme in the top copy and tease its antecedents from the stack. His daily paper might as well go from shop to pile and cut out the middle man. And yet it wasn't always like this. Evidence of past acuity is everywhere: in the marginalia of books strewn around and tidied by the cleaner. Two weeks ago he had prised one from the shelves and been surprised by the shy annotations in his handwriting: aides-memoires he couldn't remember writing to texts he couldn't remember reading. The world is being run by a generation younger than him for the benefit of a population younger still. Age is a cul-de-sac, a high tide that deposits few on a less populous shore.

It was always assumed by both that Christopher would go first. Their financial, and her social arrangements, were based on this assumption. The accumulated insurance on his life would have rebuilt a small hotel. In insisting on these arrangements she'd been swayed not so much by actuarial tables, but her envisaged widowhood, which was more of the same really but without him: whist drives, coffee mornings, bridge evenings and other outings of that ilk that Christopher had been methodically excluded from in the expectation that she'd have to go it alone anyway. It suited him.

In the light of what happened Christopher wondered if her involvement with the church was providential or ironic. She flirted with the superstructure and left dogma alone. He remembers her annual anxiety, in the atmosphere of seething competitiveness attending harvest thanksgiving and idly wondering if she believed in God, or had even considered the question, or if divinity even mattered. That had proved a watershed, prompting him to scrutinise his own soul. And all he found, in the place of conviction, was habit. 'I have doubts,' he had confessed to her. 'Don't you have doubts?' But Marjory never had doubts, not of that kind. And being in a state of doubt, he went on to explain, was not being in a state of grace, and he refused further to compromise himself by sceptical attendance.

'They're not all saints.' She said. 'I'm sure the C of E is big enough to accommodate doubts.' She said. 'Look at Thomas.'

'But he *was* a saint.'

She knew when to hector and when to retreat, and the tone of his doubts left her in no doubt. So she visited her priest and word got around. Other husbands might languish at home, in spiritual ignorance, or wash their cars with pagan indifference. That wasn't the absence of the apostate. She changed her demeanour: Marjory of the husband who had doubts.

Her stock rose. And then came the fateful day.

She returned, stiff-legged in shock. Dr Twidell, an unimaginative man wholly dependent on a limited repertoire of patented drugs, appeared as shocked as she was. Drawing forth tonight's star prize from the buff coloured envelope, unsuspected and imminent death, he steeled himself to deliver the prognosis. The question of remediation was deferred; news of hopelessness could be foisted on the locum when Marjory mustered sufficiently to ask.

But she never asked. She tottered home between suburban

hedgerows and glowing pavements, to sit dazed in the sun-drenched lounge as dandelion seeds floated past the bay window, like motes of accountable time, and tried to apprehend the scope of a lifetime that made nonsense of her new shoes. She imagined her accessories, charitable confetti, sprinkled over unappreciative single mothers on a council estate.

Christopher had to obtain the news from the hapless locum as Dr Twidell sliced on the fourth. His attempts at consoling his wife elicited a snort. He sought reinforcements. The priest made the mistake of an appeal to her spiritual side. A hackneyed attempt to relegate affairs to the context of eternity, of situating this departure in the boundless reunion to come, conjured in Christopher's mind the horror of a never-ending bridge evening. Who knows what it conjured in hers. She gave another snort and turned her face to the wall. There was no bigger picture, only that framed in the bay: the sun-drenched garden and beyond that the world that callously continued to rotate. She climbed the stairs for the last time, to bury herself among accoutrements that had lost all consolation and value. A week later she suffered a facial palsy, and behind this furious mask raged at Christopher's superfluous health, as he plumped her pillows and removed the tea tray. This accusatory glare followed him around the room for another week, till she suffered another stroke. He phoned from her room and, turning, noticed the change in her eyes. He sat on the bed and held her hand while the ambulance threaded its way. Behind the mask the moist eyes swivelled in bewilderment and began to leak. She gripped his hand spasmodically, and tried to articulate something. Venom? Affection? Reconciliation? Atonement? A lifetime of getting on, of climbing up, of things and people strategically ignored or cultivated, of things unsaid, boiled down to the travesty of two ambiguous grunts. It appeared that Marjory finally had doubts.

The congregation was smaller than he expected but select enough to obtain her posthumous approval. Several of the ladies said so. Christopher believed they were impersonating a crowd. He saw the empty pews as an indictment.

He had been alone for a week when he realised how rigorous her preparations had been, anticipating herself in his role. A cleaning lady called two mornings, and one unpredictable afternoon a week. She had her own key. Dust never settled. The contents of his washing basket emptied itself and fresh shirts appeared, stacked like bricks. Surfaces silently shone. The rumple of bedclothes pulled itself taut. A gardener appeared from the shrubbery. He also had a key, to the shed, and wielded his implements with a proprietorial air. Weeds were as absent from the flower beds as coffee rings from the occasional tables. Order reigned in Marjory's fiefdom, starting from the garden gate. He felt like a tenant occupying the premises of an absentee landlord. She would have lived in this antiseptic environment with the wherewithal to realise her social ambitions. But she had died, and he had not. Given the modesty of his requirements he found he was sitting on a small volcano of cash, erratically spewing cheques, as policies, long forgotten, matured.

Despite the self-absorption he had defensively withdrawn into he found he was curiously unprepared for the solitude that fell in lieu of dust. Her ambitions and activities, sometimes the avoidance of them, had been the armature that supported his routine. With her gone, the day sagged. 'I had ambitions,' he says to the furniture. 'I had a life. Why have I allowed this to happen?' The sterile surfaces reproach with their silence. He knows he did not subordinate his ambitions to hers, they never wanted the same thing. He allowed them to perish.

'I am not poor. I am not unhealthy.'

If anything is to mean anything he must connect.

Christopher's view of history, with extensive if eclectic reading, is of a vista of past atrocities. History is populated with the disgraces of human behaviour: ancient persecutions, mediaeval cruelty, sweeping barbaric hordes, all of these things merely lacking the refinement that advances have now lent that nasty predisposition of certain natures. Membership of the wrong tribe, or no membership at all, has proved fatal. Belief in the wrong thing, in the wrong place, at the wrong time, or even belief in nothing at all has supplied unfortunate people with the credentials to be horribly extinguished in their masses. He sees himself, standing on the pinnacle of the present tense, looking back on a soggy plain. The dry spots are pockets of safety, outnumbered by the morass of cruelty. From his eyrie it's a ghastly mosaic. In his less jovial moments he has been given to wonder if the aggregate of human history contains more grief than joy, or did people just get by – like him. The trick is to negotiate history dry shod, which is what he's done, through no effort on his part. He hasn't been called upon, his mettle hasn't been tested, which, when he thinks about it, makes him feel a number of things: relief, guilt, and sometimes a vague sense of shame when he has found himself unhappy, well fed and stable, when the television pours out daily grief, and the posthumous chorus of all the countless who got a rawer deal echoes up through the cistern of the past.

He walks out on the terrace. It's as dark as it will become. The night has a narcotic stillness. Christopher calculates the junction of both diagonals, takes possession of the long rectangle of the garden, and inspects his strip of metropolitan sky.

As a child he believed that the space above the garden belonged to his parents, as did the grass on which he stood, that space was carved into allotments and theirs was a column of air, attenuating to a tiny point, like converging rails into a flat horizon. He had tried to make some kind of order on the capricious scattering of stars by studying a children's astronomy book. Pages as thick as cardboard superimposed creatures and things, linking random points of light. Even then he had thought the selection arbitrary. Those images had faded from memory as their co-ordinates continued to burn. His abiding memory was of poring over these books, the creaking pages balanced on his mother's lap, during that interval of bed-time intimacy, when she read him to sleep. She furnished what scant commentary her knowledge could provide, inspired by the captions, with almost the same reverential tone she used when instructing him in his prayers. But she also spoke extempore, telling him of the time before telescopes, when people believed the earth was the centre of everything and everything circled round us, like ripples in a pool when you throw a stone, or the concentric skins of an onion. And she told him that these people believed everything was so perfectly balanced in this mechanism that heavenly music came from the harmony of the spheres. It was the simpler explanation that seduced him. How could harmony not envelope us when he had had a foretaste in the drowsy enclosure of his mother's arms? The evocation of her scent so impregnated his memory that he lived his whole life with the subconscious illusion that the vast distances of space were informed with the smell of lily of the valley, and the resonance of music too beautiful for us to hear.

* * *

Christopher has found a dog and lost a cleaner. The discipline of these new days starts with an early morning constitutional round the common, observing the clockwise etiquette of other like-minded individuals. And he is drawn there in the evenings too, by the fragrance of gathering dusk. He can still remember the annual fairs. Now he doesn't linger longer than the sun, as the place turns sinister in the space of ten minutes. Shouts penetrate the dark, and ponds of lamplight are bisected by hooded teenagers on unlit bikes. It was on such an outing, last week, having outstayed prudence, that he came across the dog sitting dead centre in the lamp light, an aimless bull's eye. It wasn't young, or pitifully thin. It wore no collar but gave off a slightly forlorn aura. His hesitating interest was enough of an invitation. He was only alerted to the fact that it was following him by their projected shadows. He turned with no intention of shooing it away. If he took it was he depriving the sinister nocturnal visitors to the common of a mascot? He is debating the point when the sight of its leathery testicles resting on the ground decides him.

He took it home and fed it some salami. Suddenly drained he raids the linen cupboard to manufacture a nest on the kitchen floor, which the dog occupies for fifteen minutes, before ticking its way up the stairs to lie on the bed across his tired legs. In the eerie half-light he finds his glasses and confronts the dog's blank retinas, reflecting back the sodium glare from the street beyond. They regard one another unblinkingly for several seconds till he leans forward to tousle its head. The compact is made. They fall into separate dreams.

The blanket that the dog spurned is lying portentously next to the washing machine, next morning, as Christopher and the dog come down for a late breakfast. Washing is never left in sight, one of the functions, like a healthy digestion, that goes unnoticed below decks. Mrs Griggs enters from the garden with the theatricality of a stage entrance, and stands in pointed stupefaction to labour her point. Mrs Griggs is never in the garden. It's not her domain. Mrs Griggs is ages with Marjory. By a deft inversion she had succeeded in making him ashamed of being her employer. The quantifiable effects of her dusting and scrubbing made his Civil Service scribblings seem hopelessly speculative. Since Marjory's death she has appointed herself guardian of the effects. Pretending to link cause to effect, she looks at the dog and picks several hairs from the blanket. The dog walks between them to the sunny terrace and pisses on the shrubs.

'I wouldn't have no truck with a dog in my house.' He confronts this with silence. She isn't satisfied. 'Not me y'wouldn't. Not in my house.'

'Yes. But it's not your house. It's my house.' The words seem to come from somewhere else.

'Mrs Fabian wouldn't have liked it.'

'She's no longer here to consult.'

She flinches perceptibly. He relents. She senses the advantage.

'I don't know about dogs.'

Is this, he wonders, some kind of litany? It's a tendency he's noticed with stupid people, and politicians, to hope to prevail simply by repeating the same thing. With the argument on his side he's been caught flat-footed before by belligerent perseverance. It was a technique Marjory perfected, assessing which arguments she could win by attrition. Past slights stiffen his resolve.

'If you mean you don't understand dogs then there's nothing *to* understand. I'm not asking you to accept responsibility. I'll look after him. If you mean you're unwilling to work in a house with a dog then that's your prerogative.'

'What d'y'mean?'

He rubs his eyes, imagining a blackboard syllogism with him pointing: you won't work in a house with a dog; this house has a dog; you won't work in this house. Good fucking riddance. The last sentence comes as a surprise to him again. She deserves civility.

'Look –'

'You didn't employ me. *She* did.' She points upwards, the bedroom, the firmament, he's too tired of this conversation to guess. Perhaps, Christopher thinks, she has her own blackboard syllogism: I won't have no trucks with dogs here; here is a dog; you and the dog will have to go. He has a momentary image of her as the manic housekeeper in *Rebecca*, returning to find her hysterically clutching Marjory's artefacts as the burning timbers crash down around her.

'She did take you on. And should you choose to remain, *we*,' patting the dog for emphasis, 'will be glad to have you. If it's a question of money...'

'It's not money.' The tone is almost contemptuous. 'Yours isn't the only house needs cleaning. I gave them up. I don't need to clean anyone's home. I did it for her.'

He closes his eyes to rub them again and when he looks up she's gone. A pair of rubber gloves lie flaccid on the draining board to mark her passing, this pantomime evaporation somehow in keeping with this singularly unreal person.

Half an hour later he's at the wine merchant in the high street. A worried glance from the assistant prompts him to leave the dog outside. Marjory's taste latterly evolved to an occasional glass of gaseous Lambrusco. She mistrusted anything that loosened self-control. She enjoyed disliking this shop, making his browsing a pleasureless affair. He orders a case of white burgundy, another of claret, and delights the assistant by giving him carte-blanche to compose a third. They will be delivered that very afternoon. On impulse he lifts a bottle of Pinot Noir and a box of Coronas from the humidor, another habit Marjory disapproved of. The occasional Christmas gift that escaped her embargo was smoked in the kitchen, crouching beneath the extractor hood, sucking up the perfume of Havana.

He decants the delivery that afternoon, bottles randomly littering the kitchen surfaces in pleasing confusion. He takes a cigar to the terrace. From the first fragrant puff he knows this will deliver what it promises. Marjory never did. He recalls their trysting days, turning the bend in the top landing of her parents' house. Her bedroom door half ajar, her topless reflection arresting him as the sound of placing cutlery wafts up from below, the right-angled collision of their gaze as her eyes meet his in the tilted glass and she glances downwards, directing his scrutiny to her coffee-coloured nipples. Look, she seemed to be saying, these are only for you, as she made an unseen motion with her foot and slowly closed the door, bringing down the curtain on the promise of carnality – never honoured. Given she didn't care for intimacy, he was surprised and saddened by the lengths she would go to, tending her appearance for half strangers.

A Sunday afternoon, over two years ago now. Felicity is beginning her long, long decline and George has advertised the prognosis to anyone who will listen. Marjory sits at her three-mirrored bureau, a reflective triptych giving her back her double profile. She has applied some foundation that makes her as pale as the woman they are about to meet. Christopher considers the elaborateness of her preparations an oblique insult and pointedly looks at his watch.

'We're going to be late.'

'She's not going anywhere.'

'That's not the point.'

'My face,' she says, 'I can't go without my face.'

She pads and brushes and tweaks and smudges, her blooming civic mask emerging as the growth, in the bedroom across the common, metastasises.

'Don't go overboard.'

'Someone has to.'

'Why?'

'As a mark of respect.'

'She has cancer.'

'You can bet your bottom dollar George won't be dowdy.'

He suspects this is a slight aimed at him, rather than an endorsement of her efforts, but she has missed the point again: it isn't George they are going to visit.

Marjory is right. George is wearing a blazer and a tie of subdued diagonals, transfixed with an enormous tie pin. His shoes shine like glass. Christopher is reminded of a retired wing-commander with too much consideration for his appearance. He has that over-groomed look Christopher finds disturbing in a man, and vaguely effeminate, if George's reputation didn't belie this.

George opens the door slowly. He has a new persona. His

manner is reverential. They are shown into the bedroom. One look at Felicity and Christopher wonders if she will ever see another four walls. Marjory bends forward to mime a kiss, and he is struck by the obscene discrepancy in colour. George lingeringly appraises Marjory's buttocks. Looking past Marjory's ear, Felicity catches George, and a flicker of irritation crosses her face. Christopher witnesses the whole exchange. Realising he has been caught George steps forward, takes one of Felicity's hands and turns to the visitors. He sustains this tableau for five seconds.

'Tea?' he asks, cheerfully.

'That would be nice.' Marjory answers for them both. Christopher sits on the bed as George tramps down the stairs, the reverential manner forgotten in the preoccupation of a small task. Marjory straightens some drooping daffodils.

'These want some water.' Christopher continues to look at Felicity. Marjory gives a brief roll call of the women who intend to visit, and whisks off the flowers to refresh them. She could do it in the bathroom, but they hear her footsteps following George's. She has had enough of the sickroom. On an impulse Christopher takes Felicity's hand.

'She's very attractive you know, Christopher.'

'Yes. She has all the components. Somehow the total effect is a little off true. It's her expression, I think. Took me years to notice. No doubt you spotted it immediately.'

'Yes. But then, I didn't have the distractions of a man.'

'Do you think George has noticed?'

'No. He never gets beyond the components. Are you worried about them down there?'

He laughs, briefly, at the thought of George considering whether or not to paw her as she bends across the sink, arrested by her glacial stare as she guesses his thoughts. It's not difficult with George.

'I'm sorry. I didn't mean... No I'm not worried. She's not

interested. I don't just mean George...'

'That's a shame – for you, I mean.' He shrugs. Her hand is dry, phthisic, in the sudden candour of this companionable silence.

'I take it George is interested, not just in Marjory I mean.'

'Not just in Marjory.'

'And did you spot that immediately?'

'Yes. But I was foolish enough to think I could change him.'

'Do you care?'

'I used to. But not now. I don't have the vitality any more. He's got enough for us both. What does perplex me is the complete absence of what I thought I saw in him. I don't know if he's changed that much, or if I was deluding myself from the start.'

'It's easily done.'

'Not for a woman. I think I must have refused to see.'

'I can't speak for everyone, but I don't think it's that uncommon to attribute things to people, generosity, care... whatever, because we want them to be the way we want to think about them, not the way they are.'

'And whose fault is that?'

'I never thought about it in terms of anyone's fault. I suppose if it's anyone's it's the one deluding themselves, not the others being themselves. But if it's a fault it's a very venial one. I don't think of it as blameworthy just to want to make people seem nicer.'

She doesn't say anything and gives his hand a faint squeeze, which he returns. He looks out the window, lets his eyes lose their focus till the foliage becomes a green blur.

'We married the wrong people, Christopher.' He refuses to turn and meet the gaze he knows is directed at his profile. 'I'm sorry to sound presumptuous, especially with you and Marjory in full health. I don't think of the consequences of what I say any more because I don't have to live with them.'

'Being sick still doesn't give you the right.'

'Doesn't it? You're probably right. I don't know any more.'

Nor does he, and he doesn't know if he's defending his bad choice or Marjory's reputation, whatever that might be.

'I'm sorry if I've hurt you.' she says.

He's wrung by the scrupulousness of this compassion from a failing body. In her state would he see beyond his own demands? Then there are the two downstairs, in rude health, who see the surface of their world and their bodies. He turns to tell her that she couldn't hurt him but she's asleep, her face suddenly smaller still in the frame of its pillow. He's upset that she has slid out of consciousness with the thought of his reproach. He goes downstairs and sits eating a biscuit while George and Marjory exchange pleasantries. George has formed a habit of dropping his voice when Felicity is mentioned, and discussing her prognosis *sotto voce.*

'It's all right – she's asleep.'

They are saying their goodbyes in the hall when Marjory excuses herself to go upstairs. Christopher knows she seldom uses other toilets unless she wants to appraise the fittings. They stand at the bottom of the stairs and listen to the running tap she turns on to conceal the tinkle of urine. Bereft of other company it's plain they have absolutely nothing to say to one another. Discomfited by the silence, George repeatedly touches his tie pin. Christopher is not fazed, he is too mesmerised by the sheen of George's oxfords to notice. Did he achieve this himself, or was the leather worked by some Dickensian boot boy? Do such functionaries still exist? If he leans forward he imagines he will see his distorted image in the gleaming toe cap, like the Arnolfini couple, slyly reflected, back to back, in the poised mirror behind them that so fascinated him on rainy afternoons in the National Gallery. Details, details. Life is a limitless succession. And now Marjory is at the top of the stairs, unsuccessfully disguising her reconnaissance, and George is at the bottom, unashamedly staring up her skirt, without the good grace to look embarrassed when caught by Christopher.

'Must keep up appearances,' he says, in regard to nothing at all, stroking the diagonals of his tie. No, Christopher thinks, there are other more important things you must do. You must care more for your wife than the public depiction of your own grief. You must give her private evidence that the remainder of her short life is not eked out as the fag-end of a bad decision, taken in health and optimism and the mistaken belief that you would grow as a human being. You must, in short, learn to love before it is too late for her, and worse, for you. Marjory, clopping down the stairs in her heels, nods with the jerky motion, signifying her agreement with George.

He puffs the smoke in a thin blue column, whistling steam from boyhood kettles. He returns inside and reaches for the glass of Pino Noir, clumsily nudging it and regaining balance by grasping the stem. Some liquid has spilled over the rim and continues to waver in the bowl. The geometry of its purple shadow is worth the attention of a Dutch master. What he assumed to be flecks in his vitreous humour, he now realises are motes of dust, banished from the house since Marjory's occupancy. It pleases him that the glass has left a ring in its wake that will grow sticky, and persist till tomorrow, or the next day, or the day after, until he decides to wipe it off.

* * *

Christopher is getting his car out of the garage. It is a Morris Traveller complete with a fretwork of timber, a Tudor cottage on wheels. Marjory disliked it, considering it tantamount to a van, suitable for trade. He keeps it exorbitantly taxed, insured and maintained, to languish in darkness, trundled out for the few annual excursions it enjoys. Until the wine and cigars this was his one indulgence.

He is going to visit Felicity. She has endured beyond medical expectation and has lived to see another four walls. She is in a hospice. George has modified his persona accordingly. With

Marjory's death little gossip now percolates down to Christopher, but he has seen the ostentatious flowers George stands with at the bus stop, the sombre expression broken by the distraction of a passing skirt. The hospice is awkward to get to by public transport, two buses, hence Christopher dusting off the Morris. He has been tempted to give George a lift but hasn't, for motives that disappoint him. George has a car. It's the display that public transport affords George that put him off offering. Their visits have never overlapped, more by serendipity than design. The longer Felicity lasts, the greater the chance of their meeting at her bedside. The longer Felicity lasts the greater her private candour. Christopher doesn't want her to die and he doesn't want to meet George there either.

He turns into the driveway. It curves, 'round the bend'. It's rumoured that the place was once an asylum, thus, he is told by Sister Judith, the origin of the phrase. No one wanted bedlam in plain sight. He wants to corroborate this in Brewers, but forgets each time he tells himself to remember. Sister Judith came as a surprise, as did the others. Felicity has dredged up unsuspected Catholic antecedents and 'gone home to Rome', as the High Street has it.

Christopher anticipated a staff of crones, desiccated by piety. Sister Judith is in her thirties, and follows racing form. She wears tiny earphones in the corridor to get the latest on the two thirty at Chepstow. She has the outdoor looks of a Brontë heroine, and an appetite for life that confounds him. How can this place contain it? Perhaps she is the equilibrium of vitality, as the spirits of those she ministers to fail. Christopher and Sister Judith are in silent cahoots. He knows, without being told, that she likes him and dislikes George.

She is standing at the entrance, listening to the radio, as he turns the bend. He gets out. The dog jumps down. She detaches her earphones as she crosses towards him.

'Have you named him yet?'

'No. Seems somehow arrogant. If he's this age already he's got an identity.'

'True. You can't bring him in you know.' Christopher looks at a loss. She rephrases. 'You can't bring him in the main entrance. Go round the side and I'll let you in there. He can stay outside but he'll still see you. It's better than being in the van by himself.'

'It's a Morris Traveller.'

She disappears inside. He walks the dog round the side of the building. Felicity has a private room on the ground floor, with a full-length window that opens to the lawn beyond. She was previously upstairs, and Christopher feels something ominous in the transfer to accommodation nearer the elements she is to return to. There are a number of these rooms that he passes, some uncurtained. He is presented with a series of tableaux. What would Hogarth have made of it? He is humbled by the smile of resignation from a cadaverous woman who beams at the dog. The curtains of the next window part, pat on his arrival, and there is framed Sister Judith, vital as Saint Joan, with the receding room and the tilted bed propping up its occupant, another lesson in perspective. The window opens and Sister Judith steps out, taking the length of the clothes rope from Christopher.

'You ought to do something about this. What if he gets lost?'

'I haven't really thought of him as found. He'd just go back to what he was.'

'Lost. You can't just take up with things. Not if they come to depend on you.'

'Perhaps you're right.'

Having satisfied herself that he's suitably admonished, she nods behind her. 'Not long today. She's feeling poorly. I'll take the dog. Three laps then you're out.' He hands across the rope. She takes half a dozen vigorous strides and considers the lagging animal.

'He's used to my speed.'

It doesn't seem to occur to her to slow down. She picks the dog up and turns to him as it licks her face. 'The other one was here earlier. He's tired her out. He'd tire anyone out.'

Christopher can't imagine anyone tiring Sister Judith out. She heaves the dog over her shoulder, like a burping baby, turns on her heel and strides off. The dog yawns at him and settles its chin on her bobbing shoulder. He goes in through the window. She is waiting to meet his eye, perhaps calibrating her decline from the expressions of her visitors. He was here the day before yesterday. There is a marked change. She is becoming friable. He thinks a gust of wind could disperse her, like a bad special effect.

'I hear George was here.'

'Yes. Do you wait to avoid him?'

'No.' That would be to admit he was doing something wrong. He's doing something right. 'We're bound to bump into one another. It's a matter of time.' It's said before he has realised. He sits and takes her hand to cover his confusion. They sit in silence like this for a minute. 'I think Sister Judith thinks I'm the third part of your ménage à trois.'

'It wouldn't be much of a sin it if were true and I wish it were. A ménage minus George. Pity the dog's gone. I'd have liked to see it.' It's something he has noticed before: a revelation followed by a commonplace. She's too far gone to care or calculate. There are no conversational ploys left and he finds this liberating. Marjory stuck to rules, spoke for over half a century and never said anything.

'She's doing laps. I'm only allowed here for three. The dog will be back.'

'Good. Mongrel?' and before he can answer, 'I wonder if the ability to sin disappears when you just don't have the energy to act on it. Can you think a sin?'

'I certainly hope not. If you can then everyone's tarnished. Where did all this latent Catholicism come from?'

'School.' She gestures, indicating the surroundings. The

movement exhausts her. 'Taught by nuns. Back with nuns. You never escape the vestiges of a Catholic education.'

'I suppose George thought it vulgar or something.'

'You're trying to mitigate my lapse. It wasn't George's fault. George never thought anything. George has no spiritual faculty. Not like you.'

'Please...'

'Don't be modest. Even though you are. George wasn't to blame, at least for that. It was pure apathy. Do you know there's a sin of acedia? Spiritual sloth. That's what the sisters taught us. Where's the dog?'

And on cue he appears, still bobbing on the nun's shoulder. Christopher gestures Sister Judith to come in. She is about to put the dog down when he opens the window.

'She wants to see the dog.'

'You'll be getting me the sack.'

'I thought God was your boss.'

'That'll be a joke then, Christopher.'

She brings the dog over to the bed. He has left a stream of saliva over one shoulder. Christopher wonders if he should point it out, hospital hygiene and all that. But then, no one's coming here to get better. Realising he is the focus of attention and something is expected of him, the dog wags its tail and barks obligingly. Felicity smiles. The dog is lowered to have its ears ruffled.

'I don't want dog hairs on the bedding. Hell to pay with Mother Superior. I think it's time for you to go, Christopher.'

'I must have another lap yet.'

'She's tired.' And so it proves. By curious cause and effect the dog has barked her to sleep. Sister Judith puts him down with a grunt, hands the clothes rope to Christopher and shepherds them both out the window.

'And for God's sake get him a proper lead.'

He retraces his steps to the car, winds down the passenger

window and trundles off down the drive, he, hunched forward over the steering wheel in concentration, the dog, tongue lolling, head snapping from side to side as the lamp posts pass by.

There is a pet shop of sorts in the High Street. He stands in the twittering concourse explaining what he needs while the dog savours the smells. Next a visit to the Heel Bar, shoe repairs and keys cut while you wait, a curious concept to Christopher, a man of solid welted brogues. Locksmith and cobbler. Discrete trades in his youth. What's the connection he's failing to make? Are there others? Baker and glazier? Plumber and copy editor? Gynaecologist and plumber. At least that's got an overlap. Fire eating air-traffic controller? While he ponders this the young man inscribes an address on a metal tag. And now the dog looks legitimate, with its clerical collar and authentic lead, which slightly saddens him, for, let's face it, he says to himself, such cosmetic touches are for our enjoyment.

He is walking along the pavement when the accumulated strain of the months, thinking about Felicity, imagining her departure, projecting a future without that compassionate presence, takes its toll. He is again suddenly exhausted, irritated with himself for being caught out by predictable fatigue. It is like a light going out. He casts around for a seat.

There is a fortuitous coffee bar at his elbow. If only, thinks Christopher, I believed in fate. It is a place he has passed two dozen times either without noticing or, when he does, thinking it as somehow not for him. It is a place of chrome and blonde wood that he has dismissed as ersatz Scandinavian, staffed by the young for a clientele he has ceased to understand. Tieless professionals shout for amiable drinks after working hours, a code of behaviour Christopher believes they have learned from beer commercials where everyone is remorselessly happy. He sees the café as a place of contrived bonhomie. The prices deter the hooded elements who haunt the common. At this time of day the customers are mostly young mothers with infants, whose collapsed prams clutter the entrance, and a scattering of affluent young who can afford to be redundant here in the middle of the day.

He negotiates the prams. The plentiful seating is illusory – at least for Christopher. There are a series of tall stools at the window nestled beneath a foot-deep bar where clients can perch, rest their elbows and contemplate the foot traffic. Christopher decides not to risk it. A fall from that height could prove fatal. There is a number of what look like giant leather bean bags on the floor. A teenage boy and girl occupy adjacent bladders and lean, exploiting the intimacy of gravity. To get on one of these Christopher decides he'd have to kneel down first. Getting back up would involve a block and tackle. These are more hazardous than the stools. There are a number of couches, some still occupied. These aren't hard-backed functional things. To Christopher they look more like distended marshmallows, reminiscent of American sitcoms or those dreadful morning television talk shows. He casts about some more.

The only real options are the tables with hard chairs and arms for purchase. Most of these are occupied by the sorority of young mothers. He is the focus of a number of accusatory glares. They are staring at him staring at the half-obscured bosom of one of their members, breast-feeding. The infant detaches. The nipple is mesmerisingly red and upright, reminiscent of a wine gum, the aureole huge and glistening. His eyebrows shoot up. He realises he is being watched watching, shields his eyes with a hand that shoots up like a salute, mutters a general apology and sits at the vacant table at his other elbow.

But is it vacant? There's a smouldering cup with a creamy inch of residue that the waiting staff have also chosen to leave in case the customer returns. Shifting his position he can see some official-looking papers in the chair, pushed under the table, invisible to the aproned girl spraying rainbows of antiseptic mist in the mid-morning glare and wiping the tables in moist crescents. He is about to alert her to the papers when he is distracted by the movement at his side.

It is Vanessa, as preserved and svelte as the image he is slightly ashamed of having retained in memory. She is, of course, the owner of the coffee. He doesn't know if she has come back from the toilet to sip the residue or in from the street to retrieve her papers.

'Vanessa.'

'Christopher.'

'Vanessa.'

'Christopher.'

He gets purchase from the table top and begins to hoist himself up. She puts a hand on his shoulder and persuades him back into his chair.

'Vanessa.'

'Don't start that again. It's hardly Noel Coward dialogue.'

And for the first time in as long as he can remember he finds he is gently laughing. There is no noise, just a seismic tremble of the torso and a slitting of Christopher's eyes. When it subsides he finds he is embarrassed to find he is enjoying looking at her, her body, her neck, her face.

'Sorry,' says the rainbow girl, turning in a luminous sweep of careless antiseptic, 'no dogs.'

Again he starts to stand. Again she reclines him with a hand on his shoulder. She is a woman who has learned to take her chances when she finds them and she will not have this opportunity wasted by something as trivial as a hygiene regulation. She takes the dog outside and ties him to a bin. He scratches his ear with a hind paw and his testicles vibrate. Then he watches the cars.

Vanessa returns and looks steadily at Christopher, as if willing him to speak. Realising something is expected of him and feeling unequal to the moment he peers at the chalked-up table of fare behind the counter. The array is bewildering.

'What happened to just coffee?'

'Tell me what it is that you want.'

He pauses before responding. Is this an iceberg question, seven eights submerged?

'You know...' he says.

'No. I don't. Tell me.'

'The kind of thing you used to have when you went into a place that served afternoon tea but you ordered coffee instead.'

'Those were dilute granules, unless you frequented a better class of place than I did.'

'Yes. That sort of thing.'

She smiles at the rainbow girl and orders Christopher a flat white. He doesn't see how she has deduced that from the blackboard. As an afterthought she points at her own cup for a refill.

'Things have moved on, Christopher.' Is she still talking about coffee? 'And anyway, how are you?'

'Oh. You know...' He is hearing himself say this, the kind of non-committal response he dislikes.

'No. I don't know.'

'Well, I got rid of the cleaner. The garden seems to be mysteriously sorting itself out although I haven't seen the gardener to pay him. Maybe there is a standing order to pay him I don't know about. Perhaps Marjory...' At the mention of her name he hesitates. 'I'm managing fine.'

Her steady look hasn't wavered. His sense of discomfort is lessening. He wonders if this is what prey feel like, the moment of calm before being devoured.

'I'm sorry about Marjory. I can't pretend we got on but I'm sorry nonetheless. For you I mean. I didn't know what to say when I heard. I thought of writing.'

He casts his mind back to the rank of cards on the mantelpiece and window ledges, more populous than the mourners, and tries to attribute an identity to each. He can't remember Vanessa's. He was sure it was there, now mulch, as his wife will eventually be.

Christopher has always given Vanessa the benefit of the doubt, his weakness of empathy exerting itself again. Marjory didn't. Marjory disliked Vanessa because Vanessa refused to be simply a haberdasher. Vanessa breezed into the High Street with no ring, no past, and enough collateral to open a shop. The Woman's Guild vibrated.

Perhaps Vanessa was even aware of this. She kept the rumour mill churning by saying absolutely nothing. The truth was more ordinary and sordid, as it usually is. As a young women she had cohabited with a dentist in Bristol, when such an action still turned heads and tarnished reputations. Her parents tacitly approved. They considered her a girl of limited abilities and fewer options. Of an age and class that venerated the professions, they were so paralysed by respect for the family doctor that he attributed their silence to idiocy. Cohabitation with a dentist outside marriage was preferable to working-class drudgery within it. Love didn't enter their utilitarian calculation. The dentist agreed and so, without thinking about it, did Vanessa. She paid her dues by looking nice and crouching before dinner most weeknights on the hearthrug, as he took her from behind while the Fray Bentos Steak and Kidney pie crisped to a turn. Three nights out of four he would adjourn to the local, leaving her with the cold dishes and lukewarm semen, to return for News at Ten and a repeat performance.

It's fortunate she had a libido equal to the task. It was the slackening of his penetrations that led her to believe he was otherwise being serviced, corroborated the following evening when, facing the fireguard, he breathed 'Charlotte' into the small of her back. Charlotte was his receptionist. An unscheduled after-hours visit to the surgery found Charlotte in the hearthrug posture, being pantingly referred to as 'Jane'. Charlotte accepted these confusions better than Vanessa: it was an unenlightened time and her bonus reflected the proportion of time spent on all fours. It turned out the dentist preferred *coitus a tergo* precisely because of his difficulty in putting a name to a face: one set of shoulder blades was the same as another, and pumping away doggedly from behind he could let his imagination wander. So could Vanessa. At any one time there were three simultaneous copulations: the literal participants, the dentist and his dulcinea, and Vanessa and the younger, handsomer, harder, more attentive man who existed out there somewhere beyond the rote of shopping, cooking and applying makeup, only to get fucked like this face down in front of *The Magic Roundabout*. But at least her infidelities were confined to the mind.

He had been careful to drip-feed her money. She had no bank account and no rights. She let him stew while she calculated, and wrung incremental concessions out of him each time she crouched. When he attended an amalgam conference in Galway, with Jane or one of her successors, she burnt his clothes, bent his golf clubs, poured sugar into the petrol tank of his Jaguar and left with her portable life: a matching suite of luggage and a meagre amount of money. He hadn't broken her heart but he had dented her self-esteem. She emerged from her first affair with immaculate teeth, a regimen of dental hygiene practically American, a whetted sexual appetite and a desire to get on without ever being beholden to men. She had no delusions about her employment options and held down a series of casual jobs and casual affairs, ending most liaisons when better employment beckoned.

From crouching like a tupped ewe she now preferred to kneel astride and look down. She looked down on a surveyor, a welder, a loss adjuster, the man who came to paint lines on the road, an actuary, her postman. She was a sexual opportunist and her tastes were eclectic. She looked down on her GP, but fled in panic when he declared a love so intense he intended to expose the affair and liberate them both. She didn't love anyone and liberation was not something she believed possible in male company. The type of people she attracted she found predictable and egocentric, but recognised decency when she saw it.

When her parents died her inheritance comprised a rented house she was obliged to clear. The tawdry furniture was auctioned for a pittance, and she was left with an enormous and unanticipated collection of buttons her mother had amassed. Her dormant acumen was roused. Couturiers looked for some of these older specimens. The Sunday stall in Camden Market graduated to a modest shop: The Button Boutique. It didn't take a fool to make the link from price to location, and she was no fool. She had a talent for spotting talent and delegating. A disgruntled art student with a flair for decoration was the first in a series of girls. They all left in amicable circumstances with a fierce sense of independence, the best thing she could teach.

The place modestly flourished. The nest egg modestly grew. But the pace of growth was dictated by the modest means of the local clientele, so she hazarded all on the move to the High Street, where she now sits across her replenished coffee and Christopher's flat white. The gamble paid off.

She was surrounded by people whose average age she would soon approach and whose income she could match. She had a string of liaisons behind her that she had terminated without gaining a reputation for promiscuity, and no ties. She was as respectable as her dead parents could have wished. She knew what was what in the bedroom and in the balance sheet. And she was bored.

She first met Marjory at a church function she tolerated in order to try to establish business contacts. Vanessa looked at Marjory and saw a ruthless social climber who didn't have the saving grace of humour, or of realising her own restrictions. Her only interest lay in the exemplification of a type. Vanessa wasn't interested in social theories; she'd seen plenty of types. Vanessa found Marjory a bore.

Sex never scandalised Marjory, it was just something other people engaged in, like eating liver or playing golf. Had Vanessa's past come to light Marjory would only have been disappointed that rumour fell so short of the mark.

Vanessa was still bored. The menopause had left her less urgent and more discriminating. The disadvantage of the High Street was the available men it brought within her compass: a self-publicising roué with a dying wife. And then she met Christopher.

He was married, but unaccompanied, as he guilelessly walked into her shop looking for advice on the purchase of a present for his wife. Not putting two and two together she sold him a length of taffeta, knowing it was unsuitable for the wife of the man she'd just met. She wanted him to come back and exchange it because she wanted to see him again.

But he didn't come back. Instead she was confronted by the hag of mock gentility who had sparked reciprocal dislike at the church social. She now did put two and two together, logically but not emotionally. This seasoned campaigner of erotic trysts, who had seen most things, couldn't see Christopher and Marjory coming to grips. This cheered and excited her.

'I believe you sold my husband this piece of cloth.'

'Yes.'

Pushing the bolt away with the back of her hand. 'I don't need this.'

'Of course not. Your husband didn't explain the circumstances. This will do you no favours. Perhaps something darker that will look at you, something earthy, like those delightful tea-cosy colours for that social we so enjoyed. Something *serviceable*.'

'I'll take the money.' It took her a hundred yards before she realised she's been bested.

Vanessa thinks of Christopher constantly. His fidelity in such an obviously unsuitable match serves to make him more attractive. In the few social encounters where they do meet, some force compels her to cross the room in a conspicuous diagonal to talk to him, stand near him. She is a repository of thwarted impulses, accumulated like tree rings. 'I am here!' her mind and organs shout. 'Drink deeply!' She is aware she is making herself ridiculous. That first infatuation, suppressed by her dentist, has bloomed on her posthumous fertility. He is unfailingly polite and offers not the least morsel of encouragement.

His wife dies. She phones condolences and is met with a bewildered voice that does not recognise hers. She stands outside the church, not wishing to intrude on his grief, if that's what it is, but to be acknowledged. He makes the forty foot trip from steps to hearse without registering anything in his peripheral vision. Her heart tugs at his immaculate cuffs. As the vehicle slides past he is frowning at his feet, concentrating on the day's sequence that must be got through, and she stands, watching it disappear, as the other mourners register her presence with varying degrees of politeness. She decides to wait. Time's efficacy is proverbial, but how much do they have? And now fate has delivered him, widowered, with a destitute dog and an incipient loneliness she can sense, mirroring her own, looking frankly at her across two cooling coffees and a cooling universe.

'How are you coping?' she asks.

'Well, as I said, I got rid of the cleaner but'

'No. Sorry to interrupt. I don't mean the bread and butter things. I mean how do you fill a gap made by the absence of someone who's been a part of your life for so long? I'm not trying to pry and I don't mean to make you uncomfortable, it's just that I don't know. I've never had that kind of thing taken away from me.'

In other circumstances he would think this as intrusive as dreadful morning television, prying mawkish revelations. But there's a frankness to her gaze that tells him her motives are as far removed from those people as it's possible to be. Her reputation for privacy is well known. She must have understood the adverse speculation it invited. God knows, Marjory and her ilk made interior life around here more difficult. He senses that in her last sentence Vanessa has revealed more about herself to him than she has to anyone else around here.

'"That kind of thing" is a bit of an elastic category. I think the kind of thing any couple has is unique. I don't think anyone outside can really understand.'

'I think there are lots of types who just rub along, not noticing that they have less in common.'

He decides to reciprocate her confidence. 'Marjory and I didn't have less in common. I don't think we ever had shared interests in that way.'

'You and I have things in common,' she blurts, and bites her lip, losing her composure for the first time in twenty years. She hails the rainbow girl to cover her confusion. Again he thinks something is expected of him.

'I don't know what your interests are, Vanessa.'

'I'm not talking about hobbies or superficial things like that.' She snaps it back, over her shoulder while settling their bill. The waitress is confused, believing the remark addressed to her. Vanessa smiles at her, rectifies the misunderstanding with an exorbitant tip. When she leaves Vanessa has no reason not to turn back. He knows her curt response was a defence mechanism. She takes a deep breath, lets it out slowly while contemplating her coffee and looks at him.

'I'm sorry. I didn't mean to be rude. Stop waving, Christopher, it does matter. Some things are too important to be misunderstood. I'm not talking about hobbies or all the things people do with other people just to avoid doing them on their own. I think often they're just contrivances to avoid loneliness. I'm not saying there's anything wrong with that I'm just saying it shouldn't be mistaken for something it's not. Communion. I think some people even do things they don't much like because doing something slightly unenjoyable in company is preferable to them to being on their own. You're nodding. Do you agree?'

'I've always been a bit suspicious of people who can't stand their own company.'

'And you can obviously stand yours. I'd go further. I'd say you were flourishing, Christopher.'

'I don't know about that. You seem fine.'

'Solitude has its place. But you can get too much of a good thing.'

'Yes. I'm sure.'

'Have you found that out yet?'

'I didn't need to.'

'That's the kind of thing I'm talking about. The thing to have in common is a caste of mind. Not dominoes or bird watching or... or... whatever. The rest is incidental.'

The waitress returns with the receipt. He welcomes the distraction. He doesn't think he knew Marjory's caste of mind after a lifetime of contact, such as it was. He wouldn't presume to know someone else's after the brief exposure he and Vanessa have had to one another. But, he thinks, perhaps that's him, and Marjory and Vanessa. Perhaps with Marjory there wasn't any caste of mind beyond what he gleaned. Perhaps Vanessa is emotionally clairvoyant. Perhaps she reads him like a book because he's obvious. Vanessa smiles sadly, accepts the slip of paper and crushes it into her saucer when the girl leaves.

'Thank you for the coffee.'

'Your turn next time.' It is on the tip of her tongue before she stops it. The effort of suppression has allowed sincerity to skip the queue. 'Don't you want someone?' There is an intonation, a note of entreaty, she can't take back. They both know she means 'Don't you want me?' He looks more puzzled than alarmed. Want? Want has never come into it since his mother's death. It never occurred to him since that his wanting anything could divert the world by a fraction.

'I'm sorry, I've no idea what I want or if it even mattered.'

The contents of her handbag suddenly preoccupy her. She rummages for half a minute and looks up with a counterfeit smile.

Her courage touches him.

'Your dog must be bored.'

'Oh, I wouldn't worry about that. He's beyond fatalism. However,' again pulling himself up, 'I must be going.'

Ideally he would have liked another twenty minutes to gather his strength, but he feels the most diplomatic thing he can do is leave. Having untied the dog he turns ponderously to wave goodbye. She is a vague silhouette behind the mirror of the opposite façade that a burst of sunlight intrudes between them. She smiles at his chivalry, knowing from his sudden shadow and narrowed eyes that he probably can't see her. There is a confusion in his retreat as the dog takes the other side of the lamp post and doubles back with the shortened lead, encircling Christopher's ankles.

He executes a clumsy pirouette and walks in the dog's wake to extricate them both. She feels this display of patience has aged her ten years on the spot.

* * *

Summer has arrived in a profusion of metropolitan blooms and the smell of mown suburban lawns. It is the first summer Marjory hasn't seen and, realistically, the last Felicity will endure. The departure of Mrs Griggs has occasioned more than just the mantle of dust. Christopher is now stimulated by a routine. He has discovered something known as a 'service wash', and a cheerful young woman who delivers his ironing pressed to military standard. The purchase of a microwave has opened vistas. The Hoover lurked beneath the stairs. He found it. The day starts with a walk on the common with the dog and establishes a cheerful momentum of its own, with the rota of things needing to be done. The phone rings. Usually it is someone from the Indian sub-continent trying to sell him something. It is Sister Judith.

'I think you'd better come in.'

'How bad is she?'

'Don't loiter. If you can't find someone to take care of the dog I'll do it.'

When he rounds the bed with the dog at the quarter light, she's waiting for him. As he gets out she gets in, and nods towards the building. Her abruptness forestalls further questions. Without the dog he doesn't have to walk around the outside. It's the first time he's used these antiseptic corridors. As he approaches the door George steps out, rubs one shining toecap against a calf, straightens his tie and sees Christopher. A look of anger crosses his face and he walks wordlessly past.

Felicity looks every bit as bad as he expected, although he hadn't imagined the febrile brightness of her eyes. Perhaps consciousness heightens before it fades. Perhaps he won't have to do all the talking as he has recently.

'I just met George. He wasn't pleased.'

'I don't care.'

'Even so, pretty rotten luck considering all the number of times we've managed to avoid one another.' He stops. They both know how this reasoning goes.

'Is the air nice outside?'

'Beautiful. English summer. Rupert Brooke weather.'

'Ironic, that I got to see it, such as I can, and Marjory didn't. She always looked so healthy. I've looked like a less unwell version of this for ages. I always thought she found my illness a bit distasteful, or a deliberate means of drawing attention to myself. George does too. Where's the dog?'

'Sister Judith.'

'Listen to me,' she says, needlessly. It's why he's here. Her quota of remaining words is now so finite he feels he can count them down, like clock chimes. 'I've been thinking. I used to wonder if we were kindred spirits or just similarly marooned. You don't have to say anything because it doesn't matter. I know you care for me but

I love you, and if I had to sum up the one achievement in my life I was glad of it's my time with you. This illness brought us together, and it's almost worth it. And I'm glad you've behaved impeccably and I know you still would have, even if I were in full health and you were free with Marjory gone. Where's the dog?'

'Sister Judith.'

'Ah. Can I see him?'

He is apprehensive about leaving her. How much has that just cost? He doesn't want her to go alone, without someone there, without him there, holding her hand. He goes out the window and returns five minutes later with Sister Judith and the dog. At the sight Sister Judith gestures him to stay where he is and leans over the bed.

'Is she gone?'

'No. But you both have to go.'

'Will you please do something for me? If she wakes will you please tell her I felt the same way?'

'Yes.'

'You will remember?'

'I said yes, didn't I?' She exhales, matter of factly. 'Sorry.'

He has hit the rush hour, as London debouches, and trundles home in sporadic second gear burps. He forages through the fridge and stops to open the French windows. The scent of barbecuing meat hangs tantalisingly on the evening air. It is too much for the dog, who plunges like a torpedo through the privet hedge that separates Christopher from his neighbour. Christopher groans now he is compelled to go next door and drag the dog away from two comparative strangers, who should be better known to him.

Both back gardens of identical houses are accessible only via the house, or from a gate set in the back wall which runs the length of the terrace. There is a similar wall that the rear gardens of the houses opposite back onto, the narrow lane between yielding the odd desiccated condom, and sprouting intermittent vegetation between Victorian cobbles. So Christopher is obliged to walk the length of his immaculate garden, enter theirs, and run the gauntlet of their hostile scrutiny as he approaches the barbecue. His gate opens easily. Theirs gives two inches to the shunt of his shoulder, and yields the rest of the arc with a rusty groan. Christopher stands in the gap, apologetic, glasses flashing back twin suns.

'Christopher! You've timed it well. Your dog doesn't seem to have eaten. If you haven't either come and join us.'

It is a woman's voice, floating through the smoke. She is sitting at a ramshackle table, the surface burned and scarred with usage. The man stands beside the barbecue wielding tongs that he snaps with an excess of virtuosity. He is wearing a plastic apron depicting a woman's basque and tassled breasts. As he passes the man, Christopher accepts the hand extended towards him. As he disengages he is surprised to find he is holding a bottle of beer. He puts this on the table and extends the same hand to the woman. She deflects this, stands, puts her arms around him and says, 'We were sorry to hear.'

'Hear, hear' the man echoes.

Christopher is ashamed.

They are called Deborah and Oscar Bennett. They moved in eight years ago, with two moderately boisterous sons. Marjory stood at her bedroom window, taking inventory of their furniture. The younger boy was in his late teens, the other three years older. They played their music as loudly as people of that ago do, but the volume was no cause for scandal. On chance meetings they were mannerly, helpful, articulate and, as far as Marjory was concerned, exasperatingly difficult to qualify. The parents were no better. They drove a car as ramshackle as their furniture. Marjory was happy to brand them as philistines until one Sunday morning she heard husband and wife improvise a duet that incensed her with its plangency. Further disconcerting revelations came to light. Oscar had something to do with Covent Garden. Even if only in an administrative capacity, some of the vicarious status rubbed off. Marjory's coffee morning cronies thought so. Deborah improvised some kind of studio in an outhouse, and obviously cared more about applying paint than cosmetics. She even had the temerity to go out for last-minute groceries with smudges of paint on her hands and hair. It was convenient for Marjory to brand them as unrealistic and self-indulgent bohemians, and she was foolish to hint as much to Christopher across the dinner table when he remarked, with devastating casualness: 'You don't afford a place round here with your head in the clouds. Besides, I bumped into the boys yesterday. Delightful. The older one's reading law and the younger's been offered a place at Cambridge next year. Medicine. That can't be cheap for the parents. Be silly not to...'

'Not to what?' she said, very quietly.

'Accept the place at Cambridge.'

She hated everything about them. She hated how his obvious love for his wife was compounded by his easy and public intimacies with his children: he kissed them with the verve of an Italian. She hated how these displays seemed only to gratify the neighbours, and cause them to reflect on their own English reticence, as if reserve is a sin. And if that wasn't enough the wife flirted with journalism, and supplemented their income with ad hoc pieces in women's magazines. While Marjory struggled, unsuccessfully, to publish an open letter in the community bulletin, she had to endure the humiliation of sitting in the hairdresser and having the familiar name pointed out to her from the well-thumbed page. The sons' intelligence was undeniable and, as Christopher remarked with infuriating pragmatism: 'They didn't pick their brains off the ground.'

It's hard enough to be overtaken by someone who has worked harder, run a better race. It's harder still to be beaten by an undeserving victor, whose natural ability no amount of effort on your side will compensate for. But it's intolerable to be completely eclipsed by someone who isn't even aware of the competition.

Christopher had no idea. The everyday pleasantries began to falter when Marjory stopped acknowledging their 'good morning's. At first oblivious, he continued in his affable exchanges. When the younger son left for Cambridge, Christopher met him at the garden gate with a congratulations card and a book token. He hadn't made any attempt to hide the gesture. When a thank you letter arrived and he revealed the gift, he was stunned by her glacial hostility.

The neighbours took the hint. They kept their greetings brief after that, continuing to walk while talking, so that the front door or the car marked a conclusion. Marjory pushed her advantage too far after the two couples smiled fleetingly at one another in the High Street: 'Just because their son's a doctor all of a sudden we're not good enough.'

He let her arm, which had seized his for solidarity when they hove into sight, drop. He had belittled himself even though his motives, to honour a vow, had been good. He knew people aren't revealed in the large, premeditated actions but by trivialities. He saw, fully. It was a shock. If he thought it would have done any good he would have turned on his heel, walked back and apologised. They have no reason to be magnanimous but here he is, with her arms round his old body, and the sweating beer awaiting him. She sits him down.

'Thank you for the card.'

'No worries, mate.' Oscar experiments with an Australian accent.

'Nevertheless...' His intensity is obvious.

'It was only a card. We're not going to redeem your mortgage.'

'I have to apologise for my husband. His manners are deplorable.'

'Are they fuck.'

'Oscar thinks it avant-garde to swear. He'd sound like the Archbishop of Canterbury if we lived in a slum, so he swears at a suburban barbecue with all the Volvos lined up.'

'Do you want me to take you outside and give you a slap?'

'We are outside, dear.' Turning to Christopher, 'Men go funny at a certain age. As long as he doesn't present a bad example to the boys.'

Pleased at one of the good reminiscences this sparks he asks: 'How are they?'

'Able to see through their father.'

Oscar cooks. The first experimental sausages are incinerated. They test them on the dog who disdains them too. Oscar squeezes lemon over the grilling sardines.

'Christopher, why don't you go and fetch two of those beautiful cigars you've been teasing us with for the past few months. And get one for yourself. I'll smoke Deborah's.'

Back in the kitchen Christopher picks up a bottle of white wine, less for its grassy credentials than its topaz shadow. As he reaches for the cigars he hears laughter from the barbecue. Thinking back over his marriage he can't recall a single memory of tenderness interrupted. He pockets the cigars and makes his slow way back up the garden path.

* * *

The phone pulls him from a restless sleep. Once he had retrieved one bottle he went back for another two. His sleep has been troubled and the reason for it isn't likely to improve his mood. The dog lies leaden across his legs. The ringing seems to get more insistent as he fumbles for his glasses and locates the receiver.

'Hello?'

'It's me, Christopher. She's gone.'

It takes him a minute to realise that Sister Judith is speaking. He has never heard her voice catch before, and he realises how articulate the pause is. He has been drinking and she has gone. He wasn't there, worse, he wasn't thinking about her. He has no right to the credentials she credited him with.

'I'm so sorry.'

'I am too. You'd think in this line of work you'd get used to this.' There is another pause. He tries to think of something comforting that doesn't sound trite. The phone goes dead.

Five days later he rises unusually early. Spare keys to see to the dog have been left with Deborah. He didn't want to impose on a friendship so recently re-established, but had no choice. A brief taxi ride runs him to the station. Dandelions grow in verdant sidings. A cultivated blur of colour overflows hanging baskets suspended the length of the platform. Early as it is for him, the worst of the suburban crush is over. Phalanxes of suburban gardens and intermittent park land begin to accelerate past. In the distance a brindled cow stares meditatively from an Alpine meadow, beneath a strapline advertising processed cheese. Green peters out until it becomes the exception, confined to urban rectangles, window boxes and exuberant weeds. Children, whose faces collectively exhibit all the colours of the brindled cow, vibrate on the playground tarmac. He feels a pang for them in their urban fastness, so different from the expanses that gave scope to his childhood imagination. He can still recall summer waves of itinerant hop pickers. Residential gives way to commercial. A gas works looms; an acre of flashing windscreens of deposited cars; low-rise office units and seated people in thrall to computer screens; Hungerford Bridge; the Thames rippling through a latticework of girders; Charing Cross.

He emerges from the station to a sparkling rain in the summer sunshine, waits his turn, umbrella raised, mentally rehearsing the address till his turn comes.

'St Patrick's, Soho Square please.'

He has the only taciturn taxi driver in the whole of London, perhaps disgruntled at the shortness of the fare, perhaps taking his cue from Christopher's subfusc suit and black tie. He would have walked, but lateness is one of Christopher's cardinal sins. On a card he has the address of the crematorium. He will order another taxi if necessary. Sister Judith has told him not to worry. 'All else fails, you can cadge a lift with us.' This was said two nights ago, dictating the details over the phone, while he found a pen and wrote with copperplate slowness. He is pleased her manner has reverted to its former brusque geniality.

The place is as surprising as Felicity's dormant piety. He thinks the interior would have pleased her. Had she any association with this place, or do you take what you posthumously get? He's sure George won't be able to answer. And there he is, at the front of the meagre congregation, casting intermittent backward looks, taking inventory. He looks uncomfortable in this numinous place. Behind George are a number of local people, and on the other side of the aisle, unidentifiable from the back in their drab habits, are the Sisters. He sits behind them in solidarity, trying to pick out the youthful frame of Judith, till she turns and winks at him. He smiles. From his peripheral vision he notes that George has registered the exchange.

The service is longer and more elaborate that he imagined. He stands, kneels, sits, in concert with the nuns, is drowsily mesmerised by the responsorial psalm, intones hymns he scarcely knows and feels a mixture of piety and boredom. The chink of the censer and perfume of the incense adds to the unreality of the situation. He can't come to grips with the conclusion that an entire abbreviated life is contained in that frivolous box. Marjory's send-off didn't give rise to this sense of absurdity, or existential mirth. The idea is so singular he wants to laugh out loud, and suppresses his mirth with tremors that run the length of the otherwise empty pew. He is reprieved by the sign of peace, when the clairvoyant Sister Judith turns and shakes his hand with a grip like Achilles. That sobers him.

The mass finishes. The sombre procession filters out, the pews emptying in order. Sister Judith nods in the direction of the departing cortège. He interprets this as an indication that they will meet outside. He waits until the last of the mourners passes and stands to follow. George is standing at the church entrance, with a woman who looks remarkably like a healthy version of Felicity, shaking hands with the mourners in turn. Christopher didn't anticipate this, or an undisclosed sister who has only now materialised. She shakes his hand first and seems pleased to see the end of the line. In her relief she makes some brief pleasantry he only half catches, confused by her intonation. New Zealand? He turns to George. They shake hands sombrely. He is trying to think of something appropriate to say. George speaks first.

'Sorry old boy, it's friends and family only.'

'I... I'm sorry, I don't'

'At the crematorium. It's friends and family only.'

George is watching Christopher's confusion intently. This handshaking may be a Catholic convention, but it occurs to Christopher that George has gone along with it solely to orchestrate this moment. He holds on to Christopher's hand till he's satisfied that the whole effect has been registered, lets go and turns to the woman who has the good grace to look embarrassed by the exchange. Dismissed, Christopher walks into the sunshine and Sister Judith.

'We've got a mini bus. There's room.'

This gives the lie to George's assertion.

'You're very kind but I can't...'

'I thought it was all decided.'

'George says it's friends and family only.'

'What utter bollocks! What a nerve! Friends and family? When you come to think of it he's been neither to her. Do you want me to have a word with him?'

'No. Please. The last thing I want to do is hector my way in. It's not what she would have wanted.'

'She never got what she wanted from him. I don't see why he should thwart her one more time.'

He fans his fingers apologetically and walks on. At another burst of drizzle he turns his jacket collar up. He has left his umbrella behind, but isn't about to go back and give George the satisfaction again. He reasons with himself that he's said his goodbyes, that that isn't really her, just a skin bag of organs in a box, but the colossal unfairness of it strikes him and he reluctantly admits to himself that he is hurt.

He doesn't want to go home carrying this sensation with him. He stops for lunch in a trattoria in Greek Street, eats without relish, and, still numbed from the encounter, threads his way in the direction of St James's Park, feeling the need for space among the unaccustomed crush. The park doesn't dispel his low spirits. He walks to the river, hugging it to cross at Vauxhall Bridge. He finds a bench in Lambeth for a half hour's reflection, gets up and continues walking. In his mind he is trying to revive the last few conversations he had with her, but she is already receding. With the speed of the foot traffic increasing around him, he realises both that he is completely exhausted, and that if he doesn't get a move on he'll be caught in the homeward rush.

He has made his way along the south bank, to cross at Waterloo Bridge, and stops to rest on the approach. Beside him is a woman in baggy shapeless clothes, leaning against some kind of collapsed cardboard structure, awaiting assembly once the pedestrians have passed. Her face is partially hidden by a hood. Beneath this her hair hangs in clotted points. Her movements are slow and he recognises that she, too, is exhausted. The cardboard is a beige rectangle; she is trying to improvise some kind of three-dimensional shelter. He looks at its porosity and the looming sky. She almost succeeds when a man bangs into it, collapsing the structure, walking on briskly with a backward cluck of impatience. She lets the cardboard fold to a two dimensional mat and sits, hunched.

'Why stop on a bridge?'

'Why anywhere?' She doesn't look up but has obviously been

aware of him. She now looks up, past him, wearily stands and begins gathering her things.

'Where are you going?'

'I'm being moved.'

'Moved where?'

'If you have to ask you don't understand.'

The policeman draws abreast of them.

'Move along.'

'Where? Move where? She's here because of a lack of alternatives.'

'I could give you a list of moderately priced B&Bs. Where? How the fuck should I know. Any fucking where as long as it's not here.'

He has grown up with and subscribed to the myth of the English bobby, tipping his helmet, dispensing directions, admonishing naughty schoolboys. He looks at her fatigue, the policeman's impatience, the treatment she accepts without complaint and the chasm of her world momentarily yawns. He feels a sense of horrible vertigo. He has always held an opinion of himself as a good person, but goodness is only manifested in acts of kindness. Potential goodness is of no use to anyone. His empty rooms. Her exposure. It's a tiny example of the aggregate of inequality, but it comes within his compass to rectify. He can't walk away from her and continue to think of himself the same way again.

'Come back with me. There's space. We'll... we'll work something out.'

She looks at him properly this time, intently gauging his sincerity. Perhaps, he thinks, she is evaluating the risks. He doesn't think he looks sinister, and perhaps the fact that the offer has been made in front of a policeman will weigh her decision. The policeman's growing impatience is manifest. A curtain of rain patters up the river and drums on her cardboard. In her eyes there is something terrible, a vitality extinguished, that sharpens his resolve. His anger at his treatment, by George, and hers, here, has honed itself to a single function.

'Please.'

'And take this crap with you.' While saying this the policeman prods at one of her bags with his foot. For a moment her attention shifts from Christopher to the dull boot and follows the line of the uniform up. The eyes beneath the helmet brim are slitted against the rain, the face devoid of expression. She turns back to Christopher. The discrepancy is sufficient prompt.

She picks up the various bags littered around her, folds the cardboard into a giant envelope under her arm, and nods imperceptibly to Christopher to lead. He bends into the rain checking every twenty or so strides that she is still in his wake. At the other side of the river he fully expects her to disappear. She follows at a cautionary distance all the way to Charing Cross. He buys a second ticket to complement his return.

They sit side by side, partitioned by her defensive cardboard, silent. At the other side he hails a taxi. He is so tired she has to help him with the exchange of money. Deborah must have been in to see to the dog. He is glad of the warm lozenges of light, thrown out by the stained glass of the front door. The dog greets them both enthusiastically. She leaves the cardboard in the hall and takes inventory.

'You live alone?'

'Yes. Well, there's the dog.'

He walks into the kitchen. Behind him, unseen, she opens the lounge door with her foot and looks quickly inside, glancing back to ensure her path of exit to the front door is unimpeded. She follows him warily into the kitchen and reconnoitres.

'I was going to make us both something to eat but I'm suddenly very tired.' His voice comes from inside the fridge. He is foraging. He straightens up. His tiredness isn't sudden, she's been watching it overtake him for the past hour. 'I'm really sorry, I don't mean to be rude, but I'm going to have to go to bed. Feel free to make yourself whatever you want.'

'Can I have a bath?'

'Of course. The door to the spare room's open. You can't miss it.'

The dog follows him. As it lies solidly across his legs he hears the movement downstairs, then upstairs, as she moves from room to room, stopping on the landing outside his door. Her movements perplex him. Why stop there to stare at his door?

She isn't. Directly above her head is a trap door to the attic. She suspects one of those sliding ladder arrangements. Satisfying herself it looks undisturbed, she collects her cache of bags from the hall.

She lies down in the warm water and contemplates the twin islands of her breasts. She is reasoning: his age, his fatigue; if his circumstances are as he has made out it is he who has made himself the more vulnerable of the two.

He is drifting off when he hears from the bathroom the intermittent humming of a nursery rhyme.

* * *

He wakes to a sound it takes him a minute to identify: the spin cycle of the washing machine. The dog, having other stimulation, has already gone downstairs. He can tell by the quality of light that it is late, perhaps mid-morning. The bathroom towels, piled pell mell on the wicker basket, have disappeared. Fresh towels stand stacked in the alcove. He feels slightly aggrieved. After his morning ritual he comes down to the smell of fresh coffee. She is reading yesterday's paper. The world is somehow different, less monochrome.

'What is it that's missing?'

'Dust. I don't know how you saw the telly.'

'I'll have to take the dog out.'

'He's already had a piss in the garden.'

Last night she slept with the chair wedged beneath the door handle, barricading herself against the unknown. At the sight of him she realises how unnecessary her precaution has been.

He straightens his tie, sips the offered coffee. Beneath the table her plastic bags have been replaced with new ones. He correctly guesses she has washed all the contents, prepared in readiness for an imminent departure. It seems a miserable cache. The few garments he can see looked washed out.

'If you need to buy some clothes...' disingenuously producing his wallet.

'That didn't take long.'

'Oh dear.' He whistles to the dog, and, misunderstood, takes to the common.

* * *

The warning signs around the pond seem superfluous: it has shrunk to a muddy puddle surrounded by a corona of greenish mud. He stares at the forlorn patch and wonders. Conceivably she's young enough to be his granddaughter, but more likely could have been his daughter if they'd started late. He wouldn't have minded. No – that won't do. It's not just that he wouldn't have minded, a decision of that gravity isn't made by negation, he was prepared. He would have embraced the obligations.

Leaving the breakfast table that morning something in her voice made him stop. Something had snagged, a rehearsed sentence that didn't flow as intended. He had turned, asked her to repeat it. Her use of the past tense confused him. He had touched her hand, palm downward, on the table surface. And with the slightest of motions he saw that she steeled herself for the contact and he understood. Nothing had been lost. She wasn't ever prepared for sacrifices. She had taken a decision without him and was informing him in the aftermath. The news was delivered strategically as he was on his way out, to preclude further discussion.

He had gone into the city as he had done every professional day of his life. He remembers people, hordes and hordes he saw every other day without noticing, disembarking from trains, buying newspapers, hurrying to destinations. All of these people he would never know and who, like him, had something in common: the privilege of having arrived. The buildings were grey, the sky overcast. 'This place is terrible,' he murmured to himself, without doubting his desire to introduce someone of his own. And he had disguised the vacuum within himself so competently, earning a reputation for industry because he could not tolerate the introspection that inactivity admitted, that he thought himself a fraud.

He didn't think he'd have been found wanting as a father. He imagined the care he'd have taken. And that girl, in his house, how much care has she lacked to find herself alone on a bridge keeping the world at bay with cardboard? She has the look of someone not loved enough when it matters most. It marks them, indelibly. He cannot say what it is but he can spot it without fail. He has been foolish. He has made an offer to her with the same whimsy that he adopted the dog, and a human being isn't a dog.

When he returns she is standing in the hall with her coat on, festooned with bags in readiness.

'I didn't know if you had house keys.'

'You don't have to go.'

'Thanks for the accommodation and the chance to clean up.'

'Look.' He spreads his palms, a telling gesture for those who know him. 'We got off to the wrong start. Offering you money was stupid, genuine but stupid. I didn't intend to compromise you. This house is too large for two, never mind one. You'd be going out to the same thing as yesterday. You've already dusted. If you're prepared to clean we can work something out, as long as you don't embark on the antiseptic crusade my wife did. Can you cook?'

'Bits.'

'Well, why don't you cook bits, and clean more, and if you don't like it you don't have to stay?' She turns from him to stare at the spot beneath the stairs where the dog has torn her cardboard to shreds. He presses the sensed advantage. 'Consider it a trial – on both sides. All the risk is mine. You might abscond with...' He looks around this interior, contrived for someone else, to find something he actually cares for. '...The wine.' For the first time there is the premonition of a smile playing around the corners of her mouth. 'What do you have to lose?' He waves towards the world on the other side of the door. 'It's always waiting for you – whatever it is.'

She drops her parcels, one by one, falling berries, and shrugs off her coat.

'The dog needs wormed.'

'I hadn't noticed.'

'What's his name?'

'I don't know if he ever had one and I wouldn't presume to give him one.'

'Gina.'

'He's a dog, not a bitch.'

'*I'm* Gina.'

'Oh... Christopher.'

'I know.'

* * *

Christopher now has a new routine. He is reluctant to relinquish his new-found self-sufficiency but does so for her sake, reasoning that if she opts to leave he can always go back to the way things were. She immerses herself in Marjory's cookery books, bought solely for display, and absorbs the numerous cooking programmes on television. Marjory's meals were utilitarian, prepared without relish to fill a void and minimise mess. Dishes were removed the instant the last morsel was lifted from them. Sometimes, if she finished first, he even found himself chewing quicker to shorten her wait. Gina cooks with flair and an additional ingredient he hasn't yet identified: the love of it. She's a quick learner. The meals improve daily. He senses a latent talent she has never had the resources to exploit.

'This isn't a working kitchen. It's what someone who doesn't cook thinks it is.' She's unpacking to the table as she speaks: milk, eggs, carrots encrusted in authentic dirt, a brain of vivid broccoli, purple garlic, creamy scallops fringed in orange corals, steaks bleeding lightly into their greaseproof paper, the yellow disc of a lemon flan, a truckle of cheese. There is no need to display them so, they could be packed straight from bag to fridge, but he senses this fan of ingredients satisfies some inner aesthetic of texture and colour, and perhaps the realisation of being able to spend. 'Steak all right? I've gone for sirloin. You can afford it. I told him...' she demonstrates a width with parted forefinger and thumb, 'and watched him cut them. And it's marbled, like they say on the telly.'

She is happy to haunt the food shops in the High Street, and beyond, and somehow feeds the two of them better and more cheaply than he succeeded in feeding himself. She is scrupulous with his money and embarrasses him every second night with a conscientious rendering of accounts. The coffee bar of his last meeting with Vanessa has absorbed the vacated premises next door and sprouted an adjunct delicatessen. The new staff seem a similar age to her and similarly enthused. She comes back, vivid with contained excitement and the news that they have offered her a probationary position. It is the first time he has seen that look temporarily dispelled from her eyes. Even if it doesn't work out it can only be beneficial. She returns alternative nights with artichoke hearts for him, olives the colour of aubergines that shine in their oily lustre, sun-dried tomatoes that draw saliva from his mouth, and marinated squid rings that challenge his teeth. He feels this is a protracted thank you in place of the words she can't muster, for, aside from the exchange of niceties, they seldom talk of anything of any moment. He is aware of her constant need for activity, similar to his when presented with the news of the abortion. He has observed her in the slack times, when whatever small distraction she has fastened on has worn thin, or at the end of their day, when he is watching the late news, the best of her energies gone. At such times the animation that has been slowly suffusing her over these weeks deserts her face and she can look plain, ugly even. In her abstraction she loses awareness or control of her features; vertical creases appear between the brows and the eyes adopt an expression of hopeless dismay, as if remembering a vast internal confusion. It's painful to see, and he feels he's being given a glimpse of something she wouldn't want revealed, a door left guilelessly ajar, in the absorption of whatever torments her. So he calls her back to the here and now with the offer of a hot drink, or local trivia, and she gathers herself and schools her features, until the next time.

There is an ever newer routine. Who, he says to himself, said you can't teach an old dog new tricks? He rises at eight. She has already staked her claim to the upstairs bathroom. He puffs down the stairs in his dressing gown to the downstairs toilet, and back up fifteen minutes later with two cups of Earl Grey, knocking gently to deliver hers to a disembodied hand, accepted like Excalibur through the steaming gap. He inherits a bathroom that mists his glasses on contact. He has to wipe the sweating mirror to shave. Her hygiene is obsessive, as if trying to rid herself of something. Only once has he passed to the front bedroom to see her retreating form, pulling down an inappropriately brief dress. He has reinstated the daily paper he let lapse and will read her fragments aloud while she cooks, or set the table to her shouted instructions. She settles in front of a television that bores him. He goes through to read in the front room until the last walk with the dog.

She tries to give him money. He uses the opportunity.

'I tried to give you money the first day and my motives were suspected.'

'That was the first day.'

'I don't want to offend, but you came here with stuff in bags. You need more clothes. Either take the money I was going to give you or use the money you were going to give me. You can't keep going to work every day with the same washed-out things.'

There is a logic to this fait accompli she can't take offence at. She gets the next Saturday off, takes a lunch-time train and returns after eight from the station in a ticking taxi, armed with an astonishing number of purchases. Bowed from the weight she throws the bags on the vacant sofa and seems to be filled with helium. 'Wait there,' the tone is peremptory, arm outstretched, palm toward him in the time-honoured gesture, 'for the whole ensemble.' She takes the clutch of bags upstairs, reappears, and continues to do so in a series of gaudy tableaux, each entry a new outfit. He imagines he makes a cheerful endorsement of each.

'What's wrong?'

Perhaps he has to become increasingly more demonstrative to remain plausible. This is new territory for him: Marjory only required payment, not approval.

'You think they're common, don't you?'

'No.'

But he does. He had assumed her appearance was a function of her budget. Rather than buy anything good she has bought what she already had, in quantities she couldn't previously afford, loud synthetic things guaranteed to bleed out and turn shapeless at first wash.

'Fuck! I never could dress. If I ever had anything expensive people think I stole it.'

'I like the way you look.'

'Tell the truth, you wanted me to look like something in one of your wife's magazines, didn't you?'

Remembrance of her slavish obedience to the prestige of

labels makes his sincerity blatant. 'You couldn't be more wrong.' Mollified, she begins to pack the stuff away. 'One proviso – did you buy a scarf?' Since their first meeting he has noticed her exposed neck, a trait, in his mind, associated with poverty, like lacking an umbrella. And the weather is on the turn. She flourishes some trumpery acrylic thing that crackles with static. He takes it from her.

'There is no warmth in this. Buy a good one, wool or cashmere, or take one of mine from the hat stand.'

'To keep?'

The question strikes him as odd. There are several and he can only wear one at a time. 'Yes.'

She blushes, a reaction that leaves him nonplussed. In embarrassment she gathers her things and goes to her room.

* * *

The weather is on the turn: an invigorating sharpness during the morning walk; the pre-emptive sweet smell of vegetation about to rot; an amber tinge to the evening air whose beauty compels him to lengthy contemplations from his fragrant garden. He catches himself beside the hat stand mirror and experiments with various rakish angles of his hat, before returning to his usual pose. He has thought about an ebony cane but shies away from such affectation: there will be time enough when the need for support won't be optional, and he has known poor souls who have had recourse to a stick as a cheaper alternative to a prosthesis. But why, he wonders, this inner frivolity? There is a change in both of them.

Either she has succeeded in making herself busier, or the periods of corrosive introspection are becoming fewer and further between. At any rate, he notes a lightening in her mood. He has even felt that some revelation, perhaps explaining why she got here, is about to be forthcoming. It hasn't occurred yet. He would never press. He senses she wants to talk, and wishes he had some revelation of his own to barter, but feels his circumstances, like his personality, are transparent and uneventful. They have been for three barbecues next door. Deborah was as discreet as Christopher could have wished. Oscar was agog and had to be taken aside by his wife. Christopher felt for Gina, thinking it wasn't her milieu, whatever that might be. He needn't have been concerned. Both boys were there and it occurd to Christopher how pretty she is when he saw the attention they paid her, particularly the older one. On the next two occasions the three sit together at the end of the table and he glances across, trying to remember what it was like at their age. When they go back she brings up the subject of returning the favour.

'I never thought about it.'

'Well you can't keep going round and eating their food and accepting their hospitality indefinitely. We'll have a barbecue.'

'We don't have a barbecue.'

So the Tudor cottage is trundled out again, to her bemusement, and they go to B&Q. He is presented with a series of options as bewildering as the array of delicatessen coffees. She chooses on his behalf.

'Marjory didn't like the idea of barbecues. The mess.'

'There's a surprise.'

To celebrate the purchase she suggests lunch in the delicatessen. She gestures him cavalierly to the window stool. He tackles this unobserved while she banters with the staff. It reminds him of a child's high chair. There's a low back to the arrangement and a bar to rest feet on. He imagines himself trapped in a sitting position, falling like a detonated industrial chimney, fracturing from the bottom up. He gets purchase by leaning forward on the counter and eating in a slovenly pose. She stays to finish a shift. He will have to go back to see to the dog. She sees him to the car while he makes strange noises, blowing air through his teeth to dislodge the cous

cous she insisted he try. She takes his arm for the two-hundred-yard walk, a habit they've fallen into that quietly gratifies him. On the pavement they meet Vanessa, who looks at this tableau with arresting intensity, draws her own conclusion and walks silently on.

'Who's that?'

'Just... a woman.'

'A fucking encyclopaedia, that's what you are. I think we should invite her to the barbecue too.'

'Why?'

'Because she looks like she needs it.'

That evening, while Gina assembles the barbecue and experiments with the chops brought home for the purpose, he is thinking about Vanessa, Gina, Marjory and Felicity, the quick versus the dead and the lack of cosmic order in selecting who stays and who doesn't. The first chop goes to the dog. They sit down to the successful results. Gina dresses the salad. 'I think I will invite her.' But Christopher isn't listening.

The boys abandon whatever other social commitments they may have had to assemble the following Saturday night in Christopher's garden. She has been so efficient all his efforts are ineffectual. He feels he should at least wield the tongs, like those suburban men who do nothing at all till the primitive instinct compels them to burn meat in a display of social dominance. But he's denied the barbecue by the tight-knit backs of the boys and Gina. He sits with Deborah. Oscar's entry is tardy and theatrical, flourishing two bottles.

Everyone has come via the back gate. The dog hears the front door before Christopher does. He stands, knees cracking. Perhaps that cane after all. He opens the door with no expectations whatsoever. She is holding a bunch of violets in one hand and in the other the crepe cone of a wrapped bottle. Her dress is pleasing, the kind of elegant thing he expected Gina to return from the shops with. Her mouth is fixed, as if caught in the act of practising a smile. The expression in her eyes approximates tragedy.

'You didn't know I was coming.'

'But I'm delighted nevertheless.' The automatic response of his manners carry the moment. He takes the flowers from her and offers her his arm, needlessly guiding her through the hall, past the hazard of Marjory's ghastly etargé, making a mental note to consign it to the skip. Beneath the clean lines of fabric he can't help but notice the swell of her breasts and buttocks, reduced by natural attrition and careful diet, but still shapely. On waking these mornings he is still presented with very occasional erections. They don't have the provenance of erotic dreams that he can recall, or the temper of earlier days, but are still strident enough to earn the name. Each has melted with disappointment in reaction to his surprise. And now, here, with her, guiding her swaying shape, he can feel the blood flow unsolicited. Embarrassed he reverts to the teenage stratagem of pretending to tie his laces, forcing her to make her entrance unchaperoned. They cheerfully surround her. The couple and Vanessa, it seems, have played local bridge until the competitive snobbery of the others palled. She's been more generous in her attentions to the boys than he has, giving him a glimpse of the kind of rapport Marjory stymied. Gina kisses her and is kissed in return, each unashamedly reading the other. Women – how do they do it? Oscar uncorks her superior wine and pretends to swig from the bottle. The tumid little emergency over, his sense of social obligation reasserts itself. He fetches her a glass for Oscar to fill. She accepts this, confidence restored by the warmth of her reception, and leans towards him confidentially.

'I'm flattered. You can't get many of them visit you at your age.'

* * *

The leaves turn. The pond in the common, now worthy of its name, has mysteriously filled. He is drawn to watch its morning mists evaporate. He's called out of doors by some compulsion he doesn't remember exerting itself with anything like this kind of force before. The beauty of the fading season is reaching an intense pitch that has become a narcotic to him. Perhaps, he thinks, he is calibrating these changes more diligently because there are fewer left to experience. 'This tangible world,' he thinks, and like a child wants to hold out his hand to the sky and grasp it all. And then, within a week, it's over: the leaves have fallen, are dug into mulch or swept into conical piles and burnt in suburban gardens; the trees turn black with rain; the air dries, the cold intensifies and he is gratified by the plume of his breath.

She takes him up on the offer of his scarf. She consults the cookery books and changes their diet, dismays his intestines with bean soups till he establishes equilibrium, serves up stews and roasted root vegetables which he eats with a relish he can't remember. He buys a case of Barolo, and at the first sip decides that there may be a God after all. They never did anything like this. Is this sense of awareness down to her? The only thing to disturb his peace of mind is the thought of its precariousness.

She accosts him directly one evening after dinner.

'I was going to ask you something.'

'Mmm.' He's concentrating on feeding the lamb fat to the dog.

'You'll kill him you know.'

'That's not a question.'

'But you know you will.'

He thinks for a minute. He has no idea how old the dog is but somehow now doesn't envisage being without him. 'He looks as if he did without for long enough. If I thought I could prolong my life for five years by giving up wine – I wouldn't.'

'Were you thinking of seeing Vanessa?' He is half turned towards the dog and stiffens in this pose. 'You don't have to pretend to be occupied with that. You don't have to answer if you don't want to.'

'No. I know I don't. I live here.'

'I don't want to make you uncomfortable.'

'Neither did she when we met that time in the coffee shop.'

'What shop?'

'Your shop.'

'When?'

'Before it was your shop.'

'And was it uncomfortable?'

'Yes.'

'And is this?'

'Yes.' He watches the dog gobble the fat. She hasn't touched on anything personal to him before. He thinks this is more due to the possibility of being expected to make a similar revelation than natural reticence. When he turns round she is staring at her empty plate and looks the more embarrassed of the two. It strikes him suddenly that she is guided by generosity that builds up and manifests itself in unpremeditated outpourings: hydraulic kindness. This well-intentioned intervention is her way of trying to pay him back. 'In answer to your question, I never thought of seeing Vanessa.'

Her embarrassment appears to vanish, replaced with curiosity.

'I thought you liked her.'

'I like what I know of her.'

'And how is she supposed to know that? Look, Christopher, just liking someone in the abstract and sitting in separate rooms watching telly on either side of the common isn't really much use to most people. Especially a woman. It might be to you but I can guarantee it isn't much use to her.'

'I don't know her number.'

'That's lame.'

And he concedes with a nod that it is.

'What do you think she expects of me?'

'A little company. What everyone wants. What the dog wants. Plants grow towards light.'

'I don't want to raise expectations I can't meet.'

'Talk, Christopher. Just talk to her. If it doesn't work it doesn't work. She won't die. She's seen it all.'

'How do you know?'

'How can you not? Just look at her.' There's nothing judgmental or derogatory in her tone. She's obviously looked at Vanessa and seen what Marjory did and he so conspicuously hasn't. But she's come up with an entirely different evaluation from his dead wife's. 'You owe her that.'

'Why do I owe her anything?'

'Because she's kept faith with you in the face of no encouragement.'

She's a girl, to him little more than a child. She has obviously come from some obscure and neglected background. He thinks she hasn't enjoyed the benefit of any kind of formal education that he would recognise. How can she possibly know all this? He's tempted to ask but she might have to violate a confidence. He's decided he can't possibly ask when he hears himself speak.

'How can you possibly know all this?'

'Women talk. And even when they don't they understand. At least, some do.'

When he was a schoolboy he understood early that any mathematics was beyond him. His comprehension of numbers extended to the practicality of counting his change, or working out the square yardage to buy a carpet. It wasn't laziness, or lack of application. He found effortless many things his fellow pupils struggled with, but he had to reconcile himself that there was a world of abstractions and symbols that more accurately described the workings of his phenomenal world than he could. He feels that way now. Half the human race has access to a kind of understanding denied him. And so, unpractised, apprehensive, feeling the way he did when he stared at a blackboard swarming with symbols, he picks up the telephone the following evening when Gina is in the next room, glued to *Coronation Street.*

'Hello?'

'Vanessa?' If it's her he doesn't recognise this formal phone voice.

'Christopher?' The tone has instantly changed. Somehow she's managed to infuse a three-syllable question with a note of hope. He stares, aggrieved, at the wall separating him from Gina. One word and he feels he's already raised her expectations wildly beyond his capacity to meet them.

'I was just wondering if perhaps you'd like to meet me for coffee. I believe it's my turn to buy.'

'I... I... When?'

'Well, my time's not taken up. It's you who runs a business.'

'Tomorrow? Or is that too soon?' She is speaking uncharacteristically fast.

'No. That's fine with me. Does three o'clock in the same place suit?'

'Yes. That would be ideal. I look forward to seeing you then.' Her voice has slowed. She's almost formal. He guesses this is deliberate, exhaling between clauses to try and modify the sound of eagerness. She puts the phone down, sealing the bargain before it can be revoked.

He arrives the next afternoon at two fifty-five. He hasn't mentioned anything to Gina. Vanessa is already there. Gina is sitting across from her, her long apron bunched in her lap. They appear to be talking effortlessly. At his entrance they both look up. Gina walks towards him and gently touches his shoulder.

'You kept this quiet.' She is talking into his lapel. Behind his back she waves away the duty waitress. As he takes a seat Gina returns with two cups of coffee, puts them down and discreetly returns behind the counter. He's trying to work out what to say as his spoon revolves and revolves in a small frothy whirlpool of compulsive stirring. Vanessa helps him out.

'Thank you for inviting me.'

'What on earth do women find to talk to one another about? You two have hardly met yet you looked thick as thieves. In a nice way, I mean.'

'The obvious answer would be to say we were talking about you. But we weren't.'

'Sometimes I wish I understood women more.'

'Do you?'

He thinks for a moment. What would it be like? Understanding things that aren't manifestly obvious. Not facts. He's probably forgotten more of those than many will ever know, but feelings. He imagines being helplessly receptive to the cacophony of other people's feelings, the clamour of silent wants.

'No. Not really.'

She touches his sleeve and smiles at him. He smiles back.

Perhaps this is going to be all right.

* * *

Christmas is accelerating towards them. He finds himself anticipating its arrival in a way he hasn't since childhood.

'Where are all your decorations?'

He shows her a small box in the garage that yields a paltry synthetic tree.

'Marjory didn't go in much for Christmas.'

'You don't say.'

Her response at each revelation of his married life is becoming harder, as her dislike for his dead wife grows.

'She thought a real tree caused a mess.'

'A real mess, with a real smell. Marjory didn't go in much for anything that didn't suit her, did she?'

'I don't suppose so.'

He comes home one evening to a neon reindeer in the front

garden, encouraged by a flashing Santa. Deborah and Oscar will take it in the spirit it's intended, but it will apoplex some of the other neighbours. Marjory would have died. That's probably why she did it. He goes in. She has been to Woolworths. The hall is a tacky grotto. A real tree dominates the front room.

'Good – isn't it?' She is animated over dinner. He is quiet.

'What's the matter with you?'

'Nothing. All this,' waving towards the hall and the tinsel she has hung above the pictures, 'do you believe it?'

'Does it matter?'

'I think it does.' He remembers midnight mass with his mother; her squeeze of his hand on the stroke of the hour; the candles, the uplit faces, the hymns, the goodwill on the steps afterwards, bathed in a flowing out of grace from the lighted church behind; greetings in the cold air to the same people, somehow renewed in the mystery. 'Either it's just a bunch of ornaments and over spending adding up to nothing, or they're the garland round the real reason: "The uncontrollable mystery on the bestial floor."'

'What's that?'

'A poem describing the scene in the stable.'

'Oh *that*.'

Yes, he thinks, *that*, and everything it implies. And he has wanted to believe it ever since he didn't, a birth that tilted the world.

'I don't think it does matter. And I don't think it's all just ornaments and overeating. Even if there was no stable and even no baby, where's the harm if it makes people a bit nicer to one another for a couple of days? There's the rest of the year for folk to be complete bastards. Think of all those coins dropped in all those boxes just because it's Christmas.'

And he thinks in a way she's right, the same way he's not wrong. And this Christmas he has her.

'And it's a time for families' he concedes, colossally hitting the wrong note. He's thinking of separated people given a reason not to drift further from one another, but she has interpreted this in some way that twists her mouth again as she frowns at her food. He has a sense of telescoping, seeing his predicament from afar, last experienced when confronted with another casual revelation of Marjory's smallness. They are an old man and a young woman of slender acquaintance in a suburban kitchen, one light in the hundreds of thousands in the humming conurbation. He is the last of his line. Since the death of his mother this is the nearest thing he has experienced to a family, and it's not real. He has conjured this because he wanted it, perhaps at some level even still needed it. His casual remark has distressed her and he doesn't know how to make amends, because he realises how little he knows her.

'There's fruit salad,' she says, listlessly.

On Christmas morning he wakes to a vacant silence. The dog lies across his legs wearing a sparkling collar that wasn't there when he followed Christopher to bed. He taps her door to no reply. The delicatessen is closed. The folded scarf on the hall table has a premonitory weight. Her house keys fall from its folds. The kitchen is clinically clean, with none of the aftermath of last night's meal. There are precise written instructions concerning the half-prepared Christmas dinner, but no note about anything else. He takes the dog out, scrambles some eggs, sits in front of the television and regards the wrapped presents beneath the tree. The dog makes intermittent trips to the hall and back, looking for her. Deborah comes through around lunch time with presents.

'I'm sorry. I didn't think to buy for you.'

'Gina did. She delivered them yesterday. Where is she?'

'She's gone back to Scotland... I think.'

Deborah absorbs this, pauses in the delivery of her next question and decides not to ask. 'I'll leave the presents beneath the tree, shall I?'

'Yes. If you don't mind. I'm not opening my stuff just yet.'

'We're eating in two hours. There's tons.'

'There's tons here too. She left me instructions.'

'The offer's there. There's no need to be on your own.'

'Thank you.' She kisses him.

But he is on his own. He sets the oven and times the steps as indicated. She's been meticulous in her instructions but hasn't halved the quantities. A single ironic cracker has been left out. He leaves the television at a low murmur, to give the illusion of human communion. The meal is joyless. He takes the dog out again after dark and mimes a hearty greeting to the boys next door as they wave to him from the front room. Jacob holds up a glass of beer and beckons him in. Christopher points to the dog and in the direction of the common, and walks off before the invitation can be repeated from the front hall. He returns from the opposite direction to avoid their hospitality and stumbles over the darkened reindeer.

He cracks some nuts for the sound of the detonation and then decides he doesn't want them. At the sound of the front door his heart stutters. A series of contradictory thoughts shuttle back and forth at a speed that outpaces his physical reactions. Why would she ring if she has a key? She doesn't – it was in the scarf. She's returned? Was she ever away? Was this an excursion? He yanks open the door to find Vanessa in the same pose as the barbecue evening, with the same crepe-wrapped bottle and a present under her arm.

'What's wrong?'

'Nothing. No, please, please.' He waves her in with a magnanimity he doesn't feel. The dog looks at her and is disappointed. She walks into the kitchen and surveys the remains of his meal, the solitary cracker. 'I'm sorry, I didn't think to get you a present.'

'Gina did. She handed it in yesterday.'

'That was thoughtful.'

'Where is she anyway?' This obviously isn't the time for exchanging presents. She puts hers on the floor and nudges it with her foot towards the skirting.

'I don't know. She didn't say. Her thoughtfulness seems to have been all used up seeing to presents.' It's uncharacteristically peevish. She sits, still in her coat, looking at him intently. 'Excuse me for forgetting my manners. Have you eaten?'

'Yes. But I'll have a glass of wine.'

He pours them both a glass and sits opposite her. 'Would you like me to take your coat?'

She shrugs it off and leaves it hanging on the back of the chair, arms trailing. She's about to ask if he has called the police when she realises the absurdity of it. And say what? A girl he has been looking after and about whom he knows next to nothing may or may not have decided to leave. She wonders if he appreciates how uncomfortable the attention focused on his relationship with Gina would make him. She is fairly sure that since Gina came to stay here he has become more of a cause celeb among their little tribe than she imagines she is. She also knows the decency of his intentions have shielded him from knowing any of this. Even at this age he's still reluctant to believe that other people can be otherwise motivated. Considering the length of time he was exposed to Marjory she thinks this makes him either a fool or a hopeless idealist. His look of baffled concern makes him strangely childlike. Her feeling flows towards him like lava.

'Are you going to go and look for her?'

'She hasn't been away for long enough yet.'

'If it gets to the time when she has been, will you look?'

'I don't know.'

'Do you want me to come?'

'I don't know. I shouldn't expect so. I wouldn't drag you traipsing all round the place because I'm disappointed in someone's behaviour.'

'When people say 'If there's anything I can do' they don't mean literally *anything*. They mean if there's anything I can do within reason given the extent of our friendship.'

'I know. I've got cards from Marjory's churchy stalwarts to prove it. Or at least I had.'

'If there's anything I can do. If you go and you want me to go, I will. If it will help lessen it, I'll share a disappointment. If you need me to look after the dog then say so.' She finishes the wine with a glug, stands, slides her arms back into the coat sleeves and shrugs the coat back on. 'If you need to look, and you want to do it on your own, I'll be here when you get back. Stay where you are. I can see myself out.'

By eight o'clock he is in his pyjamas, still poring over her cavalier departure, wondering why she had set so little store in what had come to matter to him. By nine o'clock he is angry at her for having disrupted the equilibrium it took him so long to establish, for avoiding the ordeal of a proper goodbye. At the very least she owed him that. He had not taken her for a coward. At the dog's insistent scratching he lets it into the back garden. The kitchen light reflects from the shrouded dome of the barbecue, glistening blackly in the pattering drizzle. The dog completes a futile round of the shrubbery, looking for her, until Christopher summons him indoors. Despite the day's inactivity the turbulence has exhausted him. He climbs the stairs leaving the dishes behind.

He wakes with a profound sense of worry. His dreams have been a catalogue of destitute scenarios. He knows so little about her, how can he be sure her motives were selfish? There may be some compulsion he doesn't know about. She may have been forced back to something sinister. She didn't say she wasn't coming back because she didn't say anything.

The shop is open tomorrow. Should he phone to see if she gave notice to quit or go on holiday? What's the point? He believes that she cares more for him than the job, and if she'd leave him without notice why would she tell the shop? She still has a coat on the hall stand. There is a greyness to everything that can't be attributed just yet to the return of dust. She has taken the colour with her. He stands outside her room and, ridiculously, knocks. He pushes the door open and stands on the threshold, peering in, as if hoping to divine something from the arrangement of the furniture.

It's tidy and doesn't show any signs of impulsive departure. There are clothes still hanging in the closet, but he doesn't know if this is a good sign or not: whatever she's taken with her is more than she arrived with. She's obviously used to travelling light. On her bedside is a book of Yeats' poems, taken from the shelves downstairs that she brought up here following his reference to the stable. Various of his other books litter other surfaces. She has pored over these over the months, when he has mentioned something she knew nothing about. Whatever haunts her, there is more than one hunger there. He didn't know his words carried this weight.

He hesitates at her bedside bureau. But he has come this far. It yields nothing unexpected. There is no money, which, he decides, is not a good sign. The chest of drawers has a rationale he can understand: socks and balled up tights in the bottom drawer, the others working their way up the body. The middle drawer has a confusion of pastel bras and flimsy things that pass for pants. He closes this quickly and looks over his shoulder, as if expecting to be caught. The top drawer contains jumpers, various tops and the acrylic scarf he derided. He picks this up with a static crackle. Beneath is a shoe box. He looks at this, blinking for a few seconds, sensing something portentous. He takes it to the bed and sits down, staring at it for a silent minute. This is a further intrusion, but he's already seen her underwear drawer. It may only be receipts.

But it isn't. It's a collection of photographs, dozens, perhaps more than a hundred, thrown in in any order. The box is battered. She must have had this with her all the time. He never noticed. He tips the contents out, turning them face upward and fanning them over the counterpane, trying to achieve some kind of perspective. The largest portion are the postage-stamp booth photographs with the same subject: two girls, individually or in combination, their faces laughingly vying with one another to command space. Every close of the shutter has caught the spontaneity and affection. They can be easily categorised by age, not just because of the transformation of the subjects, but because of the photographs themselves, dog-eared, dubiously tinted by obsolete processes, faded with time and coated with a patina of handling. Gina is obvious, the woman he has spent the past months with emerging from the adolescent face that assumes a look of humorous gravity, and a wistfulness when photographed on her own.

The other girl is a mystery to him. She undergoes a marked transformation. In the earlier photographs she is the same colour as Gina. There isn't a great distinction in their development. Their paths diverge as Gina shades into gamine. The fullness of the other girl's face is obviously part of a growing voluptuousness, made more obvious by another photograph where she bolsters her cleavage to present it to the lens like merchandise, one eyebrow raised as if appraising the viewer. Gina is a blur of hilarity in the background as she is edged out the picture. Perhaps this was for the boys. He is useless with ages, but looking at Gina he would guess they are around fourteen or fifteen. He can imagine her boy-like figure in contrast to the other.

The other girl is already changing colour. It can't be attributed to some quirk in the chemical development, because it doesn't happen to Gina and it's consistent. They can't all have been taken from the same booth. She begins to glow as she fills out. In one of the last ones her face is obscured by a turban of intensely thick smoke, suspended above the tangerine delta of her impressive cleavage.

And then there are other dual booth photographs in which she doesn't figure. Here is Gina, an animated version of the young woman he knows, holding up a baby for the preservation of the moment, again and again, in different backing, in different clothes, raising a mittened hand, laughing, pretending to scowl, smiling at the baby with an intensity of directed love that's more palpable than the cosmetic glow of the orange girl. From the elaborate outfits he assumes the baby is a girl.

There are other pictures too, dozens, taken beyond the confines of the booths. The girls at the bottom of what looks like a gangplank, everything beyond the pool of the flash in darkness, Gina, vulnerably young, pulling a coat around her, shoulders raised, hunched in the obvious cold; the other, seemingly oblivious in glowing décolletage, as they snort tusks of air in shared mirth. The baby in a swing, craning backward to smile back at Gina. Who is the photographer? Perhaps the orange girl who appears with Gina in a corner café booth, the baby bolstered in a high chair between. But then who is the photographer here? A stilted shot in a shabby room, flooded with daylight, a glimpsed bend of a river from a floor-length window behind. He guesses this is done on auto timer from the contrivance of the arrangement. Gina stands between two girls her own age, the orange one and another nondescript girl, the latter self-consciously contemplating her shoes while the other two stare out confidently, down the corridor of time to this perusal.

There are more of the same that yield nothing new. The baby grows in increments at each exposure and is eventually seen walking in the same shabby room, one foot raised in preparation for the next haphazard step, a disembodied hand hovering.

For all these photographs he pores over there is so little subject matter beyond what he sees again and again. How was her world populated? He wonders if a search through his photographs would be more edifying. At least you would be able to glimpse his antecedents. There would be his mother and father, and further back moustachioed Edwardian men and corseted women. At the bottom of the box is a small purse with a miscellany of things whose significance is lost on him: a bus ticket to somewhere called Cathcart, a card from a Glasgow trattoria, a much crumpled final demand utility bill, which he laboriously flattens beneath the angle poise, hands trembling, for its redemptive address.

* * *

The dog wants to sit beside him, is dissuaded, investigates the farrago of smells beneath the seat, accommodates himself to the movement and sways in tandem with Christopher above. He has confused the train times, the way he feels he has confused a number of things since her departure. He didn't realise till she had gone how many small things he depended on her for. Sunset is earlier than he anticipated. He envisaged some friendly metropolis, gilded with winter sunset and the incipient spirit of Hogmanay, and now he feels they are racing the fading light and haven't crossed the border yet. Like Dracula he has never been north of Whitby. He feels a sense of growing apprehension as colour drains from the passing scenery.

Above his head is a small bag with two changes of underwear and socks, some toiletries, another shirt and the dog's worming tablets, the last snatched up on a whim. The dog no longer has worms. He was at a loss what to pack because he doesn't know how long he will stay, or where, or what kind of reception he will meet if he even succeeds in finding her. His imagination has run the gamut of reactions he might or might not elicit: relief, reproach, anger, indifference, tearful apologies – he simply doesn't know. In his wallet is a sample photograph of the four faces who recurrently appeared on the scattered bedspread. The picture of her is superfluous: she is one of the indelibles on his fly-paper memory. The orange girl will identify herself. Even if the colour has faded the remarkable bosom won't have. The third girl always appears to be making for the periphery of the pictures in an attempt to rub herself out. He isn't confident he can identify her. The picture of the baby is the latest of the available selection, poised at the apex of her swing, gleeful, scant hair flying. Or is she an infant? When do they qualify? Does it matter? What age is she now? Will she have changed beyond recognition? The questions are hitting him like hail. What is he thinking, that some photo-fit family of miscellaneous parts held in his speeding wallet is awaiting his recognition? How stupid is that?

He forces down the corrosive doubts and looks out the window. The border has come and gone. With no announcement he is in the darkened Scottish lowlands. Individual lights wink in the gloom and he imagines secluded farmhouses, the terminus of inaccessible roads, whose warm interiors smell of leather, dogs and tobacco. Rural station signs, rendered a blur by the speed of the express, flit past, the train threading lights in the darkness. The stations become less intermittent and more comprehensible as they slow. The impatient gather their wares and stand redundantly in the aisle. And now they are sliding past the inevitable periphery of all cities: dormant rail stock on sidings, arc-lit construction sites, the monotonous catalogue of darkened factories, the glare of a retail park with its quilt of cars. A river arrives, leafless branches of bordering trees festooned with Christmas lights, doubled in the water, dark as oil. They slide across. The train finally stops, the dog emerging at the pneumatic hiss of the doors and the smell of food and commerce it admits. He lets them all disperse before gathering the fragments of resolution that propelled him here, collects his overhead bag and the dog, and steps off. It is a wrought iron Victorian emporium dotted with concession stands. The revellers outnumber the rest, or seem to in advertising their enjoyment. There is singing down the concourse and beyond the exit. The cold is aggressive.

He finds the taxi rank and stands, self-conscious in his difference and the uncertainty of his mission. These people all have destinations. How are there enough to go around? The dog attracts pats and friendly remarks, only half of which he understands.

The queue is raucous and good-natured and moves quickly. He is momentarily caught up in the general contagion. His taxi arrives, the next ticking black cab, and the young man behind needlessly slaps him on the shoulder.

'You're up, pal.'

He climbs in and fumbles the utility bill through the gap in the glass, pointing out the address.

'I'll get you there but I'm no payin' the electric.'

How very droll. He had heard that Glaswegians, like Liverpudlians, are always anxious to prove the comical credentials of their city, or as he recalls Gina saying at an item on the news, 'Everyone's a fucking comedian.'

'Up for Hogmanay?'

'Yes.'

'Visiting kids?'

The intercom magnifies the driver's voice and his hesitation.

'Daughter.' The explanation is too long and might show him in a sinister light.

'You'll get a good view of the fireworks from that floor.' Nodding towards the flattened bill on the passenger seat.

'Good. What floor?' He hadn't looked. Is there a loft? He had no idea how tiring uncertainty could be, and a sedentary journey has drained all his reserves.

They cross the river. He recognises the reflected trees. The high-rises loom like monoliths. They stop at the approach that forks to separate blocks. Water is welling up from a rising main like gushing ink in the pooled glare of streetlight. They can't pass. It's navigable on foot, threading through a desolate rockery.

'Sorry pal. Can't drive up. It'll come over the sills. I'll carry your bag to the door if it helps.'

Is he an ambassador of their hospitality as well? He can't recall a similar offer in London. What does he mean by door? The door to the block or the door of the final demand? What if she's there and his story is exploded in a doorstep denouement? He thinks he can withstand the driver's anger better than his disappointment, but then he's never been punched.

'I'll manage.' He peels off a large tip. The driver promises to toast his health at the bells. What he took for pockets of snow in the rockery turn out to be compressed crisp packets, sandwiched between forlorn shrubs, which crepitate as he picks his way. The mass of the block frowns at his approach. He frowns back trying to find a number or name. The fluorescent hallway is vacant. He crosses the stretch of tarmac to the adjacent block to find it equally anonymous. The hallway reveals three teenagers, who stare at him alarmingly. There's something sinister in their indolence. The sitting one, regarded by the other two, stands. The dog barks. The boy decides otherwise and sits back on the stairs. Christopher backs away.

There is a cluster of shops on the other side of the burst water main. Again he winds his way through the forlorn shrubs. On closer inspection the cluster looks like a concrete bunker. There is a graffitied concourse. Several embattled shops are shuttered closed. Only two are lit. He enters the first. An Asian shopkeeper with a turban is surrounded by an arsenal of fireworks. Aside from this the place seems to sell the kind of miscellany that the desperate need in the early hours.

'Nae dugs.'

The accent is so thick he swivels round looking for its owner. A turbaned Glaswegian does not occur to him. He swivels back to see the shopkeeper pointing to the appropriate sign. It is one of a number, warning against the purchase of underage cigarettes and alcohol and fireworks, that somehow Christopher imagines he is not as rigorous in prosecuting.

'Do you know what tower block this is?' He hands the bill across.

'Sorry, pal.' The purchase of a conciliatory samosa for the dog doesn't change things. 'I'm lookin' after this place for my cousin. Try next door – they're local.'

He trudges back into the concourse with the dog following. Both have been here five minutes and both are fed up. He is astonished at the next interior. Customers are confined within a perspex rectangle. The staff and merchandise are on the other side. Transactions seem to be conducted through some kind of hatch, like a silent order avoiding contamination with the everyday. Once again he unfolds the now grubby bill and passes it through for inspection. It is taken up by a boy in his twenties who looks as if he's seen everything. As he inspects the bill, Christopher inspects him. An eruption of retreating acne; hair combed in sebaceous furrows like a grooved cap. The unschooled eyebrows shoot back an inch before he regains his composure.

'Sorry, pal. Can't help.'

Why is everyone professing to be his pal when they are so manifestly uncooperative? If he can't help why has he passed the bill to the nondescript woman at his side whom Christopher has just noticed? Why is her transparent reaction more extreme than the boy's? Will she be of as little help as him and the turbaned man next door?

'Will you mind the shop?' Her voice is as amplified by the intercom as the taxi driver's. Despite the rising intonation Christopher can tell it's not a question. The man gestures, disgruntled, towards the responsibility of the non-existent customers. She ignores him and pulls on an earthy cardigan. There is a procedure of unlocking and locking to allow her into the perspex arena.

'Come on.'

He follows her, and the dog follows him, to the left of the tower blocks. There is an unsubmerged path after all, so they don't have to negotiate the litter. The boys in the lobby look almost affable at the familiar face, and nod in recognition to Christopher. The lift is jarring and smells faintly of bleach and urine.

'This is thirteen E.'

'That's right.'

'The bill says fourteen E.'

'That's upstairs.' He refrains from saying he had worked out as much. 'There's someone I want you to meet.'

His heart compresses but she is not there. No one is there. It looks like the aftermath of a gypsy encampment.

'Do you live here?'

'I live upstairs.'

She looks around at the carnage trying unsuccessfully to find something, finally delves into her bag and produces an old envelope.

'Have you got a pen?'

He gives her his treasured Cross. She flicks the unfamiliar nib, spotting the paper, and then writes, very laboriously. He winces at the friction. She hands back the pen and looks around for somewhere conspicuous to leave the note, finally wedging it beneath the front door number plate on the way out. They take the stairs. She has to wait for him. She has a key on a personalised fob and ushers them in. The place is scrupulous, almost obsessively tidy. She takes his coat and hangs it next to hers in the hall, arranging the four sleeves to hang in parallel. In the living room she needlessly realigns some magazines. He notices a certain custodial air to her gestures.

'Is Gina here?' The mention of the name freezes her in the act of rearranging some scatter cushions on a battered sofa. She exhales and straightens.

'No. No, Gina's not here. I was hoping you could tell me where Gina is.'

'But it's her bill. It's her bill with this address.' He sounds like a querulous schoolboy challenging an unfair mark.

'And it's over a year old.'

He blinks, registering this, corroborates it from the bill and feels suddenly exhausted. He sits, frowning morosely at the carpet. The awkward placing of the furniture doesn't successfully cover the threadbare patches.

'Would you like some tea?'

'I wouldn't want to put you to any trouble.' He has remembered his manners.

'You've an overnight bag and you don't look as if you've the energy to go anywhere.'

'Tea would be nice. Do you live here?'

'Yes. I'm looking after it for her.'

She goes through to the kitchen and he finds himself imprisoned in the disembowelled sofa whose structure was illusory. There is little support beneath his bottom and the arms have folded in like a carnivorous plant, trapping insects. He extracts himself with a lot of grunting effort and stands. He walks to the hall. The kitchen door is open. She smiles shyly at him across the warming pot and turns to retrieve the caddy. He considers the available doors in the short hall and pushes the first open: bathroom. The next: bedroom, with the same frugal scrupulous appearance of the living room, a bed with hospital corners and a row of utilitarian shoes in a rack beneath the window. This is an intrusion. He came here to find her, or something, at the expense of propriety if need be. The last room. He pushes the door open and stands on the threshold for a minute. The air inside is stale, the room dark with drawn curtains. He reaches inside the door and snaps on the light, standing stock still, taking in the implications of what he sees before venturing in further.

It is a child's room. In the corner stands a cot with an overhanging mobile, pantomime animals in primary colours swaying slightly in the unaccustomed gust from the opened door. The walls are lavender, the ceiling yellow, the cornice a bright pastiche of animals and toys, arrested in frozen procession. At his hip, beside the door, is a small coat rail with a confusion of children's coats and jackets.

On the nearest peg, in the form of a duck's head, a small scarf is draped. Hanging below is a woollen hat, suspended by ties looped in a bow over the beak. Inside the hat are tiny mittens. A collapsed pram, so different from the blunt upholstered barrows of his infancy, crouches beneath. A small bureau with a shin-high chair is littered with toys, which also sprout from an open chest. There is a matching lilac chest of drawers. A series of shelves have been fixed to the wall, adjacent to the cot, and between book ends of opposing elephants, large cardboard volumes of bright illustrations lean. The drawn curtains are a collage of happy aeroplanes, balloons and spaceships, cheerfully piloted by waving aviators, threading their way round smiling constellations and a winking moon. In the overhead light he is fixed with the glassy stare of half a dozen dolls and bears. He takes three strides into the centre of the room, the spring of the pile beneath his feet distinct from the threadbare resistance of the rest of the flat. All her money has gone into this room. There is something not quite right about the colour. It is lacking in intensity. He takes out a cardboard volume and realises why: there is a mantle of dust here thicker than that which made his house monochrome till she removed it. The girl from the shop announces her presence with a cough. She leans in and hands him a steaming mug. He moves forward to accept. He is about to apologise for the intrusion.

'Take your time.'

She closes the door behind her, confronting him with Gina, young, happy, staring at him a dozen times from the collage fastened to the pinboard on the back of the door. And in all the photographs her head is twinned with the little girl's, and she wears an expression he has never seen in the flesh.

He is absently holding the mug at the base and realises it is burning his hand. He looks around for somewhere to lay it down when he hears the front door bang open. There is a commotion in the hall and the bedroom door is flung open again, agitating the mobile. The picture of Gina he was studying is replaced with two young woman in the doorway, also now framed in the proscenium of memory. The second one has identified herself by her own illumination. She is clutching the crushed envelope. Two large rivulets of mascara stripe her face. The spectacular breasts are heaving spasmodically as she looks desperately askance at him. The kind girl who delivered the tea has now been identified as the satellite of the photos. Sad to say, he has only succeeded in identifying her as an ancillary to the other, who is now brandishing the envelope towards him. Neither has entered the room. In reply to the wordless exchange he retrieves the photos from his wallet and hands them across. They examine them and put their arms around one another. The plain girl almost disappears.

'I'm afraid I'm going to have to sit down, but please, not in that settee.'

# PART 3

Personally I didn't see what all the fuss was about and I went upstairs to tell her. Ruth's standing behind her with one hand on her shoulder. And that kind of annoyed me. 'So what,' I said, 'he was a man and it didn't work out. If you'd wanted him that much you could always have tried sex.'

'She did try sex.'

The fact that Ruth's doing the talking isn't a good sign. Gina normally doesn't let anyone talk for her.

'So once he got what he wanted he just pissed off. Typical fucking man.' And something else struck me. 'You haven't risked another...' and I nod towards the nursery. At least this makes her look up.

'Look at this place,' she says, moving a bit of carpet with her foot.

'What's wrong with it?'

'Look at it. What are the chances of it containing happiness?'

'What the fuck are you talking about? Is this some kind of *University Challenge* philosophy question? I'm worried about you being knocked up and you're worried about furniture.'

'We didn't have sex.'

'Gay.'

'What?'

'Name like Simon. Works in a *classical* music shop. Dead giveaway really. How many women go into a *classical* music shop? And now he turns down sex.'

She just sighed and got up and went into her room. If you can't raise an argument out of her there must be something really wrong. I went through her cupboards looking for biscuits. It's astonishing the amount of food and stuff you have to have around for a kid. But no biscuits. Millie woke up. Gina went through and fetched her and took her through to her own room. That's something I hadn't seen for a while. Usually she tries to settle her where she is. I gave it half an hour and looked in. The curtains are drawn against the sun and everything's shades of grey. They're lying together on the bed, face to face, like the last survivors in a lifeboat. Adrift. I thought she was asleep. I go to close the door and she says, 'I can't stay there now.'

'Where?'

'Work.'

'Fuck that. Let him move.'

'He's the manager.'

'A man or a job. A man *and* a job. Neither are worth it. Any biscuits?'

'No.'

'There's not much a Gypsy Cream can't fix. Want me to go out and get some?'

'No.'

I could see it was quite serious. I went to Davinder's for the biscuits and ate half of them on the way up while I thought about it. She once told me I wasn't a whole person. She thinks I won't remember. She thinks I've got the recall of a hamster. Some things stick – if they hurt and they're true. That was true, although I wouldn't admit as much to anyone. But she was right. I wasn't a whole person by her reckoning. And if I look at her now there's something wrong. For the first time, looking at her poke that bit of carpet with her foot, *she* looked to me as if *she* wasn't a whole person. She stepped up to the plate for me more times than I can say. I'll do it for her.

So I waited till the two posh girls leave and I breeze in. 'We're closed,' he says, and then looking up 'we don't keep money on the premises overnight.'

Fuck me. What does he think I am – a one woman ram raid? What did she see in this specimen? And that's when I saw the flaw in my plan – there wasn't one. Some kinds of men just can't be seduced – dead, gays, some clergy, happily married, and the frightened. He looked petrified. I just assumed I'd work on him, maybe a bit of office gymnastics. The outlay already offered half a dozen possibilities. And then a nice little talk. And if the fire alarm permits, a sly fag. I mention Gina and he laughs and we work something out. I go home and tell her and she's furious and then she's grateful and then we hug and she burst into tears and admits I *am* a whole person and we watch *Coronation Street* and everything's the same. Only better.

'What do you want?'

'I'm interested in...' I wave, 'Glen Miller.' It's a moment of inspiration and the only classical composer I can come up with.

'Are you a friend of Gina's?'

'Have I got a badge with 'poor' or something stamped on my forehead?'

'Not your forehead.'

That stopped me for a minute. I liked him better for it.

'Look. She just wants her job back.'

He looks shocked. 'I don't understand. She hasn't lost her job. I'm expecting her in the day after tomorrow.'

'Well, you turning her down. It's a bit of a blow for a girl.'

'But...'

'I know, I know.' But I didn't know. No one's ever turned me down. No doubt Gina would argue that I'm not that choosey. And then I hit on my plan. It was the same as all my other plans and the one I'd half an idea of when I came in. If I overcame his nerves and gave him a bit of relief in the back shop and told her, she could write him off as another one of these useless bastards she accuses me of hanging around with. And then she wouldn't feel sad because she hadn't lost out much. In my imagination I'm even telling her how he was too anxious and came all over the Jim Reeves CDs, and she's laughing, and the Custard Creams are tumbling on to the plate like coins.

'Why don't we discuss it in the back shop?'

'No,' he says, with his eyes on the door, as if he's going to shout for help from the passing foot traffic. 'There's nothing to talk about. She's welcome back, and if she's not coming she should tell me herself.'

I turn to leave and he breathes out, like a bust football.

'Tell her...' he says. I turn back. He looks as if he doesn't know what he wants to tell her, or if he does, he doesn't want to tell me. 'Just tell her to let me know...'

And she does. And thankfully it's by letter, cause I don't want her going in and finding out I'd been there. I was looking after Millie while she hauled herself back into town to see if she can get her old, old job back, when the door goes. I'm on the phone to her mobile while she stands outside the shop, working up her confidence. I can just see her, polishing her shoes against the calf of her other leg the way she does when she's nervous. 'Look,' I say, 'you're a strong confident woman,' because I've been reading those waiting room magazines again, 'you're *inpowered*.'

'*Empowered*. Who's at the door?'

'I'm not a fucking clairvoyant. They can wait a minute. I'm trying to give you confidence because, God knows why, you need it. You're the cleverest person I know. That might not be saying much but we both know you're a lot better than selling bits of ribbon or whatever it is you do down there.' As I'm saying this I'm walking down the hall. There's a pause on her side – I know she's touched. 'Look, if you come out in half an hour's time and you're still on the bru then you're no worse off than you are now.'

'It might be Dad.'

I open the door and there are the two toothpaste adverts I waited on to leave the shop before I went in. Both are staring round with the curiosity of a puppy. One opens her mouth about to speak.

'Who is it?'

'Got to go,' I say, and jab the phone. I look behind them into the landing in case he's with them too. But he isn't.

'We're looking for Gina.'

'You'd better come in.'

So they clip clop into the living room in their designer shoes and give this the once over too. One of them gives the same bit of carpet a nudge with her foot that Gina did when she talked about the chance of happiness. In a way it's a bit insulting. They've got the same kind of curiosity David Attenborough probably has visiting a flock of chimps or something. Gina said they're nice but dim and looking at them I agree, or 'concur' as they said on the *Crown Court* rerun the other day. Both their hair is so shiny it looks like fibre optic or something and I realise what it is – money. It's what Gina told me about. It's not just expensive shampoo, it's years of vegetables and stuff like that that I know I should eat instead of Pot Noodles and the like, but can't be bothered.

'I like your top,' one of them says. And all of a sudden I like her. 'Gabby,' she says, holding out her hand. And so does the other one, and I like her too even though I didn't want to like either of them. I don't remember meeting new girls and shaking their hands. You felt as if they'd learned this stuff on the hockey pitch or something and there was something fresh-airy about them.

'Mind if I smake?'

'What?'

'Smake.' The way she says it rhymes with 'cake'. I must have looked blank till she pulled out a packet of fags.

'Flash the ash.'

'What?'

'Hand them round. Let's all have a *smake*.'

So we all took the coffee table, in other words the crate, out on to the balcony and sat on that and had a pally fag. I don't know if it was the afternoon light or what but the other one, Naomi, was *exactly* the colour I've been aiming for in the past forty sessions. I put my arm against hers.

'TANerife. I can get you a discount.' I didn't say how. 'Where'd you get yours?'

'Verbier.' I ran my mind over all the tan stands around town and couldn't come up with it.

'Where's that?'

'Swiss Alps.'

'Fuck.' I could imagine her and the big-dicked ski instructor. Sauna sex. Chocolates. Fondue. The fucking lot. Suddenly draining wee Tam's pods in the back room of TANerife lost some of its glamour. 'You know, by rights I should hate the two of you from the off.'

'Why?' They're dismayed.

'Cause you're both everything Gina said you were.'

'But we like Gina.'

'Gina likes you.'

'Where is she?'

'At an interview.'

'But we don't want her to leave!' It was a chorus. A chorus of people who've had pretty much what they've wanted their whole lives just by saying so. It's what I'd have said if I'd been them. And suddenly I thought – there by the grace of God, as those shrivelled old women teachers used to say. It's not their fault they're airheads without any *real* knowledge of the world, like me, graduate of the school of hard knocks and all that. Just because they haven't had my advantages, it's not their fault they're sitting there wearing three hundred quids' worth of clothes apiece without a thought in their heads. So I get my stash out and roll us a titanic, super-jumbo, Olympic torch spliff and time just seems to melt and before I know it the front door goes and she's standing there like the angel of death, shouting through the fog at me about being the worst negligent babysitter with no sense of responsibility, doped in charge of a kid, blah blah. The full boonah. 'Keep your hair on,' I say, and explain how Millie woke up and Ruth came up and pleaded, *pleaded* to take her out in the pram, and I thought it might settle her. 'And,' I say, picking up my mobile and pointing at it, laying on the sarcasm like marzipan, 'we agreed to keep in touch with one another in case anything happened, with this little gadget you may have heard of called a telephonic device.' And that shuts her up long enough to take stock till she says 'And what if she needs you? What are you going to do, like this?' But she doesn't wait for the reply I don't have because she's distracted by her new pals being there. They're both past the point of noticing she's back and are wearing that skunked-out thousand yard stare apiece.

'Girls. Girls.' She sounds like that posh teacher in that film about Edinburgh schoolgirls. She even claps her hands and looks at me, accusing like, as if I've corrupted them or something. And I say, 'Nobody asked them to smoke.' And the one with the Alps tan says, 'You did.' And then I remember that I forgot to ask them not to say anything about me being to the shop. I don't think I've got anything to worry about because Gina's got them to their feet. She knows she's not getting any conversation tonight and I think her worry is getting them home safe. 'It's not a war zone,' I say, 'they found their own way here.'

'And then they found you.'

'Thanks for the smake,' says one.

'See you at the shop again,' says the other.

'Shop!' says Gina. 'What fucking shop? What have you done?'

And I explain. And she's so grateful she burst into tears. Well, actually, I burst into tears. And Gabby manages to miss the couch and the linoleum and every other thing that wouldn't matter a fuck and throw up on top of the telly. The only thing that works. And it's pretty liquid. There's a slow drip, drip and Ruth barges in with the pram, timed like one of those crap ITV sitcoms that depends on stupid coincidences. And I say to Gina, 'These posh girls – fucking amateurs.'

But there was one good thing that came out of it. The telly was well and truly gubbed, with Gabby's puke getting in the electricity or whatever. Two days later a titanic, super-jumbo, flat-screen, surround-sound televisual *experience* arrives at Gina's door. I know, cause I watch the progress from van to panting floor-by-floor delivery. So does half the block, their only employment guessing who the lucky bastard is who's getting it. I lean over the stairwell to all these faces looking up, like the view backwards from a cockpit when the plane's climbing vertical to avoid a mountain through the mist. 'Mind your own business!' I shout. The heads disappear. I want to lay down a marker there's nothing happening to *this* telly.

There are two guys to *install* it. My stuff and Gina's is all plug and play – previously unplug and steal. I breeze in behind the boys, ignoring the fact that she doesn't like me for a week. 'Ignore me if you want,' I say, 'but you can't be such a cow to stop me from watching this. Wee Tam's got one. You can watch *Ben-Hur* and it's as if you're *in the chariot*.'

I open the card that comes with it. 'Gabby's apologised,' I say.

'Help yourself,' she says.

'Still. Nice of her to pay,' I say, ignoring the insult.

'She didn't pay anything.'

'You could have fooled me.'

'And people frequently do.' She gives off one of those sighs she always does, the 'God grant me patience' ones, as if she's trying to explain algebra to a dog. 'Even if it came out of her wages she didn't pay for it. Things don't cost what you give for them, they cost what you give up to get them. She didn't give up anything. She meant well but it wouldn't occur to her to sacrifice a thing.'

'Sorry, I fell asleep at the beginning of the economical lecture. Look, are we watching this or not? Let's get Ruth up.'

So I called Ruth and told her to pick up some Garibaldis and Coconut Creams and beer and a movie at Davinder's on her way back from her shift. 'Nothing serious,' I said, 'no explosions or that. Just slush.' So she came up with *Beaches*, 'cause I already had it downstairs, and we sat in a sea of crumbs and howled. Well I howled, and Ruth did the discreet turn away thing and pretends to be scratching her cheek or something while she wiped her eyes. And I looked at them and said, 'You *are* the wind beneath my wings.' I waited till Ruth went downstairs before I said anything.

'What's the matter?'

'I don't know what you mean.'

'You *always* cry at *Beaches*.'

'Maybe I'm just not in the mood.'

But I knew her better than that. There's nothing better than a good cry. Well there is, but a good cry's almost up there with that too. It's the valve in the pressure cooker, the bursting boil. It stops sad things building up.

'I defy anyone to sit dry-eyed through that and say they're not holding something back.'

'I'm not holding something back.'

Then she fetched Millie, even though she was asleep, and took her through to sleep with her. Adrift. Again.

She went back to her old new job but something was wrong, and I don't think it was just boredom with what she was doing. She knew I knew, and tried to avoid talking about it about as much as anyone around me can avoid talking about anything I want to talk about. Aside from Millie, me and Ruth, in that order, she didn't seem to take any enjoyment out of anything. She never wanted to go out. I said, 'I said it before and I'll say it again – he was just a man. It was just a job. Move on.' She said she had moved on, but I don't think she had. She'd made the fatal mistake of letting someone else's view of her become her view of herself. She said she hadn't. But I could *see* it. I told her as much. 'Imagine if I did the same,' I said. 'Here's me, a healthy girl with healthy appetites and a healthy tan. So – I might not have done so well at school or read many books, or any books really, and my career might not have taken off *yet*. So what? If I thought of me the way those bastards,' pointing out the balcony at the world, 'thought of me, I'd have myself convinced I'm an overweight orange dole tart. And how stupid is that? You're not what he thought. Who gave him the right?'

'I did.'

'Then you're stupid. You're special. Even more important, you're special to *me*.'

But some kind of mood descended on her, like one of those times before it rains when you feel the clouds are pressing down on the air. And it didn't break. And one time I got her on her own for two hours, and got two drinks down her, she said she was 'only going through the motions', whatever that meant. Motion is life. Death is the big stop.

It's one afternoon. Nice light outside. I'm half watching the telly, *Columbo* or *Murder She Wrote* or *Ironside* or *Quincy* or who cares what. Ruth's at work. I hear her upstairs, moving about, and that sets me easy in my mind because I feel more comfortable with the thought of the little family above me. I'm dozing. And then I'm awake and I hear a noise. It sounds like it's outside the building and it take me a minute to realise it's coming from upstairs. It's regular, almost mechanical, but I know right away it's not coming out a machine. It's a kind of chant, but there's something terrible about it. I burst out the front door and burst into hers. Millie's door's open and she's not there. I run into the living room. She's sitting, with *her* on her lap on the balcony, rocking, making this terrible high drone that wavers as she leans forward and back. The only thing I can compare it to is those women in the news, African probably, headscarves, after a war, or a famine, or both, kneeling over a lump in a shroud, wailing something, a high warble that sounds like pure distilled grief. It's the worst noise I ever heard and I hope I never hear it again.

It was truly – fucking – terrible.

* * *

There were all these arrangements to be made. How can someone who never got to reading age cause so much paperwork? Ruth was a star. I did everything I could but I felt as if I was living under water, not least cause I couldn't stop crying. Stuff happened in slow motion, till it didn't. Gina's dad was totally useless. I prized him away from his drink one night to try and get information on her mum. I was holding the back of his hair and I thought that if I let him go, his head will hit the table. We had no way of finding her. It was Ruth's suggestion. I didn't see the point. She was as useless last time as he was now. Would she even want her here? I didn't think so. Gina wasn't really there to consult. From not sounding like a machine she became one. She was totally wooden. I cried enough for the both of us because she didn't cry at all. Or talk. Or eat – unless we made an issue of it. I could tell that in her mind she was away in that lifeboat. Adrift. With *her*.

We had a Humanist ceremony. The poor bastard did his best but what are you going to do? If it had been religious he could at least have said something about Heaven and stuff, all meeting up again. I think of Heaven, if I think of it at all, as a dingy waiting room, at the train station or the ferry terminal, where you meet all your old pals. You all squeal when you recognise one another again, cause it will only be the ones you want there. And then you go on out to a supernatural knees up. I don't know if there's a God, but if there is I don't think he'll begrudge me this fantasy. I'm not doing anyone any harm when you look at other religious fantasies that are out there. But this ceremony just seemed to say we should all be nice to one another. Fair play to him, and I don't doubt *she'd* have grown into the kind of woman who'd get his approval, but *she* didn't even get to the age where *she* got the chance to be nice to anyone. When we talked about it in front of her beforehand Gina stopped being a statue for two minutes. I said we should go for the full regalia, priests, ministers, whatever. She looked at me and asked me if I believed in a God who took *her*. That was the first time I ever felt there was nothing I could say that would get through.

And then she stopped being wooden – when we weren't looking. We were taking turns at being with her during the day and I was sleeping with her at night. And then she was gone. Just like that. I went rabid, tearing through her things for clues, trying to work out what she took, as if that would give me a clue to anything. Ruth looked worse than I'd ever seen her – which *is* saying something. We trawled every place we could think of she might be, and then we did it again. I thought her dad was useless before. He was even worse now. The talk in the scheme is that he fell to bits when Gina's mum left him. Personally I always found her a bit common.

We went through the same routine as last time, where I held his hair to stop his face hitting the table. It wasn't just that he escaped from his life into the bottle, he was now abandoning hers for the same hole. I could forgive him for the past bits of her life he ruined. But not this. I let go.

I mobilised all those guys, I suppose you could call them boyfriends, to look and ask. If there was a rock in Glasgow she couldn't have hidden under it. Nothing. Fuck all. Ruth even suggested phoning the police. 'I've got a better idea,' I said. Wee

Tam's either a mason, or he's got a pal who's a mason, or he's got a pal who's... and so it goes. None of them admit to it. I explained it to Tam. The masons is heaving with police. Tam walks into the pub this night with this specimen. Six two. Farm boy hands.

'Plain clothes,' Tam says.

'Not so plain,' I say.

'Not plain clothes,' he says, 'off duty.' So I give him the once over and fill in the details. 'Has she been reported missing?' he asks.

'I'm telling you,' I say.

'Maybe she's just gone,' he says.

'Well fuck me, Sherlock. Two years' training for that. Glad to see all our tax was well spent.'

'Let me see what I can do,' he says, turning away. And I just *knew* it was the brush off, and he was losing interest and he'd be stone cold after a pint. The same way I knew I had to do something to keep his attention on this.

'No,' I said, 'let *me* see what *you* can do.'

And I did. And he did. And in other circumstances I probably would have anyway, so I didn't feel as if I was cheapening myself or anything. All in a good cause, like putting nicked money in boxes in poppy week. I don't know what I expected – posters on lamp posts or what – but something. Two weeks later I'm crossing the zebra and I see him stopped in the squad car with a woman police officer. I tap the window. It rolls down on his sneer. I ask him what's happening. 'What d' y' expect,' he says, 'top billing on *Crimewatch*?' He's showing off to her.

'So what's the total of your efforts?' I say.

'There hasn't been a crime,' he says.

'I'll tell you what's criminal,' I say, 'you calling that thing the other week a hard-on. I've seen stiffer six-pinters before, when they can't raise a smile. I've bent them in with the best of them. That felt like a marshmallow pushed into a piggy bank. You'd be done under the trades an' descriptions for calling that a soft-on.' It wasn't true but it's the easiest way to hurt a man. His mouth had disappeared into this line and he was breathing through his nose. If she hadn't been there he'd have got out and slapped me around – and not in a nice way. I leaned in and spoke to her. 'If you're thinking of giving him a bit of hand relief behind the lock-ups, then make sure it's a double shift, love.'

He roared off. So much for the fucking authorities.

Ruth, God bless her, didn't have my gifts when it came to getting men to do what she wanted. She hadn't a net to cast. She wore out shoe leather asking around, and this from a woman who starts to blush handing across the bus fare. I don't know if it was the constant rejection, or the gloom of missing her, but she looked like shit. And I suppose I did too, under the war paint. Nobody was seeing me like *that*. Gina's absence seemed to get worse, not better. Her not being here, day after day, became like an actual *thing* in the room with us. It turns out Ruth did visit the police. I found out long afterwards. And she got as much joy as me – without the joy.

Bad as it was we were diverted by another problem her leaving had caused. We were completely, utterly skint. I don't claim to be any economist, but even I could see how desperate it was if we were to keep the place for her. And on that we both agreed. Instantly. We *were* going to keep the place for her. She was going to have a place to come back to. To give it up was like somehow giving up on her.

'I'll move upstairs,' Ruth says, 'keep it nice for her.'

'It's not the occupancy you stupid cow – it's the double rent!'

'You think I don't fucking know that?'

'Stop the world – I want to get off. That's the first time I've *ever* heard you swear.' And we looked at each other. Her swearing set the seal on it – the seriousness of the situation. Our determination. 'Come here,' I said. And I gave her the kind of hug I usually reserved for Gina. And it felt right.

We both agreed we wouldn't touch *her* room.

Ruth took on extra shifts. It wasn't as if her life wasn't dreary enough already. It wasn't fair. She was dragging herself home night after night looking more and more like a refugee. I bit the bullet and got a job as a hospital orderly in the Victoria Infirmary. I don't know why they call it 'orderly'. The place might run well but nothing I could see was orderly about *my* job. There was always the thought, in the back of my mind, that I might snare a doctor, some young guy with a shiny stethoscope, clean habits and prospects.

Not a fucking chance. I think there's a caste system in bits of the NHS that'd put India to shame. I felt like an untouchable. I spent my breaks smoking outside with the porters. It reminded me of Gina having *her*. I'd walk back into the antiseptic smell with a lump in my throat.

At the end of the first week I'm worn out after my shift, eyes gritty with tiredness. I'm walking to the bus stop to go home. I've been working from an hour that a month ago was the middle of the night. It's still bright daylight and I'm blinking in the glare, when I see a big shapeless sack staring back at me from the glass. I stop dead. So does she. A week and this is what I look like. Other shifts have finished too and a lot of women, cleaners or auxiliaries or orderlies or whatever they are, are all gathering at the bus stop. There are about fifty separate conversations going on at the same time. The noise is tremendous and it makes me feel better. A 66 draws up and the first woman pays to go into town. 'I'm no' goin' to town,' says the driver. He looks about fifteen. All conversations stop. We all want to go to town, or that direction.

'What d' y' mean?' says the woman.

'This bus goes to Shawlands.

'But it's a 66.'

'It's a 37.'

'It says 66 on the side.' And so it does. She points. But it also says 37 on the front. Some useless bastard, probably him, sent it out the garage with two numbers. This is pointed out to him by a chorus of women.

'Well,' he says, 'it says 37 on the front. And this bus goes frontways – no' sideways.'

'Sonny,' says the first woman, 'I've been wipin' arses all mornin' and you're the first one that's talked back.'

And we all just about piss ourselves laughing and he shuts the door and escapes to Shawlands. And before you know it a 66 has arrived and we're all feeling like one of the gang and the driver, who looks like the last one's younger brother, watches me fumble for my pass and says, 'On you go missus.'

And then it hits me, like a bucket of freezing water. I *am* one of them. First of all I've got a bus pass, cause I can't afford a daily return. Then the driver calls me 'missus'. He sees me as one of the herd, and no harm to them, but that's what they are. You see them at break time, in uniform, taking up a quarter of the canteen, their noise drowning out everyone else's. And they drift together, like wildebeests, from work, to shops, to bingo, to wherever, before they all go their separate ways to go home and come back and club together tomorrow to start all over again.

Well that's not me. It's just not. I've never been a member of any gang in my life. You can take your Girl Guides with your knot tying and your star gazing and your map reading and shove them up your arse. I know fuck all about the team spirit and that's the way it's staying. I couldn't dump the job flat, cause we need the money, so I took another job – on an ice cream van. I'd come home from the Victoria and change, just to tinkle round the housing estates, announced by *Greensleeves* that got faster when he got the revs going. The owner, Pavel, was decidedly dodgy. I don't know where his family originally hailed from, but he spoke pure Glasgow at Gatling-gun speed. He used every excuse to rub against me. As far as I could see, all his transactions were on the black. If they looked at his books he probably said he spent a hundred quid on petrol and drove five hundred miles to sell two Magnums and a ninety-nine. That didn't bother me. I could put up with the groping and him swindling the taxman. It's the other trade I couldn't abide. There were certain customers, most of them older than sixteen, he always served himself. Almost nothing was said. He'd hand out tea-bag-sized sachets to them and take the cash. You could spot the type a mile away. They're *waiting* for you to turn the corner. When you get close you realise it isn't an earth tremor, it's them who's shaking. They'd all complexions like Gina's dad, but there's a difference between drunks and druggies. It's hard to explain but you can see it a mile away. Druggies are always skinny, more desperate, *sinister*.

That bastard would sell anything to *anyone*. He went out with sub-standard ice cream and soggy cones and came back with *thousands*. For the first time *I* was the respectable front. I was thinking about chucking it when a brick came through the side window, and *Greensleeves* upped tempo, like the *Keystone Cops* or fast motion bit at the end of *Benny Hill*, while we made our getaway. Maybe it was an unsatisfied customer, who'd just found out that the flake in his 99 wasn't Cadbury's. Who knows. Who cares. Not the police, who called Pavel to tell him that the overnight lock up had been jemmied and the van was up on blocks. Oh, and the wheels were stolen. And the contents stripped out. And it had also been torched. Out of curiosity I went round to see it. They'd driven it out to strip it down. It was still smouldering. Pavel's leaning against the lock-up running his fingers through his greasy hair looking like some refugee who's lost his whole family in a tidal wave. I'm wondering how much of someone else's merchandise walked, the kind of stuff you don't insure. From the look of him you can tell that *they* won't be understanding about it. He'll be avoiding any high-rises in the near future in case his investors help him find the quick route down. There are some kids throwing stones at the only window that somehow didn't cave in. The police aren't even trying to stop them. *They* don't give a fuck. Truth be told, neither do I. That was the end of my career in retail.

After that the hospital didn't seem so bad. I still knew nothing about the team spirit but the older women seemed to like me. It's as if I became their mascot. They kept asking me about my social life. Mostly they were settled, with kids and stuff, in various stages of happiness, like the rest of the world, but they liked to hear what I had to say. Maybe they liked imagining themselves in my place, if this or that hadn't happened back then, if their lives had taken a different turning. I used to pile it on. 'Men are like Alton Towers,' I said, 'some rides are tame and some rides are scary.' They loved that kind of thing. I had them all round for a knees up. When they all arrived they thought the place had been ransacked. Ruth came down at the noise, which was good because I was going to invite her anyway. Somehow she managed to be nice, shy and disapproving all at the same time. After they'd gone she offered to help tidy. 'Don't bother,' I said, 'stuff takes up the same amount of space whether it's over there or over there.' But she hung about anyway, like this cloud of gloom, blaming me. She didn't say a thing, and the more she didn't say it the worse it got. I don't know how long I lasted but it was quite a long time for me. 'Look,' I shouted, 'I can't bury myself. I just can't. I'm not like you. Life can't stop. She *chose* to leave *us*.' But what I couldn't bring myself to say, because it was too harsh, was that Gina was her only cause because nothing else was happening in her life. 'Just cause she's your only cause cause nothing else is happening in your life...'

She stopped dead still with the tights she was holding. Something was stuck to them. It looked like a trapped bat but it couldn't have been. And then she started speaking and got quieter till I was holding my breath to hear the end of the sentence.

'You're probably right. She is my only cause. She came and found me when I was rotting away with loneliness. She didn't need me. She had you, and *her*. She went out of her way to find me and I'll return the favour if it's the last thing I do.' And then she burst into tears. Well, actually, I burst into tears at being cruel. I'm not like that. Well, actually, I am – but only to people who deserve it.

And she didn't. Well she did a bit for having the nerve to come down here, like some ghoul, all silent blame for me daring to enjoy myself. But still I shouldn't have said it. Or maybe I should have, but only in a nicer way. I couldn't catch a breath or find a hanky so I snatched the tights from her and blew my nose into them and said, 'Do you honestly think me looking this way and acting like this make me miss her any less?' And then she started to cry, really quietly, and I looked at that sack of a person and saw what Gina saw worth prising away from that selfish cow Moira. And I realised I loved her.

'I love you,' I said. And a look came over her face that I don't think any man's succeeded in putting on mine. And before she could say anything I handed her back the tights. 'They're for the bin,' I said.

I finished a back shift, and for the first time in years I thought it might be nicer to walk for a bit. That's what wearing flat shoes during working hours does for you. I was passing one of the churches, because they seem to be a religious lot around here, when this thought suddenly struck me. I'm nice to people who deserve it, but maybe I'm not as well-behaved as I like to think I am. I can't think what I might have done, but maybe Gina's departure is some kind of *punishment*. And I ran into the church. There was light coming through the stained glass in shafts, like some old religious film, and when I turned to all the empty pews, all silently shining with devout polishing, I came over all religious and a thought struck me.

Sanctuary! I don't know if I just thought it or I actually said something. Anyway there was this polite cough from the back. And this guy came forward. He wasn't wearing a funny collar or anything, but you just knew he was one of the clergy. He was holding a rag like he'd been polishing the brasses. He didn't look old enough to hold down the job, hardly older than me. He had a nice face, a kind face, the kind of face you'd be prepared to take home to your mum, provided she didn't behave like Gina's. It was the sight of that face, kinder than mine, that suddenly made me think it was all my fault.

'I want to confess!'

'We – we don't actually believe in confession here. Not the way I imagine you're referring to.'

'A child was delivered unto the womb of my pal and smitten by death and I can't help feeling that it's all my fault!' God knows where I got 'unto' and 'womb' and 'smitten' from. It's all those big-beard Charlton Heston Bible epics they show at Easter and Christmas. He retreated to the front pew and took all this in. Then he wiped his face with the rag and left a streak. Somehow I couldn't help liking him for that. It made him look like a wee boy. And then he says, 'I always find this place a bit sombre. Would you like a cup of tea?'

'Any biscuits?'

Fondant Fancies. Gone soft. You could tell he was a bachelor. His house was at the side of the church and he had this family kitchen he didn't know what to do with. He sits there with the streak on his face and asks me what's wrong. 'Where do I start?' I say. It turns out that he wants what I want – to make *me* feel better. You don't come across many men like that. I start off with Gina and me as kids and he starts this kind of rolling his hand, like he wants me to fast-forward till we get to what he calls the 'spiritual crux' of the matter. So I tell him about Gina and me and *her* and Ruth and he says it can't be punishment. 'Because,' he says, 'by extension,' he says, 'Millie's death would be part of that punishment, visited on you, and God doesn't work that way. I don't believe in a wrathful God. I believe in a God of infinite compassion, and I don't think you've done anything wrong and even if you had, it isn't anything that He can't forgive. You're no worse, or better, than me. There's a purpose behind all this. I don't pretend to know what it is, but I know it's a good one.'

You look at a man like him, Mark, his name is, and you look at Quick Nick and Wee Tam, and you can't believe they're the same *species*. I was tempted to lick my hanky and lean across and wipe his face, make a joke about mark and Mark, and take it from there. But I didn't, cause with ten sentences he made me feel as if I'd fallen in love and climbed Everest at the same time. I floated home congratulating myself on how I'd held back. I always knew I'd a spiritual side.

He phoned me up a week later and I thought – here we go. But I was wrong. I'd told him about our money worries and he'd got me an opening in a chicken factory. The shifts were better and the money more than the hospital, so it was goodbye to all that. When he got me the job I don't think he quite knew what was involved. There's the ethics of animals and stuff to consider, but if it means half your day with your hands up a chicken's arse pulling out innards to keep the flat for her, then I can only say tough luck for the chickens.

We'd to wear wellies and coats and hairnets and latex gloves and the whole nine yards. Every last man of us on the production line was a woman. There was a bit of banter in the canteen with some of the guys who worked in other parts of the plant, but you trudged in there, still wearing half the stuff, looking about as sexual as a Dalek. I couldn't employ my assets. Looking round you could barely tell one of us from the other. Well – Danny could. He came up to me and said he needed to take a swab.

'Is that code?' I said.

He ran some kind of lab in the place, or said he did, to make sure we don't all die, or kill the customers, with some kind of bird lurgy. There wasn't much of me he didn't investigate.

'Is this standard procedure?' I said. He was very, very clean. I pointed it out.

'Scientific protocols,' he said. I'm not sure I was so flattered by that.

'And so, what can you do for *me*?' I said. And lo and behold I became a receptionist – just like that. If that's all it took then I could see my career in the place going up like a meteor. Half a dozen office parties and I'd be vice president. But the truth is I *liked* being a receptionist. You get to meet lots of people and you can chat and be nice to them if they deserve it, or send them in the wrong direction and make things generally rubbish if they're not. I phoned Mark to tell him I got a promotion. I didn't tell him how I got it.

'That's marvellous,' he said.

'Too right,' I said, 'beats the hell out of fist-fucking dead poultry – excuse my French.'

Reception was a place where I could employ my assets, and I made the best of it. If we were really pushed for money I could get time and a half for Saturdays, or pull an extra shift downstairs with the buggered birds, which I did sometimes, just to keep up with the girls and the factory floor chat.

All in all things were going very well. I couldn't have been happier. Well actually I could. Well, truth be told, I wasn't happy at all. I was fucking miserable. My first ever Christmas without her was looming. I was dreading it. I told Ruth one titanic thing was missing in my life. 'Kids?' she said. 'No – Gina!' I said. She made a point of cooking Christmas dinner. I offered.

'I'm thinking of something more substantial than Pot Noodles,' she said. Since I told her I loved her she seemed to be taking certain liberties, but I couldn't take it back because it was true.

'Fair enough, but don't go all sanctimonious about it. And another thing – no poultry. I've shaken hands with enough wishbones from the arse up to last me a lifetime.'

So she made a pot roast. And we sat, the two of us, upstairs, at a table she laid out in the living room, some collapsible Formica thing she'd rescued from a canteen clear out. It sat four, and you could see the four placings where the veneer had been worn out by countless plates and elbows and cutlery, like rocks rubbed out by geology. So we sit across from one another, beside the two ghost settings. And suddenly I get this vision of what it would have been like, five years from now, if *she* hadn't died and she hadn't left. The four of us round the table. Laughing. A little girl with her mum and two aunties who love her to distraction, confident as the focus of all that feeling, sitting with her own special paper hat. And a big tear plopped off the end of my nose into the gravy. And I was just about to say 'I can't do this' and get up from the table when I realised that would have been selfish. She was going through this too. This was her way of coping, the way mine was to paste some slap on and go out for a knees up. And she had made this effort. She leaned across and rubbed my hand and said 'Eat up' and I said 'Merry Christmas' and we pulled two crackers and put the hats on and read the jokes and she put on a CD, *Dean Martin's Christmas Extravaganza* or something. We were halfway through *Have Yourself A Merry Little Christmas*, that I must have heard a million times without listening when, for the first time, I actually pay attention to the words. He croons out 'Faithful friends who are dear to us, gather near to us once more'. I smile across at her but I swear to God I felt like one of those chickens, that some gigantic hand had just taken a hold of my insides and pulled them out.

And then it became that kind of timeless holiday time, the no-man's-land between Christmas and New Year, when you watch *Jason and the Argonauts* and stuff like that, and eat chocolates you don't want. Ruth worked. The factory was closed. I moped about the flat. I've always avoided my balcony. I've only ever used it during parties and never, ever, gone out on it alone. It's because it's directly below her balcony, and if I were to stand here I'd see her with *her*, rocking, ten feet above my head. It's been a timeless day and I've run out of fags. It's getting on for the early winter sunset, and I remember the way she was always drawn to stand out there at this time and look at – what? And I think that maybe if I go out there, on my balcony, I'll see what she saw and maybe I'll understand better why all this happened. Why she went. So I brace myself and go out. The cold is shocking. I look around. Everything's gone kind of red. There's just the river and the windows across the way reflecting light. Nothing to look at really. What did she see that I can't? What? What? My heart's battering and I want to shout. I do shout. 'What?' and 'What?' then 'What?' leaning on the railings, craning out as far as I dare, trying to catch something. Anything. The sound disappears with my breath. Nothing.

I wipe my eyes and blow my nose. The cold drives me in and I look around at the mess. Light's flooding the room. It's almost the colour of a blood orange. But it doesn't really matter. She took all the colour with her. And suddenly I realise what she meant, and I know that *I'm* only going through the motions. And I can't bear this anymore. I just can't. I go out for fags for something to do.

I draw out the conversation at Davinder's as long as I can but they're not interested. Chit chat obviously doesn't cover their overheads. For the first time I can remember I don't want to go back, but I don't want to go anywhere else either. If nothing else the cold drives me back. There's a folded envelope under the number plate. The sack? The place is closed and they wouldn't do it this casually. There'd have to be a proper postman and everything. I unfold it. The writing's on the folded part but still on the outside. It's too dark on the landing. I take it into the hall. Ruth's writing's crap enough to recognise. I don't know if she signs it cause I don't get any further than the first couple of lines. And suddenly I'm at her door, at electrical speed. Either she's been waiting or she hears me coming. She opens the door and points along the hall. I take her hand and drag her with me. I practically boot open the door, like troops on the telly. I don't know what I expect. If I'd read the letter right to the end, instead of stopping at her name, it might have explained. I might have an image in my mind that the scene fits onto, like tracing paper or a brass rubbing. The last thing I expect to see is this vague-looking older guy, staring at me and taking stock. He reaches into his pocket and pulls out his wallet. And he takes out some photos and hands them across. And although he doesn't say anything Ruth and me know, we just *know*, that the thing we've dreaded so much we were afraid to say the words out loud in case it came true, isn't true. She *isn't* dead. And I don't remember anything about the next half hour at all till somehow *I'm* nominated to fix *him* a fry-up.

# PART 4

He is seated in the most reinforced corner of the sofa with a plate of food on his lap. It consists of fried eggs, fried bacon, fried sausages, two hemispheres of a fried tomato and fried bread. All these ingredients appear to have been made in the same pan, at the same time, by simmering everything in half an inch of hot fat. The egg whites have run to embrace their shipmates, before coagulating, and the entire ensemble lifted out with a spatula. On investigation the egg yolks burst open and now flow, lava-like, over the rest. The whole thing is delicious. He had not realised he was as hungry as he was tired. Now that the uncertainty of his reception has been removed, tiredness has hit him like a wave. The mug of tea is replaced twice more. The cupboard won't yield anything to the dog's taste, so Ruth returned to the firework emporium to buy him half a dozen samosas. Lolly made the fry-up with great gusto, shouting staccato questions through the open kitchen door. What does she look like? Is she happy? Miserable? Has she asked for her? Why did she leave like that? Who the *fuck* does *she* think *she* is worrying *her*, worrying *them*, like that? Does she know her dad's been drunk since Christ knows when, and tortures himself to stand looking like death warmed up staring into that room? Can she not see what they, gesturing with the pan in a tidal flip of hot fat, have been through? Does she know that she's even been to a fucking *clairvoyant* to try and find her, and has even been thinking about going to church, or worse, the *polis*? Does she think the electric pays for itself and that they've got nothing better to do than be fucking *caretakers*? At this there is a conspiratorial nod above the pan towards Ruth, patting the dog, making Christopher complicit in the secret that she probably hasn't anything better to do. Where does she get off treating them the way Nick treated her, evaporating like some fucking panto genie? Who, Christopher wonders, is Nick? Doesn't she know that she'd give anything, *anything*, to see her walk in that door right now and put her arms round her and...

The sob is like a detonation, so sudden he thinks the pan has caught fire. He has been craning from the sofa, unsure of what's expected of him, but thinking that this tirade might merit eye contact. Unsure of what to do he stands. Ruth's beaten him to it. They hug in the kitchen. The outburst stops as quickly as it starts. He is startled. Is that all it took, an instant of human contact to diffuse that much grief? Ruth comes back. He hears the rasp of a match and Lolly is smoking a cigarette over his bubbling dinner. She deftly picks some loose tobacco from her bottom lip, and something else from the fry-up. The whole lot is shovelled onto a plate and presented with another cup of tea. The dog is gnawing a stale samosa.

She plies him with questions while he eats, and, inexplicably, turns on a gigantic and disproportionate television at the same time. He finds the background flicker and drone a distraction, but it seems this is another form of human contact she somehow craves. There is something so compulsively tactile about her that he wants to reach across and stroke her, but thinks this might be misinterpreted. She picks up the dog, samosa and all, and sits so suddenly on the sofa that his meal is nearly catapulted. He answers between slow mouthfuls. She can't conceal her impatience, or disappointment, at the inadequacy of his answers.

'Yes – but what's she *like*?'

'In comparison with what?'

'Was she happy?'

'Sometimes.'

'Was she sad?'

'Sometimes.'

'Well that's no fucking good!'

Ruth moderates her with a touch. He wonders if this is a safety valve against more tears. What cost his antiseptic life, practically hermetic since his mother's death, punctuated by loveless pokes at Marjory?

'If you don't mind me saying so, you look as if you've had more fun than me.' He doesn't know where this non-sequitur comes from: thinking aloud, tiredness, age. It silences her for a moment only.

'If you don't mind *me* saying so, the Count of Monte Cristo on the telly last week looks as if he's had more fun than you.'

But the break in her flow has allowed him to ask questions and he perseveres, doggedly, in the face of their halting replies. What was she like? Happy? Sad? Because these questions weren't nonsensical the first time round and he does have something to compare it with. He has the woman in the photographs, the woman fixed to the back of the nursery door who gazes out on that small mausoleum. Because of course the child, Millie, whose name causes them the same difficulty as entering the room does, is dead. And that one deadening fact explains everything: the clotted points of her hair on the approach to the bridge; the vacancy, remoteness, sense of reproach at enjoying anything; the discrepancy, between then and now, of depth in the eyes whose cherished object has been rubbed out of the foreground. It explains everything except where she has gone.

'By the way, your wee dog's lovely but a bit rancid.' She pushes him onto the carpet, causing Christopher's tea to spill.

'Perhaps the samosas?' he suggests.

'We'll find him something more suitable tomorrow.' Ruth says, on her way for a cloth.

* * *

Despite protestations he is given Ruth's bed. Lolly offers her spare and again he is made complicit in another wary exchange, this time from Ruth. There is abundant green around the flat to walk the dog, and abundant blowing crisp bags to pick up shit with. Their chimed insistence that he stay longer sways him, particularly Ruth's appeal. He somehow feels Gina's proxy, that they feel nearer to her when he is here than when he isn't.

'But I haven't enough underwear.'

'Buy more.'

So the next day he is taken by bus to the city centre, and trundled round Marks and Spencers to buy more of whatever else he needs to postpone his departure. They buy proper food for the dog because he is, as Lolly says, a bit rancid. He is surprised at the Victorian splendour of the buildings. Unknowingly he has lived with the perspective that nothing really exists beyond the capital, except dormitory areas that feed it. If nothing else, the sudden dip in temperature would have told him this is a different country. The atmosphere he encountered, getting off the train, seems to prevail even at midday, a growing boisterousness anticipating Hogmanay. The lacklustre hawker, selling cheap cigarette lighters and cheaper sports socks, sports a halo of glitter.

They take him out one night to meet some other young women of their age, a local place of latent menace he feels thankfully insulated from. These other women go into hysterics at every second thing he says, as if he's contrived an accent and manner of speech for impromptu performance. Lolly has, it seems, memorised some choicer quotations and trots them out with a passable impersonation.

'Hey, Christopher, what was that thing you said the other night?'

'I'm sorry but you're going to have to be more specific.'

A round of titters.

'What was it you called that politician guy on that party political broadcast? The one that came on instead of *Emmerdale*?'

'Unctuous.'

More laughter like party poppers. What she doesn't say is that he didn't volunteer anything but gave opinions to her questions, posed, it now seems, to supply humour. He isn't offended but feels like some prop from an Ealing comedy, wheeled out for archaic laughs. Emboldened by three spritzers Ruth rubs the back of his hand. They are all nice to him. They call him 'sweetie', and 'darlin'', and ply him with drinks to prompt more nuggets of received pronunciation. The smuggled dog, beneath the table, contemplates a ring of garish footwear. They say their goodnights and on the way home the three of them suddenly become four, as a taciturn young man appears, perhaps from the shrubbery, and wordlessly accompanies Lolly as she gestures to him. He says nothing the whole lift journey and follows her out a floor early.

The next day, during an unintended afternoon nap when he has slouched into one of the sofa's depressions, he is roused by the bell. Ruth is working. Lolly has her own key. He feels it takes an age to escape the upholstery. He opens the door with an apology. He hasn't seen a face this lined since he was eight, a photograph of a Red Indian in the *Children's Britannica*, features as rugged as his environment, sunk in a creased moccasin. He had an excuse. This man has an indoor complexion. He brushes past, seemingly unsurprised at a visitor, and pats alternate walls as he sways along the corridor to the nursery door, pushes it open and stands on the threshold, oscillating with grief, or drink, or both, till he turns back and leaves the way he came in, closing the door behind him.

She had to leave. He can see that now, the enveloping hopelessness. And so must he. He breaks it to them that night over an Asda curry. Thankfully he isn't expected to eat from his lap, poised on the carnivorous sofa. They sit at a Formica table Ruth has produced from somewhere.

'But she might come back,' Ruth says, 'and you'll miss her.' He holds back the obvious remark that if she was going to return she would probably have done so before now, and here is precisely what she ran away from.

'Too many memories,' Lolly says, nodding in the direction of the nursery. Tears well in her eyes.

'If she comes back here you can tell me. If I'm at home and she comes back there then we have two options covered.'

The logic is compelling. Lolly dries her eyes on some kitchen roll and focuses her attention on the poppadoms. Ruth prevails on him to stay one more night for the bells.

The following night sees all the girls in the local pub, and later the same crew, with yet another mute male satellite of Lolly's, crowded on Ruth's frosty balcony, counting down the seconds. He is worried the structure will give: some of the girls are almost as well upholstered as Lolly. She is already drunk. On the stroke of midnight they burst open plumes of cheap Cava as the fireworks from Glasgow Green burst on the still air. Between explosions, outrollings of the tolling bells pass them in waves. Fizzy wine is sloshed into their meagre selection of glasses. He has a chipped teacup. The dog barks in recognition of the electricity. Lolly calls for silence and shouts over the cacophonous backdrop.

'Gina.'

'Gina.' A collection of clunks as the glasses and cups collide. Lolly hands hers to the mute boy and puts her arms round Christopher's neck. She is big anyway, and her heels make her of a height with him. The pressure of her forearms force his face into her bare neck.

He can feel the heat and vitality rising from her breasts. She holds him at arm's length, the collision with his back pushing the boy behind indoors, takes both his cheeks in her hot hands, stares into his eyes, pulls him forward and kisses him fully on the mouth. Her lips are cushioned. He closes his eyes instinctively before impact. Now he opens them and finds the boy has insinuated himself back on to the balcony and is observing the exchange sadly. She lets Christopher go, retrieves the glass and takes another swig of Cava. He wanders away, into the living room, not wanting a repetition of the embarrassment caused by Vanessa. He totters slightly. She is potent even at this remove. He feels as if he has been given a glimpse of a carnal vista he should have wandered down as a younger man. He drinks thirstily. Ruth, seeming to understand, refills his teacup.

Twenty hours later he approaches his front door. The reduced service vindictively called at every hamlet on its way south. He was surrounded by crapulous Glaswegians making the same commute and, for the first time in his life, felt a sense of camaraderie. Again the harlequins of light are thrown onto his lawn. He posted keys and a cryptic note through Oscar's door on his impulsive departure. They were out, thankfully. He imagines Deborah will have collected the post, and lit the place to deter burglars. He sees the blurred shadow of a figure flit past, and recede towards the top of the glass as it climbs the stairs. The dog has sensed it and barks in recognition. The figure stops. So does his heart. He reaches the handle as the outline grows. His key grates in the lock and is pulled from his hand as the door opens. They stand on either side looking at one another. She is wearing his dressing gown. His first reaction is mechanical.

'How did you get in?'

She points to the planter. He remembers the key beneath.

'I'd say that shows a chronic lack of imagination. Something out of Cluedo.' She stands aside. 'Come in.'

The invitation to his own house sounds strained to both of

them. From the speed of his movements she sees he is exhausted, helps him with his things and sits him at the table while she busies herself preparing something.

'Please, no more fry-ups.'

She looks bemused. He abandons the hard chair for the sofa, luxuriating in sprung upholstery. There is a period of accounting but it can wait till tomorrow.

'Lorraine says hello.' It slips out. He realises he has been rehearsing this on the train, envisaging all the permutations of this encounter in the desperate hope that she would be here. She puts down the whisk. 'And so does Ruth.' She turns round, gripping the surface behind her for purchase, and takes stock.

'You... you went through my things?'

He is back in the Glasgow flat imagining the broadside this would elicit from Lolly: 'Who the hell do you think... worried fucking sick... cried for two months solid... and now you've the fucking nerve...'

'It went against the grain, I'll admit.'

'But you forced yourself.'

'No. You forced me. You lost the right to privacy when you left with no forewarning.'

She returns to beating the eggs, the strokes marking time in the brittle silence. He tries to read her back. She won't face him even when there's no need to supervise the toaster. Assembling the things she finally turns and presents him with a tray.

'If it makes you feel any better then I'll apologise.'

He considers this while he tests the eggs.

'That's the kind of offer that puts the onus on the other person, and it's not really an apology at all. I'm not looking for contrition. I imagine that might be considered weakness where you come from. I'm not. Lorraine is.'

'I can't stay forever.'

'Forever is terrifying.'

'I never said I would.'

'No. You didn't.'

'I didn't break a promise.' Her voice is rising. He has seen her despondent but never agitated.

'You didn't do that either but you did offend common decency. And not just to me.'

'I don't owe!'

'But of course you do. We all do. You can't sever everything. We're all implicated in ties. It's what it means to be human.'

His words collide. She stands stock still, like some charging animal stopped by a shot before it slumps, and sits opposite him. He starts to eat.

'Where did you go?'

'Newcastle.'

'Why?'

'Mum.'

He has a childish image of passing her on the way up, waving from the carriage to a lighted window framing a Christmas tree, the woman an older version of Gina.

'You never mentioned your mother. You never mentioned anyone.'

'Neither did you.'

'I'm not complaining. I'm not the one who left. I'm just trying to understand what compelled you to go.'

'You did. Your talk. Christmas. Families. She left us. That's why Dad is the way he is, or one of the reasons. I never forgave her. I had a brother, Kevin, and he died... He died you see. And she left. And I thought it couldn't have come at a worse time. I thought she deserted a sinking ship. I never realised what it does to you. Not until Millie.'

'Was she any help?'

'No.' She turns suddenly bitter. 'You'd think being mother and daughter was enough. It was with me and Millie. But not her. And even if blood wasn't enough in common, we've got the same loss. But she's a drunk and she's trapped inside her own hurt. Nothing exists outside. No one else is allowed to be sad. It's like a tragic film she just keeps playing over and over in her head, cranking up the pathos till she batters it down with drink. She needs it now because it's her only story. It defines her. She doesn't ever think she needs an excuse. Any other sad story is just a distraction she doesn't need, even if it's me.'

'Did you talk about Millie with her?'

'You don't understand. She doesn't talk. She puts up this front, like she's insanely happy. I think she needs the drink to keep it up. She's done it so long I don't even know if there's anything left behind it any more.'

'Would you like to talk to her?'

'I'd like lots of things. I'd like ordinary parents. I aspire to ordinary problems.'

He eats the remainder of the meal in silence. The presents still lie unopened beneath the tree. They unwrap them in turn. When finally he climbs the stairs she watches anxiously from the bottom. His pyjamas seem more of an effort than normal. As he lies down his organs sigh in a chorus of relief.

Before he falls asleep he decides on a better present for her.

* * *

She returns to work next day. She'd phoned from Newcastle, working on the basis that it was easier to seek forgiveness than permission. He makes the phone calls while she is out. It's difficult getting any information from Lolly. Rather than answer any of his questions she deluges him with questions of her own. She says she's on the point of putting some slap on and running to Central to get a train right *there*. He has to tell her what he intends to forestall her. She snorts down the phone. Ruth offers more encouragement and even provides a phone number.

He makes that call the following day. He introduces himself and explains his proposition. There's an almost narcotic tardiness to all the responses. He apologises if he's woken her up. She asks if she can take his number and call him back. Of course she can. When he replaces the receiver he realises he can't infer anything about her from the call, not her age or appearance or enthusiasm for the invitation.

He waits.

Two days later he calls back. This sounds like a totally different person. There is music in the background. She gushes excitement down the receiver. He apologises if he's interrupted a party, but she says there's just her. She says she lost the bit of paper. She says she's glad he called back. She says can he send her the train fare because she's a bit short just at the moment. Before he can agree she provides an immediate list of contingencies. There's the electric, and the physio for her back because it'll be locked solid before the NHS appointment comes through, and unspecified prescription costs, and the washing machine's gone on strike, and the TV people are cracking down so she might finally have to bite the bullet with the licence thing and isn't it just like the thing with one thing after another and she says she'll have it for him when she gets there.

He says he'll send her the tickets and she says the money will do instead. He realises he has no leverage at all. They agree a date.

She's due the following Saturday. The night before he summons himself.

'I hope you won't be angry with me.'

'I don't think you'd even know what that would be like. Has anyone ever been angry at you for long?'

'Not really. But there's always a first time.' Pause. 'Your mother's arriving here tomorrow night.'

She absorbs this in silence, stares at the table. He has no idea what her real reaction behind this assumed composure is. Finally she looks up.

'I know you intended it kindly. Don't hold your breath for her coming here. I don't think it's possible for her to disappoint me anymore. I wouldn't want you to get hurt.'

Despite what she says he waits in readiness the following evening. The mother doesn't arrive. Gina has only laid two settings. He doesn't know if there's an additional portion heating in the oven. She goes to bed before he does.

'The trick of getting by,' she says, from the bottom of the stairs, 'is having low expectations.'

He thinks of phoning but thinks better of it. He's written his little investment off when almost two weeks later a taxi rolls up at ten o'clock at night. Gina, unsurprised, finds her purse before answering the door.

'Could you bring her in and I'll see to the taxi.'

'How do you know it's her?'

'How many visitors do you ever get, never mind at this time of night?'

'Perhaps she's already seen to the taxi.'

She ignores the remark and pulls the door open. Over her shoulder he sees a woman leaning on the cab talking amicably with the driver through the open window. She shrieks at Gina's approach and stands. There's something overtly theatrical in all this. Her manic enthusiasm and Gina's reticence results in a stilted embrace. Gina, behind her mother's back, deals with the fare. He trundles out for her luggage. In the dark interval between the door and the gate the mother somehow manages to flit past him without noticing her host. He swivels, undecided, until he sees Gina attempt to lift the case.

'Please.'

'I'm not the one risking a hernia.'

'Please. I invited her.'

It clinks very obviously and he is obliged to put it down twice before reaching the door. They find her in the lounge, appraising the fittings. She's standing directly beneath the overhead light she has put on. The columnar glare is unflattering. She reminds him of a pantomime dame. She's wearing sling backs, maroon leggings and some kind of tight acrylic top patterned like leopard skin. It is the kind of outfit designed to accentuate the curves of a zaftig teenager. She's stick thin. There are hollows at the backs of her knees he associates with photographs in African aid literature. Her legs do not meet at the top. Her hair is pulled up into some kind of arrangement that resembles a foreshortened palm tree. The dry ends look electrified in the harsh glare. The upward tug of the hairband is so severe it appears to have pulled back her eyebrows in an expression of permanent surprise. Her eyes are liquid bright.

'She's drunk,' Gina observes. If she hears she doesn't register.

'You've got a lovely...' a pause while she gropes for the appropriate word. He finds himself leaning forward, '...room.'

'I'm glad you like it, Mrs...' He realises he doesn't know her surname.

'Betty.'

'Betty.' He shakes her hand. It rattles like dice, all jewellery and bones. 'There's a spare room been made up for you upstairs.'

The dog sits neglected. He stoops to tousle it. When he turns back Betty is rifling through his music collection pulling out CDs at random and discarding each on the floor after a cursory glance.

'There doesn't seem to be any *order*.'

'They're ordered by composer.' Within categories they are further subdivided by dates of recording, one of the foibles that survived Marjory.

'Any Julio Iglesias?'

'No. Sorry.'

'Frankie Vaughan?'

Again he's sorry. He further apologises in turn for the absence of Engelbert Humperdinck and several names he doesn't know.

'I love Julio, me. It's that accent. Listening to him is like being licked all over by a big Latin dog. Never mind.' She rises from the mess and walks from the room. He looks from the scattered collection to the door. Her manner baffles rather than upsets him.

'Is she all right?'

'I told you, she's drunk. Don't worry. She won't fall down the stairs. She can take enough to stop a regiment and still keep up a conversation of sorts. You get to know the signs.'

They find her in the kitchen, opening cupboards at random, apparently pleased with the number of bottles.

'Good to know it's not a dry area.'

'They're waiting to go downstairs. I haven't had a chance to put them in the cellar.'

'The cellar. Posh.' She's looking at Gina.

'It sounds much more grandiose than it is. It's just a few wine racks the merchant put up for me as a favour.'

'Posh.' Betty repeats. He doesn't know if this refers to him or the wine downstairs. 'Has this room been knocked through?'

'Yes.'

'Nice. More space. I love space, me. I mean living space, not outer space.'

'Of course.'

'What's that?' The finger points, almost accusingly.

'It's the bottle of wine you just took out the cupboard.'

'Is it any good?'

'I'm no connoisseur. I like it. Would you like to try some?'

'What I always say is, why not? Eh...?'

He realises Betty is waiting for a response. The remark is so banal he's stuck for a moment. Gina just looks tired.

'It would cover most situations – if you're game.'

She laughs uproariously as if he has said the funniest thing in the world. He uncorks the bottle. Betty waits with an outstretched glass.

'Would you like something to eat?'

'Maybe later.'

In the next few days he will be astonished at her ability to live on fumes, caffeine and alcohol. Food is something haphazard, eaten distractedly and without relish.

'I've got work in the morning. I'm going to bed,' Gina says. Christopher offers to show Betty her room.

'Just leave the door open lover, I'm sure I'll find it.'

Christopher stays till his head is drooping and finally, apologising for the bad form of leaving a guest alone, excuses himself. As she requested, he leaves the guest door slightly ajar, the night light on. As he shuffles along the hall he hears a distant rumble of recorded laughter. She has turned the television on. He is trying to gauge the disruption of the volume to Gina when he hears the popping of a second cork and the closing of the lounge door.

He expects to find her crapulous the following morning but she's animated, sitting cross-legged on a kitchen chair, the ashtray before her already quarter full. She wears another gaudy and unflatteringly tight outfit. He notices there is lipstick on her teeth as she drains her third coffee.

'This coffee of yours doesn't touch the sides.'

As soon as she is upstairs Gina outlines the arrangements.

'I'll take her into town.'

'The High Street?'

'Town. I'm not advertising her in the High Street. If we're back early afternoon maybe you could distract her for a couple of hours. Then dinner and a video and that's tonight taken care of.'

'That sounds like surveillance.'

'No it isn't. I just want an eye kept on her every moment she's awake. You've no idea what that woman can get up to.'

This isn't turning out to be the purging resolution he had hoped for. He realises how hopelessly primitive his private equation was: intimacy plus him as some kind of emotional umpire equals reconciliation.

'I'd like to help as much as I can.'

'Get one of Dorothy's boys to put the wine in the cellar.'

The week is one of alternate supervision. Betty is tractable with Gina but won't be supervised by him.

Next afternoon she gives Christopher the slip three feet from the fishmongers. Worried about Gina's disappointment he trudges the streets until exhausted. When he gets home Betty is unconscious at the foot of the cellar steps. He assumes she's fallen till he sees the discarded bottles. He hauls her into a sitting position, crouches behind her and loops his arms under hers, hands clinched on her concave stomach. He can feel the articulation in her joints, her washboard ribs, the prominence of her shoulder blades as he slowly stands, ignoring his back, shuffles towards the stairs and hauls her incrementally up, reversing step by step. He knows he's only capable of doing this because she weighs nothing.

On the last step she opens her eyes, twists round and looks at him levelly.

'You know Kevin's dead.'

'Yes. I know. I'm sorry.'

'You an' me both.'

There is almost a tragic dignity. For a moment he's confused into mistaking her sudden reminiscence for sobriety, the shock of the old, as if the gravity of what she has just mentioned has traumatised her out of her stupor. She gestures to be left alone. He lets his hands fall to his sides. She lurches and nearly falls down the cellar steps. He clutches her arm. Her head lolls against his neck in a blurt of sound. He can feel the spasm pass through her. He guides her towards the stairs and the spare room, steers her towards the bed. She sits resignedly. He waits, entirely at a loss. Her shoulders and head droop in complete dejection till he realises she is asleep. He rolls her onto her side and covers her with the duvet.

He anticipates an embarrassing exchange the following day.

If Gina is there and witnesses it he'll be obliged to tell her what happened. Betty is carelessly cheerful and seems to remember nothing. He doesn't get the impression of a woman suppressing embarrassment. The same afternoon, stoking an unseasonably cold barbecue to produce a surprise meal for her host, Betty pours lighter fluid to enliven the coals and sets the whole affair ablaze. She tries to extinguish it by kicking the barbecue over and succeeds in burning a hole in the fence separating Christopher's garden from Dorothy's. There's now a blasted patch that looks like the aftermath of small meteor collision. They couldn't be nicer about it.

'Convenient access for the dog,' Oscar says.

He receives a call from the wine merchant.

'Excuse me. A lady here is asking us to let her have some merchandise 'on tick' as she puts it. She insists we charge your account.'

'I'll be right there.'

She isn't cowed by the interrupted fraud and companionably takes his arm as they walk back. He's astonished at her resourcefulness. She can manage to sustain a state of near drunkenness for the best part of an afternoon and evening with no visible means of financial support.

'Sub me for some fags, Christopher.'

'Would you prefer a cigar?'

'No. Fags.'

He gives her money. He only has a twenty. She comes out the shop. He gives it five minutes.

'Cigarettes?'

'Filthy habit. I'm thinking of chucking it.'

'She only ever smokes other people's,' Gina confides, when he tells her. 'She's got a boyfriend in the merchant navy. Polish or something. Long name with a 'z' in it somewhere. He brings her duty free when he's in port and she obliges in the usual way. You can just see her, can't you, puffing away on a Polish fag leaking tobacco, and watching the telly over his shoulder while he bangs in six months' ballast?'

Christopher confesses that he can't.

'And she's got some Asian guy. He's got a corner shop near her digs and a battalion of kids. Mum told me she goes round early closing and he keeps her in fags and samosas. You can just see them too, going at it on the basmati sacks.'

'If you don't mind me saying so, her transactions add up to prostitution.'

'I don't mind. Don't let her hear you say it. She's not shy at raising her voice and what's obvious to you would offend her to the point of going supersonic.'

He's in the music shop, browsing when he feels the pressure of someone clumsily brushing past, recording, from the corner of his eye, a familiar stagger. It's impossible not to hear with the volume and careful tipsy enunciation of each individual word.

'Do you have any Julio?'

'I'm sorry, we operate a strictly no-smoking policy in this shop.'

'Never mind that. Any Julio?'

He makes his escape unseen.

'Sometimes cowardice is the better part of valour.'

'You're speaking in code again, Christopher.'

'Your mother was in the music shop this afternoon. I ran away.'

'Did she steal anything?'

'Does she steal as well?'

'As well as what?'

'As... things...'

'Where's all your loose change?'

'I don't know. Around.' He habitually leaves loose change and crumpled notes on convenient surfaces.

'Look around. How much change do you see. I've put all the notes I could find in a sock in your sock drawer. I'm sorry to have to do it but there's no point in tempting her.'

He's even sorrier. Betty fails to return one evening. This only becomes apparent the following morning when they awake to an absence of cigarette smoke. He lets Gina go into the guest room. He's on the point of calling the local police station when they call him. She's been found lying in a garden in the early hours and detained in custody until sufficiently sober to recall his address. He prevails on Gina to let him go. It's all gone horribly wrong and it's his fault.

When he gets there he realises Betty doesn't subscribe to the same view of the police that he used to hold, before encountering the constable on Gina's bridge. He's expecting a subdued woman behind bars. She's leaning on the counter regaling the desk sergeant with some vulgar anecdote that's proved so contagious everyone is listening. She sees Christopher and finishes her story quickly. The sergeant convulses in a wheezing laugh that's taken up by unseen staff behind the partitions.

'Here's my lift. Must go. People to meet, things to do, gardens to sleep in.'

Another appreciative burst of hilarity. It's he who is subdued in the taxi. She chats incessantly, an inane backdrop to his musings.

'Can I use your mobile?'

'My?' He's forgotten its existence. She takes the phone from his pocket.

'Chokey always gives me an appetite. Never any other time. Don't ask me why.' Assuming permission she dials Gina to order breakfast. For the remainder of the journey she regales one of her cronies, presumably in Newcastle, with her previous night's activities.

'...And then I woke up in a rockery. Gnomes an' stuff. Ornamental pond. Garden centre advert.'

Artistic licence. Wheezing smoker's laugh for the next suburban mile. Meter ticking up more ignored indebtedness. A week and he's now more tired of her than he's ever been of any human being ever.

This hasn't worked. He blames himself. He had hoped her visit would produce some kind of catharsis. It hasn't up until now and he now knows it won't.

By the time they get back to the house Gina has made French toast and a reservation for Betty on the afternoon train. She takes news of her imminent departure without rancour.

'He's really nice,' she says approvingly, referring to Christopher in the third person despite the fact that he's sitting beside them. She leaves with his blessing while a taxi throbs at the same gate she walked through a lifetime previously.

'I want you to take this bottle of wine for... the journey.'

'She's already got two bottles in her luggage...'

'What I always say is, why not?' She pinches Christopher's cheek as if he's an endearing schoolboy and then gives him a searching kiss that causes him to stumble back against the Welsh dresser.

'Why not?' he finds himself repeating, as another taxi ferries another person out of his life.

Gina sees her to the taxi and returns with a look of strained relief on her face. She goes to her room and only comes down to cook. They don't talk properly till after dinner.

'I suppose now, having met her, you can see some things more clearly.'

'You mean about loose change disappearing and that sort of thing.'

'I mean how I came to be on a bridge trying to sleep in a box, or didn't you ever wonder how that state of affairs came about?'

'I still think it strange to find someone as resourceful as you on the street.'

'So you did wonder?'

'Yes, I suppose I did.'

'Didn't it occur to you to ask?'

'If you thought it was necessary for me to know I think you would have told me.'

'Is that an answer?'

'It's not my place to ask.'

'Yes it is.'

He makes a baffled gesture, palms upraised, as if lifting an invisible plank. 'One doesn't like to intrude.'

'Meaning?'

'Meaning... one doesn't like to intrude.'

'You've more right than anyone else in the world. If it's anyone's place to ask it's yours to ask me now.'

A pause while he sits considering. He is about to lift the invisible plank again when she interrupts.

'So are you?'

'Am I what?'

She leans across and knocks on his forehead. 'Hello? Anyone home? What have we been talking about? Are you going to ask how I came to be destitute?'

'If you want me to.'

'What do you want?'

'I want people to be nicer and for you to be happy.'

'For fuck's sake, Christopher! Haven't you ever eaten the grapes in the supermarket before you get to the checkout?'

'No. I don't see what that's got to do with anything. And I'm not going to apologise for not having shoplifted.'

'The first night I stayed here I put the back of a chair underneath the door handle. I thought you might try something on. Call it rent. You don't have to put that expression on. Much as it might surprise you that kind of behaviour isn't unknown. I wouldn't put it past George Coleman to expect to get the leg over. Mum came back briefly, a couple of years after Kevin had gone. It was just for a while. I even stayed with her, to see if we could maybe make a go of it. Whatever I had to offer it wasn't enough. She disappeared again. I wasn't sad to see the back of her boyfriends. Most didn't have George's subtlety.'

Next to Betty George is the person Christopher would least qualify as subtle.

'And did any of them... try?'

'Yes.'

'You weren't... hurt?'

His euphemism touches her. 'I was agile. That helped. Most of Mum's men were as much of a lush as she is. I'd hear them fuck through the wall when their periods of consciousness overlapped. But a couple of them, if they were up for it and she was out the game, came tapping on my door.'

He has an image: a bloated man with fat hands and venous nose leaning over a sleeping teenage Gina.

'Don't worry. I wasn't Fay Wray. I didn't lie back with big shag me eyes looking helpless. Most didn't get near. One broke my nose to slow me down...'

He takes off his glasses and massages the junction of his eyebrows.

'Mum woke. Guessed right first time and slapped him. It would have been poetic justice if she'd broken his nose, but he cracked two of her ribs on the way out. We were three up. If we'd had a handy chip pan on the go I'd have poured it out the window and scalded the fucker on the doorstep. Like one of those mediaeval sieges. But we didn't. She never cooked. She never eats. She's the only person I know who thinks you can get vitamins from smoke.

'So we never saw *him* again. Can't even remember his name. Punches my face, kicks Mum's ribs and I don't even know who he was. Says something somehow. Doesn't it?'

'If it hurts you don't have to say this.'

There's nothing self-pitying. Her disclosure has found a momentum of its own.

'I saw Mum on her feet. A couple of weeks till she could get to the shops on her own. But I knew that even if *he* didn't come back there would always be another. There would always be someone knocking on my door. I was sixteen. I left. Sixteen. I can't even think of that now. Sixteen. I still think of Millie. I never stop thinking about her. I wonder what she'd have been like when she was five, and ten, and fifty. If I ever thought of her at sixteen, standing on a pavement, carrying everything she owns, I'd probably burst into tears.'

Which is exactly what she does the moment the last syllable is out. He doesn't imagine she cries easily. He wonders how she held out for so long. What chance did she have with that raddled phantom of a man he saw in her hall, and the woman who has just left in the taxi. He's seen women cry before; he's seen tears of wounded vanity, he's seen Marjory's tears of social frustration, but he's never seen anyone cry like this. The violence of these tears is vehement and purgative. He puts his arm around her. She spasms at each inhalation. He feels something entirely unexpected: privilege. Since the death of his mother he has skated, living on surface tension. If it had been someone other than Marjory, someone who gave back, it might have been different. There was never any immersion till she arrived. He feels the privilege of this vicarious pain. She has lent him depth.

He fishes in his pocket for the ubiquitous hanky. She rests her face against his neck and sobs till his collar is saturated and mascara-stained beyond repair. He waits till the heaving shoulders subside. When she finally pulls away from him to accept the hanky, a long loop of catarrh attenuates from the tip of her nose to his ear lobe. Her head looks full of water. She blows her nose, a foghorn at this proximity. He winces at the noise. The dog barks.

'There must have been some happier times?'

Phrases come out in a hot rush, thickly.

'There were in-between times, times that seemed good till I look back, only good because of what came before and after.'

'You weren't always on the street?'

'No. But what you said,' her speech is becoming more uniform, coherent, 'about being surprised about me being resourceful and on the street. Sometimes it's having nothing that's the test of your resourcefulness. You see, I wasn't frightened of it. It became a place to go. There was never a home to go back to.'

She has clarified his intention.

Her breathing slows while his arm grows slowly numb. He guesses the effort of this revelation has exhausted her. His bladder competes with his shoulder for relief. He disentangles himself with a muttered apology and returns fifteen minutes later with a tray. He's made a pot of tea and a pile of hot buttered toast. She rouses herself and puts on the television. There's an old black and white film, *I Know Where I'm Going*. They sit side by side watching it in silence.

* * *

It's a week before he can countenance another interruption to his routine. He's more tactical this time and waits till she's going up to bed.

'You can always invite your friends down here, you know.'

'I don't know if you could stand it. I don't know if I could stand it.'

'Well, the invitation's there.'

She doesn't mention anything for the next few days. It's Vanessa who puts the thing in perspective for him.

'She probably feels she wants to see her friends because she's indebted to them.'

'So she should. They kept faith. They kept that flat going and that can't be easy on their combined income.'

'I don't blame her that she doesn't want to go back. From what you tell me it sounds like a museum to the past that she's just recently gotten away from.'

'She's been in the house for a while.'

'I mean that she's just gotten away from it in her mind. Don't be so literal, Christopher.' He understands how far they've moved that she can chide him. 'So it would be good for her to see them but not go there. So they need to come here. But Gina's hesitant to invite them because she thinks it might be too much for you. The answer's obvious.'

'Not to me.'

'You need to go away.'

'Away where?'

'Will you leave it to me?'

He ponders the implications of this while the Gaggia stutters out another espresso. Gina's not on shift so they won't be caught conspiring.

'You don't mean on my own?'

'You mean do I propose to send you away somewhere on your own? That's seriously what you're asking me?'

'Yes.'

'No, Christopher. I don't propose to send you somewhere on your own.'

'With you?'

'No. George Coleman. You can find your inner gay together. Of course I mean me!'

He ponders some more.

'Some women would find this hesitation very,' she lowers her voice in mock gravity, 'very,' she lowers it further, 'insulting.'

'Sorry. I'm not trying to offend.'

'I know. Don't take this the wrong way but you're not the first man I'll have ever been away with.'

'Gina said you'd seen it all.'

'Did she now?'

'Yes. Not unkindly.'

'Gina's almost as incapable of being unkind as you are.'

'You know it was her idea to invite you to the barbecue that time.'

'Yes.'

'And for me to invite you out for coffee.'

'Yes. There's this mysterious form of communication that women practice. It's called talking. You should try it some time. And not just about the Middle East or architecture or whatever it is you do. You know, you may not be the first man I've been away with but you're the first who didn't jump at the chance. Most of the others did the inviting too.'

'All right,' he says decisively. 'I'll do it!'

'Good for you. Have you got a passport?'

The decisive look vanishes and then reasserts itself.

'If not I'll get one. Let's make it a long weekend.'

'A week. Give them a chance to spend some time together.'

'Five nights. I don't want to leave the dog too long. And not too far mind.'

'You're so masterful. I'll even book us single rooms.'

This aspect of the trip hadn't occurred to him. Something suddenly does.

'Do you think I should invite her friends as a surprise?'

'No. Look what happened with her mother. I think we should give her dates and let her know it's an opportune time for her to have the girls there. I'm only sorry I can't meet them myself. They sound good fun. And I'm stuck with you.'

* * *

On a Tuesday night in mid February, two taxis arrive. One rolls up to Christopher's front door and spills out two girls who abandon the luggage and driver to run towards the figure standing framed in the lighted doorway with the dog sitting at her feet.

The other makes slow progress up the ascent of the Malá Strana in Prague. The night is crystalline. The stars look brittle. Frost coats the cobbles.

Lolly's stumbling because she's been crying on and off since Euston. The preliminaries are nothing compared to what happens to her when she recognises the lighted silhouette. She can barely see as she runs towards the light with Ruth at her elbow, and kicks over a potted conifer in her haste. The driver purses his lips and blows air through them. He can just tell that this is going to be one of those reunions. Women are the worst. If only he'd kept the meter running.

The concierge from the small hotel carries Christopher and Vanessa's luggage from the taxi into the vestibule. Christopher pays the driver off while Vanessa registers for them. She borrows his passport to pass across the details. The same porter follows them with the luggage to the tiny lift. He presses the floor button for them and retreats back. He will have to follow because there's not enough room for them and the cases. The little cage is a gem of Art Nouveau intimacy, hoisting them up. They wait outside the room till the porter arrives. He opens the door and gestures them inside. Subdued lights have been put on and the large window purposefully left with the curtains open, giving a view down the hill. Steeply gabled roofs descend towards the river in tiers of glinting frost. The crescent of lighted globes arching across the Charles Bridge forms an irregular oval with its reflection in the dark water. Behind the blazing river frontage twin spires of the old town square are illuminated against the night sky. Beyond that Prague hums. He thinks if someone contrived to manufacture this panorama it couldn't be bettered. It's improbably beautiful. He hands the porter a note without turning around and misses the snort at the derisory tip. Vanessa hands him another on the way out. She always gets the best out of people.

He turns and is arrested by the prospect of the enormous double bed, commanding half the floor, that he somehow missed in his preoccupation with the view. He looks at Vanessa.

'I lied,' she says, imitating Gina.

Lolly has cradled Gina's face in her hands. They're all crying – with the exception of the taxi driver. No one has said anything. In a moment of profound awareness Lolly becomes conscious of the fact that this drama isn't restricted to her and Gina. With her left hand she reaches across and cups Ruth's right cheek. Then she gathers her in and leans towards Gina so that their three faces form a triangle, each with a cheek touching the other two. Thinking that this will be a long fucking night the driver gets the luggage from the boot. He crunches across the driveway towards them, cases dangling from either wrist. Within twenty feet he can tell there's a different quality to this. It isn't the excessive hen-party explosion of shrieks, recriminations and tears he's seen more times than he can care to remember. None of them is making a sound. It's not his fault he misjudged. That orange one with the big tits has been crying on and off since the station. No, there's something different to this. Something he feels he's interrupting and shouldn't. He drops the bag on the stones and clears his throat almost apologetically. The one who had been standing in the door hands him a crumple of notes. They're hot. She's been holding them for some time. The tip is excessive. He's about to ask her if she's sure when she smiles at him through a face he won't forget for a while. He's sure she's sure. It's some kind of delivery bonus he knows he'll never understand. He's trespassed long enough.

Christopher looks at the bed, and at Vanessa, and feels both flattered and apprehensive. What does 'seen it all' really mean? What is his capacity to disappoint? But then she did choose him.

'Dinner?' she suggests.

It's a basement place of vaulted ceilings that looks as if it's been here for centuries. The menu is carnivorous. They eat duck and wash it down with a local tannic wine. It's only a five-minute walk back up the hill, past frontages that have seen out the Hapsburgs, the Nazis, the Communists and now bear witness to an old man ambling up the hill to a nervous tryst.

When one starts to talk they all do. Three conversations pile in from the front door to the kitchen. The two Glasgow girls are too preoccupied, or happy, to notice anything. The three of them eat defrosted and scorched pizza. Gina didn't have it in her to cook tonight, or to time the cooking. Before they sit down Ruth flourishes a piece of paper.

'A letter,' she announces.

'No one's ever written me a letter,' Lolly complains.

'Did you ever write anyone a letter to expect one back?' Gina asks.

'Not so much a letter as a note,' Ruth says. Even in this state of being happier than they've ever been the other two have it in them to start an argument. She flattens it out in front of her and reads, very slowly.

'If you're reading this then you've opened the envelope (obviously) and that was under the strict condition you are all three together. There are three special bottles put away for your reunion. They're in the shed. Gina knows where. They should be cold enough.'

They rush out. The dog rushes with them and barks. They rush back. The dog rushes back and barks some more. They open three bottles of Veuve Clicquot almost simultaneously, racing drivers on the podium, soaking one another. There isn't much left to taste but there are lots of bottles of Prosecco downstairs.

'That Christopher,' says Lolly, turning the bottle upside down and draining the frothy drips into her mouth. 'Diamond geezer. He didn't...' she makes poking motions with the neck of the bottle. The look she receives back leads to the second moment of awareness she has had that night. 'All right. Keep your hair on. Only asking. Since when did you become Mother Superior?'

The bathroom is an acoustic cavern. He waits till she uses it first, looking down the hill. Will she have packed a negligée? When she comes out he can see her reflection, behind his reflection, superimposed on the roofs of Prague. She is wearing some kind of simple slip.

'Close the curtains, Christopher.'

He takes his pyjamas into the bathroom. There isn't the same unflattering overhead glare of the bathroom at home, those intense lights he replaced once Marjory died. She had insisted on their installation. Why? They compelled remorseless scrutiny. He doesn't remember her ever knowing herself any better as a result. If she ever did she was ready to forgive herself, exonerate all those faults she itemised so scrupulously, without acquittal, in others. Why is he thinking about her now? Perhaps because she is all he knew. And on the other side of that wall is a woman of vaster experience. He reminds himself that this isn't a competition. And it suddenly occurs to him as sad that his only touchstone was as grudging in this as in all the important things.

He thinks, I'm glad I've still got my teeth, as he rinses and spits.

Lolly has found the Prosecco. The blaze of emotion has died to something less combustible, more capable of being managed. Gina knows this is Ruth's doing. Something about her presence is soothing. She can see the change a year of Ruth's company had brought about in Lolly. If it had just been the two of them here, without Ruth, then on Lolly's side there would have been tears, tantrums, recriminations, reconciliation, elation, despair and relief all in the first half hour.

Lolly hasn't noticed anything of their surroundings yet, besides locating the booze. Ruth's been looking around. She goes to the French windows and steps outside, takes in the darkling trees, swaying in whispers. Gina joins her.

'It's beautiful,' Ruth says. 'He's kind. If you can't be with us I'm glad you're here.' They stand side by side, looking. Lolly feeds the dog some chorizo she has found in the fridge.

Christopher emerges from the bathroom.

'Who were you talking to?'

'Was I talking?'

'Something about your teeth.'

'I didn't know I said it aloud.'

'You've been alone too much.'

He pushes aside the duvet and climbs in. The light is on his side. He reaches across to turn it off and turns back towards the centre of the bed. She rolls towards him in synchronisation. It is all easy, effortless, the unlearned automatic dance. He is so relieved there is nothing to worry about that the pleasure takes him by surprise. His body has been so clamorous of late he is surprised at how it works by itself. This, he thinks, is as easy as easy digestion. She is generous.

Lolly pops the Prosecco in another frothy burst.

'Well that's that then,' she says afterwards. 'No need to be nice to you anymore now that I got what I wanted.' And she bursts into a raucous laugh that he's never heard before. It's so full of life it makes him even happier than his relief at their successful rhythm. She props herself on her elbow. He can sense she is looking down at him in the darkness. 'You lovely... no, *my* lovely man.'

He feels he's spent his life pursuing the path of least resistance. He doesn't see what he's done to deserve this.

The next afternoon Gina drags the girls into the city. On point of principle she's determined to show them some culture. She suggests the National Gallery. Lolly puts up a fuss. There *are* paintings back home, she reminds them. And what's so good about art? It's all a bunch of wank. They settle for St Paul's. It's quicker to get round. Lolly bridles at the suggested donation. It echoes down the Nave.

'At least the other place was free. *And* they had paintings.'

After a shower and breakfast the couple find themselves on the pavement. The sky is clear. Their breath levitates. Behind them the hill rises to the Castle, site of three 'defenestrations' that excites Christopher, not for the building's historical significance but as the pretext for including a word he's only ever encountered in dictionaries. Below them is the baroque froth of St Nicholas he has been reading about, five sauntering downhill minutes, and beyond the prospect of the undiscovered city, to be explored in café-stopped instalments. She is smiling at him in the sunshine. Her grooming is perfect but he is pleased to see she looks older in the morning light.

'What would you like to see?' he asks.

'What would *you* like to see. This is more your thing. I've watched you absorb that guidebook and all the plaques we've passed so far. You have to find yourself in a setting. I don't care. I'm just here for the sex.'

She takes his arm. They begin to walk towards the dome he can see rising from the surrounding rooftops. She's right. She knows him better than he suspected she did. He does have to locate himself, in a place, in the context of its past, at the bow-wave of its history. This is middle Europe, a place of intermittent purges, of soaring buildings to the glory of God and horrors enacted for the sake of liturgical niceties. Blood has run like gesso down the walls around here. And yet, with her at his side, he can't feel the sense of thwarted expiation, of something seeking atonement that such old places usually inspire. It's a beautiful morning. They'll amble in a radius dictated by his hip and bladder till their first coffee, or drink.

And there's something else the weight of her arm in his makes him realise. Being with her has freed something else. Suddenly he doesn't feel the same obsessive concern for Gina. He doesn't love the younger woman any less, but he has the compensation of knowing that if she were to leave again he wouldn't feel as if she had taken all the colour with her.

* * *

When he gets home she's at work. He puts his case in the hall and sits to pat the dog. The place gleams. He imagines Lolly's departure had required a complete cleaning. After he has rested and had some tea he takes the dog out. He is walking towards the common when he sees her coming from the opposite direction. The dog has rushed on to greet her. He stops about ten feet from them and looks at her intently. She's in a half crouch, patting the dog. She looks up. Nothing has prepared him for the onrush.

'What's wrong?'

'Nothing.'

'How was Prague?'

'I'll tell you tonight.' She slits her eyes appraisingly, the way he imagines George Coleman would enjoy being looked at. 'What are you doing?'

'I'm on my lunch. I just wanted to check you'd got home and were all right.' She straightens. 'No need now. Walk me back. I'll bring in dinner. Should I bring enough for Vanessa?'

'Not tonight. Perhaps tomorrow.'

'Or perhaps you'll go there?'

'Perhaps.'

A week later he visits the building society. The mortgage is long since redeemed but they continued to make deposits, saving up for Marjory's ostentatious widowhood. The office paraphernalia he was once familiar with has vanished. No staccato typing. He misses the tactility of passbooks, of banknotes transacted, the solidity of cash registers, of jingling coins in the shunted drawer. He's invited to sit at a veneer desk among muted office furniture. He imagines cables underneath carpet tiles, the hum of subterraneous transactions, of electronic money, flowing like corpuscles.

Two days later he follows this with a visit to his solicitor to instruct on the terms of his codicil.

He decides to confront her head on.

'I hope you won't be angry with me.'

'Last time you said that Mum arrived. She's not coming back?'

'God no!' The shudder dispels his awkwardness for the instant it lasts. 'I'll come straight to the point. I'm old. You're young. My wife is dead. I have no dependents. I want you to stay for as long as you want without you feeling you have to stay out of a sense of obligation. I wanted to put some wind in your sails. You always have a place here as long as I'm here, and it's yours when I'm not here anymore. By that I don't mean moving out or emigrating or anything...'

'I know what you mean.'

'The thing is'

But she has abruptly interrupted him by standing and walking out. She goes up to her room to think. The dog follows. She sits on the floor, back to the bureau, stroking the dog beside her as she tries to digest what she's just heard. She's trying to comprehend the extent of her indebtedness to him, not just for this latest thing but for everything. Even before this she knows she couldn't adequately repay him for the restoration of herself. The seriousness of this is too great and she finds herself taking inventory. She thinks about Nick, useless, vain, flimsy Nick, that stick-on transparency of a man. Perhaps he unintentionally established a prototype in her mind or perhaps her dad had already done that. She knows she hasn't experienced a fair cross-section to generalise, but it doesn't prevent her. Besides her dad there is the limitless succession of Lolly's admirers. Simon was the best of a limited lot, and he didn't even have the courage of his inclinations. She's experienced or met the kind of man who fertilises, or in Simon's case doesn't, and runs. They've all been disposable. She can admit to herself now that all along she's held a low opinion of men. None of them remotely stacks up. Except him, sitting downstairs, probably bewildered at her reaction and wondering if he's done a good thing or not, or if he should come upstairs and offer some tea, his only reaction when he's emotionally out his depth.

What's so difficult to accept is the event that would have to happen for her to come into all this. In her mind it's impossible to disassociate him from this house. And this house without him is unthinkable. She sees an image of herself, face down, the top half of her body sticking out from under the front doorstep, the rest of the masonry bearing down on her back. He's worked himself up to this and she's walked out. She might have hurt him. She knows there's nothing she can begin to say. There isn't any combination of words, or any that she can think of that comes close. She drags herself to the top landing. He appears at the bottom with the wobbling cup. She bursts into tears and sits on the top step. He makes his way up, tea slopping into the saucer at each creak of the treads. He sits beside her. The dog insinuates itself between them yet again.

'Deed's done,' he says. 'Papers are signed. Welcome to the middle classes. Can't say it's ever made me any happier.'

* * *

It is her second summer in the house. When she returns from work she shouts through to the back garden, imperiously summoning him upstairs. He's building the charcoal in a conical pile. They have this arrangement now timed so she can walk onto the terrace to glowing embers and start their meal. He dusts his hands ineffectually, one against the other, as he goes upstairs. She's in the top hall taking something out of a Boots bag.

'I've always had Lolly around at every crisis in my life. She's not here. You'll have to do. Wait here.'

She goes into the toilet. Rustling. A pause.

'I can't, with you listening.'

'I should point out that you asked me up. I've no desire to listen to your functions. I'll go downstairs.'

'No. Wait.' The noise of a woman pissing that Marjory tried so very very hard to conceal. Now the tap and not before. She comes out and stands beside him as he tries to grasp the significance of the blue line.

'I'm not sure I understand.'

'For God's sake, Christopher! It's a home pregnancy test kit.'

'I understand that. And I can guess what the line means. Is it an accident?'

'No.'

'Did you want this to happen?'

'Yes.'

'Was it deliberate?'

'Yes.'

He puffs like a stranded fish for three exhalations before the obvious question. 'Who?'

'The boy next door.'

'Literally?' For one dreadful moment Oscar appeared in his mind as a candidate, before being replaced by the two boys, equally fertile.

'Literally.'

'Which one?'

'Does it matter?'

'Of course it does. He has responsibilities.'

'He's a child. He's a nice boy and in time he'll meet a nice girl. He doesn't know.'

'He will.'

'He'll know that. He won't necessarily know it's him.'

More baffled breathing. 'Where? How?'

'You've met Lolly. She's got a gift for improvisation in these things.' He remembers the balcony kiss. 'The weather's been good. I just imagined how she'd go about it and did the same, minus the precautions. And there was all the time you've been out at Vanessa's.'

'It all sounds a bit clinical.'

'I got what I wanted. Don't worry, Christopher, it's good stock. Look at that family. Look at the parents. It'll dilute the genes on my side.'

'You can't mean that. He might *want* to know.'

'If he comes up to me and asks I won't lie.'

'He gave you a gift.'

No, she thinks, he didn't give me a gift. He just did what they all do. What we all do. That dance. That itch the unborn make us scratch just to keep this show on the road. You, Christopher, gave me the courage to ante up again, to want to try, to have a place, to keep *my* show on the road. You, Christopher, you gave me a gift.

* * *

Christopher is on the common with the dog. He could calibrate the day by the foot traffic. Give him a snapshot of the people and he'll guess the time. Early morning are the vigorous employed who walk faster than their loitering pets and stand vigilant with poised plastic bags over shitting dogs. After nine are the young mothers, supervised crocodiles of nursery children and the elderly. The unemployed emerge around noon and sleep off their indoor complexions in the long grass. Three until four thirty the successions of children as the schools stagger their release. Then a miscellany: older children with kit bags crossing the grass after practice; an elderly couple, touchingly congenial with library books; a belated nursery teacher, vexed as she searches the grass for something valuable dropped. Around seven or seven thirty the same vigorous employed appear with new plastic bags and the same pets, dogs costive through the long day, bursting with energy and more shit. And at any time after school the ball kickers, hide and seekers, kissers, promenaders.

The turning of the light is later each evening. Sometimes he loiters for the cavalcade and the spectacle of dusk. She understands. Either they'll eat early or late. Today he left before the evening news. She'll delay the dinner until his return and their visitor arrives. The workers are out for their evening constitutional. Half a dozen ball games are going on in adjacent stretches of green. There are vigorous shouts, different people encouraging different people kicking different balls, groans and burst of laughter. It's intoxicating.

He sees George. He's seen him before, on the opposite side of the High Street, gliding past on occasional buses and once, standing indecisive among the potted shrubbery of the garden centre. He's seen him also, solitary on the common. Unless one of them takes evasive action this is the first time their paths will cross since the funeral. George hasn't yet seen him. He has the opportunity to study the other man. He has aged, markedly. Somehow he looks chronically lonely in a way that Christopher knows he does not. Although fastidious as ever, there's now a whiff of desolation coming off George that he can sense at this distance. Somehow the louche outings never materialised. There's something of the fallen streamers and flaccid balloons about him, of the party that happened next door and abandoned the paraphernalia of gaiety to fade. It's so obvious that people don't want to be contaminated by proximity. He's not the neighbourhood roué, just a sad old man without the comfort of past compassions to console him. Perhaps, Christopher thinks, this is no more than he deserves. Like Marjory, the limits of his concern stopped at the epidermis. Christopher is thinking of turning round, or drifting off into the copse and escaping detection, but thinks better of it. The funeral was one in a succession that will eventually include both of them. There is too little time left. If he had gone to the crematorium he probably wouldn't have met Gina and had the light introduced. George did him a favour.

'Hello, George.'

'Oh... hello, Christopher.' He is startled and wary. Their last real exchange was the calculated snub at the funeral. George is thinking that perhaps Christopher crept up on him to return the favour. 'And how's the bonny wee Scots lassie?'

'Pregnant.'

'Oh.' There's a grudging admiration injected into this single syllable. Christopher knew he would jump to the wrong conclusion, ascribing to him the torrid afternoons George aspired to, that singularly failed to happen.

'Three months.'

Gina has talked about the chattering classes. There is a purpose in telling George. He'll pass on the news in the spirit of randy camaraderie.

Having exchanged these greetings he and George are at a loss. He has assumed that the momentum of his good intentions would follow through. He was wrong. George, jealous in his wrong conclusion, is somehow suddenly lonelier. One thing Christopher has come to realise since Marjory's death, and Gina's departure and return, is that there are strata of loneliness. He thinks it a shame that having for so long shared this tiny portion of the surface of the earth, spoken the same language, trod the same byways, known the same people, they have so little in common. Out of sympathy he is almost tempted to invite George to tea – but doesn't. Both Gina and Vanessa dislike George. Neither would make any attempt to disguise it. George would misinterpret his motives as flaunting his advantage, as he sees it. His sympathy for George doesn't extend to disrupting the hard-won harmony back home.

'Goodbye, George.'

'Regards to your wee Scots bidie-in.'

He's glad he didn't invite him back. He leaves the path and wanders through the longer grass in the direction of the swing park. He often comes here, to sit on the bench nestled among the mulched bark, but waits now till the younger children have gone. He can sit just now because it's empty. The days of a solitary old man blamelessly watching children are no more. He checks his trousers and the dog for burrs.

Perhaps next year he can bring the baby here and speculate

with impunity. He finds it sad that the future scenarios of her and her child don't seem to include a man, at least not in any of her discussions with him. This exclusion seems to be voluntary. He's noticed the attention she receives. The postman, a chronically shy man in his early thirties who delivered Christopher's mail for five years with disembodied efficiency now finds the letter box unassailable and hovers, uncertain, hoping for something that has nothing to do with Christopher. If Christopher's blurred outline appears in the opaque glass the correspondence arrives on the hall carpet in a decisive clump. He's only one of a number. They won't all be dissuaded by a child. Perhaps she'll meet someone.

Her accepting the house thing has given him an inner warmth. He hasn't felt this gratified since primary school, when Miss McGuire rewarded his spelling with a long red tick. He was eight and she in her early twenties. He can still hear the score of the pen on paper, the short forceful downward diagonal and the tangential flick, fading to infinity. She used bath salts and some sort of lemon cologne that wafted, femininely. He thought her culture personified. He remembers flawless nails with half-moon cuticles. Beside her he felt small, grubby and inconsequential, caught in the searchlight of her sophistication when she looked at him, forgave his awkwardness, and moved on. In her twenties, he reflects, Gina's age. I would pass her in the street, if she was now as she was then, and think her a child. She probably had children of her own, scarcely younger than I am. Grandchildren. She is probably dead now. Her lustrous hair grown dry, the skin papery and striated, the cuticles faded to the pallor of the surrounding quick. Why do we spend such a disproportionate portion of our life being old? Why grow up so fast? Why sprint to the tape to stand two feet away and loiter?

The cigar in his immobile hand has burned down to a grey cylinder. The swings are empty and sway with a tiny forlorn metallic creak, like the chirruping of a tardy cricket.

He knows he has been sitting too long, thinking too much, making himself indulgently sad, for no real reason other than the pleasant melancholy of nostalgia. The dog clairvoyantly stretches. He braces hands on knees and stands. The ash disappears into the mulch. His strides are short, lengthening as his joints loosen. He opts for an unobtrusive entrance and makes for the back lane. He reaches for the latch, stops, looks around. Irregular weeds sprout from ruptures in the cobbles. Overarching trees from gardens on both sides cast patches of green shade, a shifting mosaic in the evening breeze. Drooping telegraph wires cradle the light in receding curves. Something which has been gaining ground for months overtakes him. For the first time since listening to his mother read, he realises he is completely happy.

They are in the back room. He isn't going to manage a quiet entrance. He can hear the voices from where he stands. They are too preoccupied to notice him yet. Vanessa is gesturing, the other hand holding the largest of his glasses of wine. Gina tilts her head back in laughing profile. Vanessa notices him and smiles, complicity. Gina's glance follows Vanessa's. She waves.

He catches a pitch, faint, personal, circumambient, as he acknowledges their smiles and walks towards them.